the sweetest thing

christina mandelski

EGMONT
USA
new york

EGMONT

We bring stories to life

First published by Egmont USA, 2011
443 Park Avenue South, Suite 806
New York, NY 10016

1 3 5 7 9 8 6 4 2

www.egmontusa.com
www.christinamandelski.com

Library of Congress Cataloging-in-Publication Data
Mandelski, Christina
The sweetest thing / Christina Mandelski.
    p. cm.
Summary: Fifteen-year-old Sheridan, a master cake-decorator like
her mother, loves her small Michigan town so when her father
announces they will move to New York City, where his dream of host-
ing a cooking show will come true, Sheridan fears for her budding
romance and becomes desperate to contact her long-absent mother.
ISBN 978-1-60684-129-7 (hardcover) — ISBN 978-1-60684-253-9
(electronic book) [1. Cake decorating—Fiction. 2. Interpersonal
relations—Fiction. 3. Single-parent families—Fiction. 4. Television
programs—Production and direction—Fiction. 5. Family
life—Michigan—Fiction. 6. Michigan—Fiction.] I. Title.
PZ7.M31245Swe 2011
[Fic]—dc22
2011002494

Book design by Torborg Davern
Printed in the United States of America

CPSIA tracking label information:
Printed in March 2011 at Berryville Graphics, Berryville, Virginia

To Michael,

Best friend, husband, voice of reason, and soul mate.
You *are* the icing on the cake.

Chapter One

OUT OF THE FRYING PAN, INTO THE FIRE

I make cakes. It's what I do. It's what I love.

But today, I'm standing over a mermaid, wondering what's wrong. She's as long as my arm, and beautiful—no doubt about that. Carved from devil's food, she's got a cute face, pouty red lips, fierce blonde hair. And her tail fin is nothing short of amazing.

It should be. Last night, while most girls my age were panting over their boyfriends at the Grand Rapids Cineplex, I was sculpting fish scales out of fondant.

The colors are perfect: shades of teal, indigo, and turquoise. On the board beneath her, there's an underwater garden on a cobalt blue buttercream ocean. There are coral-colored gum paste anemones, green royal icing seaweed, graham cracker sand, and silver oysters made from modeling chocolate. And inside each oyster, a single, edible pearl.

But something is definitely missing, and it's making me nuts.

Plus, we're late for church, and when Dad gets here, he's sure to be in a wonderful mood. The man's obsessed with getting his own cable cooking show, and now it looks like it might happen. You'd think that would make him sort of happy, but instead he's a moody ball of stress.

I turn away from the cake, hit Next on my iPod, and randomly land on "It's the End of the World as We Know It," which seems like a bad sign. So I yank out the earbuds and wait for inspiration.

In the meantime, I lean over and pipe "Happy Birthday, Tara" in fancy purple script across a delicate white chocolate banner. I carefully lift it off the waxed paper and place it in the mermaid's hands.

Tara McIntyre, birthday girl, is a junior cheerleader who I don't know at all, except as an object of envy. She dated Ethan Murphy for about six weeks last year. I don't know *him*, either, except that he's the most perfect guy I've ever laid eyes on. I've seen him at my dad's restaurant a few times, but for the most part, he sticks with the ultra-popular set and whatever lucky girl he's dating at the moment. In a nutshell, he doesn't know I exist.

Slam! The back door flies open. My thoughts of Ethan fly away. Dad's here.

"Oh, come on!" he roars. "You're not done yet? We're late!"

I straighten up and throw him a dirty look. "Good morning to you, too, sunshine."

He glances at his watch.

"Come on, Sheridan. Much later and we might as well not bother."

"Fine," I say. "Then let's not bother. Not like going to church twice a year counts anyway."

Even the great chef Donovan Wells can't argue with that. We're only going today because the Bishop is in town for Palm Sunday mass, and he's my dad's biggest fan.

Dad huffs, pulls out his BlackBerry, and leans against the counter. "We're going. So please hurry," he says, cranking out a text.

I step back and survey the cake again, tapping a finger on my lower lip. He reads another message and is suddenly standing next to me.

"What's the problem? It's done, it's great, fantastic. Let's go!"

"It's not done," I whisper.

His phone vibrates and he walks away.

What's missing? I stop and close my eyes. I hear the doorbell jingle over and over again at the front of the bakery as customers stop by for their Sunday muffins, pastries, and coffee cakes. It's a happy sound that reminds me of better days.

"We are so late!" Dad rails in a deep vibrato, like he's going to blow.

Better days. When my father's voice was not volcanic; when my mom was here for me. I picture her. Soft hair, streaked golden. Long fingers with trimmed nails painted cotton candy pink. Pastry bag in hand. Always smiling.

It's all in the details, Cupcake.

That's what she'd say.

And then, like magic, I know what's missing. Shimmer dust. Yes.

I make a beeline for the supply shelf, grab a jar and a small paintbrush. A light touch with the fine glittering sugar on her scales and the apples of her cheeks and the mermaid comes to life under my hand.

Now she's done.

Thanks, Mom.

I push the cake toward the corner of the stainless-steel counter. It must weigh at least fifty pounds.

"Dad? A little help?" He's sending another text.

Finally, he pockets the phone and lifts an end. We move Tara's mermaid into the cooler, where she'll wait for someone to pick her up.

Poor thing doesn't have a chance. She'll be ravaged by the St. Mary High varsity football team while the birthday girl and her fellow cheerleaders munch on carrot sticks and watch.

Makes me sad, but it is part of the job. Cakes are made to be eaten.

Dad is already at the back door, holding it open, waiting. Just once I wish he'd take some time to look at my cakes. Notice the details, maybe compliment me. But he doesn't do that, ever.

I tear off my pink polka-dotted apron, grab my winter coat, and stick my head up front.

"See ya, Nan!" I yell to my grandmother, who owns the place, but she can't hear me because her head is in the muffin case. Sweetie's Bake Shoppe is bustling, and I smile. I love this place, where I've spent a part of almost every day since birth. Where I learned how to decorate cakes and discovered that it's what I do best.

These days, I'm the go-to girl in town for awesome cakes. I can make anything, for anyone, for any occasion. I am Cake Girl.

"Oh my God, Sheridan. Let's go!" And then there's my father. In his world lately, I'm barely a blip on the radar.

As we walk in the freezing cold to Blessed Sacrament, Dad mumbles that he needs to get in and out because he's expecting a call from Sebastian. Sebastian is the agent from New York who is trying to make my dad a TV star.

The church is only two blocks away, but by the time we get there, it's standing room only. It looks like everyone in St. Mary is here.

But we're okay, of course; the Bishop has reserved seats for us. In the front row.

Walking up the center aisle of the jam-packed sanctuary

twenty minutes late is utterly mortifying. Almost every face is familiar, and I can see the words *Who do they think they are?* floating in the air like a cartoon word bubble.

The Bishop smiles and nods at us, probably imagining the dinner Dad will make for him later. But Father Crowley (aka Growly), who is here every week and knows we never come, watches us with his fire-and-brimstone eyes.

We excuse ourselves past Mr. and Mrs. Durbin, who are sitting in the front row because they were on time. Then Dad and I settle in and listen to the end of the sermon about Jesus's final ride into Jerusalem, when all the people waved palms and screamed at him like he was Elvis or something.

Nanny took me to her church a lot when I was little, so I know some Bible stories, and this one always bothered me. I mean, these people got all excited about seeing the Son of God and then a few days later they killed him?

The lesson here: even Jesus couldn't count on people. How sad is that?

I'm contemplating these deep thoughts when an ear-piercing ringtone jolts me back to reality. It's coming from Dad's pocket. You can hear the collective turn of all the heads in the place. Even the Bishop looks a little annoyed. But Dad doesn't notice; he opens his jacket and pulls out his phone.

He peers at the screen and stands up. *Don't do it, Dad. Don't take a call during church.* Surprise: he pushes his way past the Durbins without a word to me.

I grab the thick hymnal in front of me and flop it open to a random page, hoping it will suck me up and spit me out in some alternate universe where my father still behaves like a human. I look up and see Growly's forehead vein popping out as he prays for our doomed souls.

The choir starts singing, and I rise to join the communion line. Mrs. Faxon stands behind me and gives me a sympathetic squeeze on the arm. She's been the secretary at the elementary school since the beginning of time and was there the day Mom didn't come to pick me up. That afternoon, Mrs. Faxon held my hand and let me eat some of the dusty conversation hearts from the dish on her desk. She knows the whole sad story.

I make my way up to the altar. Growly stares daggers into my eyes as I stand in front of him, my palms open.

"Body of Christ," he says, jamming the wafer into my hand. He's probably surprised that I don't burst into flames. He's one of my grandmother's best friends (don't ask me why), so he knows the whole story, too: my mom ran off with a stranger, leaving Dad with both a crazy busy restaurant and a really confused seven-year-old.

"Amen," I say, trying to look as sorry as I feel.

When I get back to the pew and lower myself to the kneeler, I squeeze my eyes tight, thankful that this is almost over.

The Bishop says the closing prayer, and I feel my cell phone vibrate in the pocket of my dress. I ignore it and sneak out the side door as quickly as I can, trying to avoid Growly and anyone else who just witnessed my father's horrid behavior. Outside, I dig under my thick white parka for the phone and see a text from Dad.

Come to S&I now.

My heart falls with a plop into my stomach, and I walk down the hill toward Sheridan & Irving's, the restaurant that Mom and Dad opened before I was born. It's named after the street corner in Chicago where they met. Romantic, yes—minus the fairy-tale ending, of course.

The redbrick mansion swallows me up as I climb the front steps and push through the heavy oak doors. The restaurant is closed today, but Dad is in the kitchen. As always.

When I walk through the main dining room, I smell something wonderful. He's cooking. I sniff. Pancetta? My favorite Italian pork product. Like bacon, only better. Sniff again. Garlic, oregano, basil. The air swells with this heavenly scent. My mouth is watering.

I walk through to the kitchen. He's behind the counter, suit jacket off, white chef's jacket on.

"Hey, kid, what's up?" he says. This is most likely a rhetorical question, so I don't answer.

"I can't believe you left in the middle of church," I snap.

"Oh, relax." He laughs, rolls his eyes, and throws something in with the pancetta that makes it sizzle. "It was important. You know Sebastian—no such thing as a day of rest. But . . . he had good news." Dad picks up the pan, thrusts it forward with a pro-chef flick of his wrist, and replaces it on the burner. "They want me."

He dumps the contents of a small bowl in with the other ingredients. A shock of black hair falls onto his forehead. He looks young, even though that hair is flecked with silver. And he seems happy. Really happy.

"Good. That's great," I say, unenthused. "What are you making?"

"Frittata."

Yum. Frittata, an Italian omelet-like thing that may be my favorite food in the world. I hope I get to eat it.

He looks at me. "So you're not even going to ask?"

"Oh, sorry." I lean against the prep table on my elbows and look at him sideways. "What? Someone wants you to teach a flambé class in Timbuktu or something?"

"No." His eyes twinkle. We have the same eyes: big and brown and almond-shaped. But mine are definitely not twinkling at the moment.

"I finally got a show. My own show." A smile threatens to overtake his face. I raise my eyebrows as he circles the prep area and leans on the counter next to me.

"ExtremeCuisine TV. They're giving me my own series." He waits for me to react, but I don't. "They're gonna call it *The Single Dad Cooks*." He crosses his arms, still waiting. "Isn't that amazing? And they want to film the first episode here." He stands up tall now, puts his hands on his hips, and gulps. I can see his Adam's apple bob like a sinker at the end of a fishing pole.

I reach over to the other side of the counter, pick up a basil leaf, give it a sniff. "What's the catch?" I say, real casual, sure that there is one. I can see it in his eyes.

He laughs. "If it's a catch, it's a good one. One that you need to be open-minded about." He eyes me warily, clears his throat. "If it all works out, they want us to move to New York." Another hard swallow. "The city." He looks a little scared of me right now. And he should be.

"Wait, wait, wait." My hand is up and my mind is swimming. He's been talking about having a show forever, but he never mentioned having to move. "New York City? Why wouldn't they film it here? This is where you cook."

"Because they're serious. This isn't a onetime thing. They are hiring me to work for them, in their studios."

Now my arms cross. We look like a couple of wild animals staring each other down, waiting to see who strikes first. "Well, I'm not moving anywhere." My words are sharp, each syllable distinct, so that he'll understand me.

He squints his eyes up really small and mashes his lips together. "Sheridan, why wouldn't you want to go to New York? It's a great city. Museums, parks . . . bakeries." He must be desperate to mention bakeries, since he thinks I spend too much time in ours.

With a weak smile, he stretches out his arm to touch my shoulder, but I step back before he can reach me.

"Why would I want to go to a bakery in New York?" My voice goes squeaky. "The best bakery in the world is right here. And there are parks and museums all over the place. Right here. Where we already live." I wave my arms in frustration and turn around to leave. I can't listen to any more of this.

But Dad stands tall and grabs my shoulder. "Sheridan, don't walk away from me."

I spin back around, stick out my chin, and stare directly into his eyes. His posture relaxes, just a little. "Just hear me out, okay? Please?"

I shrug.

"Look. I really want this for you. It'll be a good thing—I promise. You could stand to have your horizons broadened a bit."

"Oh, gee," I snort. "That's really nice of you, but my horizons are just fine the way they are."

As I work hard to maintain my determined expression, I think of how Dad and I have really gone downhill over the last few years. When he's not at the restaurant, he's traveling all over the world, cooking at conventions, judging contests, trying to build the Donovan Wells "brand"—that's what his agent calls it, like he's a bar of soap or something.

Now he's totally branded, and he's got a show and big plans to turn my world upside down. "I'll stay right here, thank you very much," I say forcefully.

"You'll do what you're told," he says, like one of the

communist dictators we're studying in world history.

"No. I won't. I need to be here." I look away for a second and gulp, then meet his stare again. "For when Mom comes back."

He laughs out loud. "Seriously?"

"Don't laugh at me."

"Well, don't bring *her* into this," he says like he's just tasted something nasty. He hates my mother and he'd love it if I forgot about her altogether. But that's not going to happen.

I take a step backward, lean in just a little. "She *is* in this, Dad." My words hiss out, like steam from a pressure cooker. I get a whiff of the frittata, though I have a feeling I'm not getting any now.

There's a flicker in his eyes. Did I just win this argument? Or did he just realize that he could easily leave me behind?

Not that I couldn't live without him, but the thought makes something inside of me crack, like a tiny fissure in the earth. If he left, everything would change. And I've had enough change to last a lifetime.

We're still staring at each other, an ocean of silence between us, when I hear a battalion of footsteps heading toward the kitchen. In bursts his crew: his waitstaff, bartenders, sous-chefs, maître d'—even the busboys. They start clapping, whistling, and hooting.

As if someone just picked up a remote and changed his

channel, Dad's eyes reignite and his scowl morphs into a cheesy grin. I watch him as Danny the sous-chef pops open a bottle of champagne. Dad winks at the new waitress, who is giggling in his direction. It's like he's been waiting for this moment his whole life.

Someone starts a toast. I make my way toward the door and back into the dining room unnoticed. As I step onto the front porch, I pull my coat tight around my body and peer into the gray sky. Looks like it's going to snow, even though it's supposed to be spring.

My stomach is rumbling. I'm starving. God, I really wanted that frittata.

I reach inside my coat pocket, pull out a small red heart cut from construction paper. It's the note Mom slipped into my lunch box the day she left.

Love you, Cupcake, she wrote, in perfect, curly script.

I fold the note and slip it back into my pocket. An hour ago my biggest problem was getting her back here. Now I've got to worry about Dad leaving, too? Or worse, forcing me to go with him?

I walk around the restaurant to the carriage house behind it. That's where we live. I take a few deep breaths and try to calm down; to think of things that make me happy. Cakes. My friends, this town where I've grown up, where I have a life.

But I keep backtracking to the things that make me unhappy. Like ExtremeCuisine TV and New York City and

Dad taking off, with or without me. And the fact that I have no idea where my mother is. She had sent me a birthday card every year since she left. And my fourteenth birthday, she wrote this:

Guess what? I'm single again. And I'm finally coming to see you!

That was the best news ever. The guy she left us for was some crazy world-traveling businessman. Always in South Africa or New Zealand or some weird place that made it impossible for Mom to visit.

But no card came on my fifteenth birthday, and now I'm about to turn sixteen. It's been almost two years since I've heard from her. And now, more than ever, I need to know why.

That's the problem, I think as I force cold air deep into my lungs. Like those losers in Jerusalem who crucified Jesus, or birthday cards, or fathers who want to be famous. You can't count on anything, can you?

Except for this one thing: I am not going anywhere.

Chapter 2

WAKE UP AND SMELL THE COFFEE

I wish I could convince myself that the world is not spinning off into the stratosphere, that it will all be okay.

But honestly, I'm freaking out. I know my dad. This show means everything to him.

I cross the parking lot to the house. Directly behind it is an alley, hidden by a row of cherry trees.

The alley runs along the back of a row of two-story businesses on Main Street, and one of those businesses is Sweetie's. I can see the windows of Nanny's apartment above the bakery, just over the treetops. A fire escape leads to a narrow balcony where she sits in warm weather, drinks sweet tea, and thinks of Texas. She was born there but moved to Michigan after she met my grandfather and fell in love.

From where I stand, I can see the hopeful pot of yellow pansies on the balcony, and I feel a little better. Another deep breath, and another.

Having her so close, looking down on my entire life, has its drawbacks. But sometimes knowing Nanny's always there is just what I need.

I walk up the front steps of my house, feeling calmer. I dig the key out of my pocket.

Tonight we'll eat dinner at Nanny's; we have standing plans every Sunday night. When we get there, she'll talk some sense into Dad. She'll convince him that the Wells family belongs in St. Mary. If he wants a show, they can film it here.

Still, his words rattle in my brain. *Broaden my horizons?* What's wrong with my horizons, anyway?

I push open the door. This was once the gigantic garage of the house that is now Sheridan & Irving's. My parents renovated it when they bought the restaurant and turned it into our home. The cavernous front room (where the carriages once lined up) is usually full of sunlight, but today the drapes are closed and the heat is turned down. It's dark and drafty.

It's only noon, still an hour before I meet Jack and Lori for coffee. Just enough time for a run. So I flick on the lights and search the foyer for my Nikes. A run is just what I need right now, to get my mind off things.

I spot the shoes under the sideboard, grab them, and

sprint up to my room. Last year, as a freshman, I joined the cross-country team but missed too many practices. I loved running and being part of the team, but cakes don't decorate themselves, and I had to quit. Now I run by myself or sometimes with Jack if I want company.

I reach around to unzip my dress, then toss off my heels and slip into my St. Mary High running pants, a long-sleeve turtleneck, and my fleece jacket.

Carefully, I place Mom's heart-shaped note in my jewelry box. When she left, Dad got rid of all her stuff: pictures, books, clothes. Now there's barely anything left to remind us she once lived in this house. But I've got this heart and the cards that came every year. I quickly rummage for the box, deep in my closet, open it, and pick out the card on top, the one from my fourteenth birthday. There it is, in blue ink.

Guess what? I'm single again. And . . . I'm finally coming to see you! I've been all over the world, but I was happiest there. Wouldn't it be fun if we could work together in the bakery? Although by now you could probably teach me a thing or two. As soon as I can, I'll be home. I can't wait! I love you, Cupcake. —*Mom*

I close the card and stash it away again with all the others. How can I leave when she's coming back?

Before I head out, I sneak a peek in the mirror above my dresser, run a brush through my hair. Somehow, between my father's black hair and Mom's blonde, I ended up a redhead. My hair is dark auburn, actually. I like it—it's unusual—but it can be too wavy and hard to control. So I throw it up in a ponytail, then swipe on some Chap Stick and pull on a headband that will keep my ears warm.

I sigh. Leaning toward the mirror, I look deep into my own eyes and tell myself that everything is going to be fine.

I walk out the back door, then start down the alley, purposely avoiding Main Street. The last thing I need is to run into a well-meaning neighbor who wants to make small talk.

So I stick to the edges of town and head to the water. The St. Mary harbor is always crowded in warmer weather, but today, there's a brisk wind coming off Lake Michigan, too cold for most people. I hope.

The steady *pound-pound* of my feet fills my ears, and I force myself to stop thinking about the show, about Mom, about New York City.

I think about cake instead.

There's a big order next weekend for the Bailey wedding. Nanny will have to help me with this one; they want four tiers covered with gum paste lilac blossoms. I need to start making the flowers on Thursday after school. I can't wait.

My mind moves on to the cake for prom as the wind whips my ponytail into my eyes. I'm not going, of course, being only a sophomore, but the committee has already placed its order. The theme is "The Time of Our Lives," after that old Green Day song. I sketched them a cake of the high school's clock tower, and they loved it.

I happily plan cakes as the town drops away and I begin to hear the gentle ping of metal on mast, the dull thud of boat against buoy, the high-pitched squeal of gulls. All as familiar as the sound of my own voice.

The harbor walk is empty. I creak onto the docks, head down to the last slip, where we once kept our sailboat.

There's a wooden plank near the edge. Carved into it are the initials *DW* and *MT,* in the middle of a lopsided heart. Donovan Wells and Margaret Taylor, my parents.

Dad etched it in the wood the first time he brought her sailing, after they met in college.

We used to sail all the time. But after she took off, he put the boat in storage.

I sit down, my feet dangling over the water. I turn toward the lake, so big, constant, dependable. My heart twists. God, I want my mother back so bad that the longing has become a real thing, like a giant suitcase I lug around with me everywhere I go. A minute doesn't pass that I don't wonder where she is and why the cards stopped. Not one minute.

When Jack's ringtone blasts from inside my jacket, I jump. I look around and grab for my phone clumsily like I'm waking up from a restless nap. How long have I been sitting here?

"Hey!" I answer.

"Where are you?" he asks, sounding impatient.

"Why? What time is it?"

"Um . . . time to be here."

I lift myself off the pier. "Okay, give me a minute. I'm at the harbor."

He hangs up and I get ready to run, but not before I bend over and touch the initials, reminding myself that once we were a family.

Geronimo's Coffeehouse and Gift Emporium sits on the north side of the town square, between Mrs. Trang's Pilates Palace and Animal Cracker's Day Care. This is where every teenager in St. Mary hangs out, and Jack works here, too, to keep his broken-down Corolla up and running.

But today is his day off, and now he's annoyed that I'm late.

As soon as I walk in, the smell of coffee drives its way up into my cerebral cortex, or whatever part of my brain makes me crave a nice latte. Nanny says they'll stunt my growth, but I'm already taller than most of the boys in tenth grade, so that's fine with me.

Mrs. Davis, the owner, is busy behind the counter foaming up a cappuccino, but she still smiles and waves when I walk in. "The usual, Sheridan?"

"Yes, thanks!" I smile. No one in New York City would even know my name, much less my preference for nonfat vanilla lattes.

I can see Jack at our table near the register. He's wearing

a T-shirt that reads, I RODE THE MIND MELTER AND LIVED TO BUY THIS T-SHIRT. We both have one from last year's state fair.

"Hi," I say.

"'Bout time," he gripes without looking up.

"Oh, shut up. I have a good excuse." I take off my jacket and hang it on the coatrack behind me. "I just found out that my life is over."

"Right." He straightens some papers in front of him, takes a sip of his coffee.

I pull out a chair and sit.

"So," Jack says, "your life is over. What'd you do—break a nail?"

"Yeah, right." I hold up my nails, all of them chipped and stained purple from coloring the fondant for my mermaid. I shift in my chair. "No. Dad finally got a show. A cooking-slash-reality show on ExtremeCuisine TV."

Jack's eyes bug out, and he slaps a hand on the table. "What? Are you kidding me?"

I look at his angular face and scowl. "Do I look like I'm kidding?"

Why in the world does he look so happy?

"That's awesome! I love that channel!" He grabs my hand and waves it in the air, making a whooping noise. I yank my arm back and glare at him.

"What's wrong with you?" he asks.

"He says we have to move. To New York City. Both of us." Jack's mouth snaps shut. Yeah, that got him.

"Well, maybe you won't have to. *Hopefully*, you won't have to." He looks worried.

"Oh. I'm not moving; I don't care what he says."

"You could live with Nan until you graduate. Or you could live with us!"

I'd rather use store-bought tub frosting than live with Jack's family, though of course I'd never tell him that. He has three little brothers who are constantly farting and burping.

I smile at him as sweetly as possible. "Thanks. But I'm gonna talk to him. I mean, what's going to happen to the restaurant? He can't just leave."

Jack's got this faraway look in his eyes. "Although, think about it; he's pretty well known now, but if he had his own show, he could be *famous*. You guys could be *loaded*." He leans back in his chair and grins. "Not Michigan loaded, either; I'm talking Hollywood, baby. Ferraris, indoor pools, maybe a butler . . . Maybe you'll end up with *your* own show. They can call it *Cake Girl*. Now *that* I would watch."

"Oh my God, can you not sound so excited about this?"

The corners of his mouth fall in a dramatic frown. "Sorry. Who would want a Ferrari, anyway? Cheap-ass car."

"Jack. Come on. I'm not going anywhere. What about my cakes? What about Mom?" Doesn't he realize if Dad forced me to New York, I'd be leaving behind everything that is important to me? Even him. I've known him since preschool. I can't imagine life minus Jack.

He touches my hand. "Hey. Relax. Why don't you just

wait and see what happens instead of flipping out right away?" I look into his eyes and calm down a little. He's right. Maybe I don't need to panic. Not yet, anyway.

He looks down at the paper in front of him.

"What is that?" I ask.

He smiles wide and lifts the top page by the corner. "This, my friend, could be what we've been looking for. I think I might have found your mom."

"What?" I grab the paper out of his hand and try to focus my eyes on what's in front of me. "What is this?"

"It's a picture of a cake from a contest in Ottawa. Look at it."

It's got three tiers, covered in white fondant. And it is positively crawling with sapphire-colored butterflies. My mother was known for her sugar butterflies. They looked just like the real thing. These look just like the real thing.

"So? Lots of people make sugar butterflies." I let the paper fall onto the table.

"People named Maggie Taylor?"

"What?"

He hands me the next page in his pile. "Yeah, look."

I see a list of names. Next to the words *Grand Prize* is the name Maggie Taylor. That was my mother's maiden name.

"It makes sense, Sheridan. Last time you heard she was in Canada, right?"

I nod.

"Ottawa is in Canada, right?"

I nod, trying to pace my excitement. "But that's a common name."

"Yeah, but then I found this." He hands me another printout from a Web page. It's almost the same cake, but this one is covered with monarch butterflies.

"What's this from?"

"It's from a hotel on Mackinac that does wedding receptions. Read the caption."

"Cake by Maggie Taylor."

For the first time in a long while, I have this funny feeling deep inside my gut. Like this time it's really her.

I sit back in my chair. "Wow."

"Yeah, wow. What do you think?"

"I don't know. Maybe?"

Jack's smile is big and bright. "Could be a coincidence, but Mackinac isn't that far."

Mrs. Davis walks over to our table. "Here you go, kiddo." She puts down a cardboard cup. "So, how you guys doing today?"

"Good, thanks." I pull a five out of my front pocket. "And thank you for the latte." I grab the coffee and take a hot sip.

"Oh, no problem. And keep your money." She leans forward, her huge bosom nearly touching the table. "I heard there's reason to celebrate? There's a little rumor floating around, about your dad?"

What? My mouth turns up in an insincere smile. I shake my head. "Not a done deal yet, Mrs. D." I hand her the five.

She straightens up and refuses it again. "Oh. I shoulda known. But that's one rumor I wouldn't mind coming true. God knows your dad's worked hard enough for it." She smiles. "He's done a lot to put this town on the map. But his own show, on ExtremeCuisine? Now that would be exciting."

I shake my head. "Yeah, right. But no, it's not for sure."

"Well, keep me posted, will ya?"

"Yep."

She walks back to the counter.

I get right back to the matter at hand. "Maybe I should call that hotel. Maybe they can tell me about her."

Jack's mouth is set in a firm line. "Sheridan . . . slow down." He's thinking of the other near misses over the last year. "You need me to remind you?"

Um, no.

He counts off on his fingers. "Huh. Let's start with Margaret Taylor of Omaha, Chinese American—definitely not your mother. Or Maggie Wells in Boulder, who called the cops because she thought you were stalking her? Or should we just skip to Maggie Taylor in San Diego, who was, what . . . was she in the first or second grade?"

I cross my arms and slump in my chair. "I hate you."

"Sheridan, all I'm saying is be careful."

"Well, calling the hotel is being careful. I'll just find out where she's based and if they have her phone number."

He shakes his head. "Just don't do anything stupid. Yet." Jack folds the paper, gives it to me, and glances over my head toward the door. I follow his eyes and see Lori winding through the maze of chairs and tables.

"Hey!" Lori says, unraveling her scarf and sitting down. She scans our faces. "Who died?"

Jack grins. "Oh, Sheridan's just pissed off because she might have to get a butler." I give him a good kick in the shin.

"Yow!" he wails.

"Well, one of you better tell me what's going on." She fluffs her dark hair and stares at me.

I lower my voice and tell her about the show, but I also say that she shouldn't worry, because we are not moving anywhere—I'll talk my father out of this.

"Talk him out of it? Are you nuts?"

I smack the table. "Jeez, I'm glad you guys are so excited." I stand up and go for my coat. "If you want to get rid of me so bad, I'll just leave now."

"Oh, give me a break. Where do you think you're going?" Lori asks.

My face is hot and I'm flustered, angry. "I have about a million things to do at the bakery."

"Sit down," Lori says. "You're not working on any stupid cake today."

Jack laughs and leans back in his chair. He's got this confident look that makes other girls go wild, but it just makes me want to punch his face. "No one wants you to move," he says. "But you may be the only person in the world who wouldn't be excited about your dad getting a TV show."

I plop back down on my chair. "Well, I'm not, okay?"

"Fine," Lori says. "You are entitled to act like a complete idiot, and for my own selfish reasons, I hope you stay put. If I'm stuck here in the fourth level of hell, you should be, too."

That's more like it. I can't imagine not seeing these guys on a daily basis. I take a sip of my latte and tell myself to mellow out, relax—be happy, even. We might have found Mom.

Lori brings up Thursday's big history test, and then talk turns to hot guys, much to Jack's disgust. After a while, I am able to forget about moving and my missing mother. Forget that New York City exists. I smile and laugh and soak in the coziness of this place.

"You guys want a muffin?" I stand up during a lull in the conversation, my back to the counter. When I turn around, I walk directly into a wide expanse of black wool coat.

"Excuse me," I apologize. The back I've run into twists to face me, and I find myself looking up at Ethan Murphy in all his blazing hotness. Our eyes fuse for a millisecond.

"Hey, don't worry about it," he says, with a voice that could melt steel. He doesn't turn back around but lifts a finger and points at me. "Do I know you?"

I just look at him, dumbstruck. His hair is longish, messy blond. The kind that makes you want to run your fingers through it. I'm suddenly afraid that I won't be able to control myself, so I clasp my hands behind my back, just in case.

His eyes are so blue, his smile flanked by gorgeous dimples, his shoulders broad under his thick peacoat. And then there's that voice. Hot lava. Rumbling thunder. These are the images that spring to mind.

I need to speak, to answer him, but my tongue feels like a rock. Maybe I'm having a stroke.

"Dude, you comin'?" some random jock shouts in his direction. Ethan smiles.

"Gotta go," he whispers, just to me.

"Uhh . . . ," I say, like a Neanderthal.

That's when I hear the high-pitched screech. "Come on, Ethan!" Without looking, I know that it's Haley Haversham. His current girlfriend. And the closest thing I have to an archenemy.

"Why don't you go and decorate something, Cake Girl?" She laughs at her clever comment from the door, and a few girls in her mindless entourage laugh along with her.

Haley is a Harpy, a Gorgon, and all the other awful female monsters we studied in ninth-grade English rolled into one.

But Ethan ignores her shrill wailing. "Ahh," he says, quiet enough so that only I can hear him. The warm air coming out of his mouth makes me blush. "Cake Girl."

My heart beats faster, but in a good way. I smile. "Yep."

"Eeeeeeethaaaan!" Haley again, the she-devil.

He smiles once more, winks, then turns and walks away. His arm swings up and around Haley as she glares at me. They move toward the door, and I watch as she sinks her head into his Superman shoulders.

"So I guess I'm not getting a muffin?" Jack breaks me out of my trance.

"My God, Sheridan. Why don't you just get it over with and jump his bones?" Lori laughs.

I fumble for my chair and sit. "Jump his bones? Could you be more crass?"

Lori nods. "Oh, yes. Yes, I can."

We laugh. But not Jack.

"That guy is a loser," he proclaims.

"Who cares? He's hot," Lori counters.

"Could you be more pathetic?" he says, looking at me.

"What?" I ask.

"Could you be more jealous?" Lori says, scooting her chair back and standing up. "I'll get the friggin' muffins."

"You know I'm not jealous," Jack says to me after she's gone. "But that guy has gone out with at least one girl in all the major cliques. Next it's band geeks, chess club, and cake decorators."

I laugh, sincerely amused. "First of all, Jack, thanks for making me feel so supercool. Second, I am not going out with him. Not a chance. He's dating *her*. And I'm *me*. No one wants to date Cake Girl."

He sighs and shakes his head. "Man, you've got some serious issues."

I nod in agreement. "Don't I know it."

A few hours and too many cups of coffee later, the three of us jitter out the door. Lori waves good-bye, heading off to a babysitting gig, and Jack and I stand in the frigid air. "You wanna go work on the art project?" he asks.

Ugh. The art project. A series of nature sketches, due in three weeks. I only took the class because Jack said it would be an easy A. He didn't mention that Mrs. Ely is a pain in the butt who seems to think we should spend all of our free time drawing pictures for her.

I hang my head. "No. I don't want to work on the art project."

He tsk-tsks.

"Don't worry. I'll get it done." I glance at my watch. "But I gotta go." If I get home soon, I'll have time to sit with my laptop and search for Mom in Mackinac before I head to Nanny's for dinner.

Jack looks at me and digs his hands into his pockets. Something's wrong.

"What is it?" I ask.

"Nothin'. Just . . . promise me you won't do anything yet?"

"Sure. I promise." I lift my hand and force my fingers into the Girl Scout salute, or what I remember of it, anyway, since I was only in Brownies for one year.

"Let me keep looking for information. We don't need a repeat of Boulder," he warns.

"Yeah. That woman was crazy."

His wide smile spreads. "Right. *She* was the crazy one." His nose is turning a little pink from the cold. His dark eyes sparkle.

"Of course she was. I am completely rational." I smile.

He turns and walks the other way, toward his house. "Keep telling yourself that," he shouts over his shoulder.

I zip up my fleece and pull on my headband. It's totally freezing, and the town square is Sunday-afternoon empty, but I am warm from the cozy coffee shop and an extreme caffeine buzz.

I look up to the hills that surround the eastern edge of St. Mary, covered with trees that are still bare from winter. I love this place: so safe, always the same.

If I can just find Mom, things won't seem nearly so bleak. Or if Nanny and I can talk to Dad, convince him that we belong here, that leaving is not an option . . .

So many ifs. The wind blows, and I hang on tight to the printouts Jack gave me. They're like pages of hope, right here in my hand, and I'm not letting them fly away.

Chapter 3

PIECE OF CAKE

$\mathscr{I}$ slide the folded papers into my coat pocket. By the time I get home, it's colder and my lungs are sore from breathing the frosty air. I run up the back steps and slip the key in the lock, ready to get warm and boot up the laptop, and then . . .

"Sheridan!" Nanny shouts from her balcony in that thick Texas drawl. "Get over here, darlin'. I need some help." Aw, crap.

Fine. Key in my pocket, I look up at her. She's smiling, apparently clueless about Dad and the show.

"Well, don't just stand there starin'. Get on up here!"

I walk to the opening in the chain-link fence, cross the alley, and climb the stairs. At the top, she catches me in a big hug.

"Hey." I hug back.

"Well, hey yourself." She grabs my shoulders, holds me away from her, and looks me in the eye. "You look sadder than a flounder at a fish fry."

I shake my head. "I have news." I move past her and step into her warm kitchen. "Bad news," I add.

"Oh. Dear. That's the worst kind, ain't it?" Nanny follows me inside and closes the door. "Well, you can tell me all about it while we get busy. We got us a cake to decorate."

"Who for?" I ask, pointing to the plain white nine-inch round cake in the center of the kitchen island.

"Who do you think?"

My eyebrows crinkle together. "I have no idea."

"Well, your father, of course."

"Dad? You mean you know?" I ask, shocked.

"Of course I know. You think I don't know things? This is a big day. For all of us." She's bustling around the kitchen like it's Christmas.

I am officially paralyzed. "Are you serious? Did he tell you?"

"Yes, indeed." She pulls a pot out of a cabinet, the corners of her eyes all wrinkled up like it's the happiest day of her entire life. "And that phone hasn't stopped ringin'." She laughs. "Good old St. Mary telegraph. News round here hops from one person to the next like a frog on fire."

This cannot be happening. She hasn't thought this through. She doesn't know all the facts.

"But you don't know. He says they want him to move to

New York!" My voice reaches up an octave. "And he thinks I'm going with him!"

"Oh, calm down." She opens the fridge and hands me a plastic container full of pastry bags. They're stuffed with different colors of buttercream. She waves me over and stares down at the cake.

"Whaddya think? The ExtremeCuisine logo? We can pop it up on the computer. Or you think we should go simpler?"

"Nan? Are you kidding? How about a one-way, no-return ticket to New York City?"

She turns to me, purses her lips. "How about a nice sentiment? Nothing too smart-alecky." She nudges the container of buttercream wedged under my arm. "Do your thing, girl."

I shake my head. Fine. I tear open the lid and search for black. Perfect.

I look down at the circle in front of me. The white field of icing makes me think of Mom. When I was little, she'd level her cakes and give me the leftover crumbling humps for practice. There's nothing like staring at a blank cake. She'd also let me sit in on her cake decorating classes. I was young, but I listened to every word she said. "The cake is a blank canvas, and you are the artist." That was one of her lines. "Follow your artist's heart." That was another.

Of course, right now my heart is telling me to write, in my best curly script, *You suck, Dad!*

In black, of course.

I pick up the sleeve and squeeze the icing to the top. Nanny's still bopping around the kitchen like a spaz.

"Why are you so excited?" I say, frustrated. "There's no way I'm leaving my customers. Who am I gonna make cakes for in New York City? I'm not going." I bend over as a delicate trail of black sweetness emerges from the bag.

"Oh now, stop it." She's at the fridge again. "All that business will work itself out. I'm just goin' to enjoy the moment. It's a dream come true for your daddy."

"Dream?" I put the bag down. "What? To leave St. Mary and get all rich and famous? Great for him. What about the rest of us?"

"Oh, Sheridan, good Lord, don't get your drawers in a wad. I don't know about the rich and famous stuff. But I *understand*. He wants something bigger for himself. And for you. He's had a truckload of hurt here. Maybe he's finally ready to let go and move on."

That's it. She's talking crazy now. "Are you kidding? He let go of Mom a long time ago. Just ask all his girlfriends."

Nanny laughs again. I am offended.

"Please don't laugh at me."

Suddenly, she's at my side, her arm around my shoulder. "I ain't laughin' at you. And just because someone goes and gets himself a girlfriend don't mean he's moved on. That whole mess with your mother near killed him."

"Whatever."

She walks to the sink with a colander full of green beans, starts snapping off the ends. "You know, most kids would be over-the-moon thrilled about their parent gettin' a TV show."

"Well, I am not. Just because everyone thinks I should be all excited doesn't mean that I am."

I put down the black and pick up the red. The colors of blood and death. Perfect. I squeeze the red now, follow the line that the icing is making beneath me, but my mind is somewhere far away.

"Well, we're going to talk him out of it," I say. "People here depend on him. He has a restaurant, you, me. He has responsibilities here."

Nanny watches me, snaps a few beans. "Oh, *we're* going to talk him out of it, are we? You think that's the right thing to do?"

My stomach flips. "Why not? What about me? What about my cakes? If he really cares about what I want, he'll stay. What about you? You need us here."

She keeps on snapping. "Oh please, listen to that giant pity party you're throwin' yourself. Maybe he just wants you to see that the world is a little bigger than St. Mary."

"That's not true, and you know it." I stand back to survey my work. Very boring. "If I move to New York, I won't see the world at all; I'll be locked away in some tiny apartment, alone, making cakes for nobody. No trees. Gangs. Rats. Drug dealers right outside the door. You think that's what I need?"

Nanny sighs deeply. "Do me a favor and turn down the

drama just a tad. And don't make up your mind about this just yet."

My face is only inches from the cake as I add shadow details to the letters I've piped. Not my best work, that's for certain.

I think of the cake that I made for Libby Carman's fifth birthday a few weeks ago. An entire barnyard complete with cows, pigs, horses, dogs, ducks—all sculpted from modeling chocolate. Now *that* was a masterpiece. Where in the world would St. Mary go for cakes if I lived in New York City?

I straighten up, put down the red buttercream. This cake is so dull. As an afterthought, I add black and red polka dots to it, because, let's face it, I don't do boring.

"Voilà," I say, with little enthusiasm. I lift the cake at an angle for Nanny to see.

"Good luck." She reads it in her flattest drawl and frowns. "Yes, well, that's certainly heartfelt, isn't it?"

"Totally." I push the thing to the center of the island and start cleaning up.

Once everything is put away, I walk to the sink, where Nanny is filling the pot with water. She looks at my puppy dog eyes and stuck-out lower lip, turns off the faucet, and lifts my chin. "You know, dear, you could look at this like it's a good thing. Like maybe the man upstairs has bigger plans for you than you might have for yourself." She tilts her head upward.

Great. Now she's going to get all Baptist on me.

I turn my face away from her. "Right. You might want to ask Father Crowley about that. The way he looked at me this morning, I'm pretty sure he thinks God's written me off completely."

"What?" She flips on the stove, hoists the pot onto the fire. "That old coot has nothin' to do with it. Neither does your father. And neither, I might add, does your mama. Your life is yours to make the most of, or completely screw up. Your choice."

She whips open the oven, where a huge roast is starting to brown. "Although I'd recommend letting the big guy take the lead." She jerks her head upward again. "Way better than the alternative. Trust me."

"You know, it is true. . . ." I lean on my elbow, chin in my hand, and watch her as she bastes the meat. "This plan is awesome so far. Dad barely notices me. Mom is who-knows-where. I can't wait to see what happens next!"

Nanny stops and grabs hold of my wrist. Her eyes are so fierce I can't return her stare. "Now you just stop that kind of talk, girl. You have so many gifts. A tender heart. More talent than you know what to do with. And"—she loosens her grip—"you're a true blessing of a granddaughter."

I look at her. She's as sweet as can be. I can't imagine not seeing her every day.

"I just don't want things to change, Nanny. Not again." A tear pools in the corner of my eye. "Everyone thinks something's wrong with me because I'm not excited. Isn't it okay that I just want things to stay the way they are?"

"Well, of course it is. This is your home, and it is part of you." She wipes away the tear that's falling down my cheek. "But darlin', that will always be true. No matter where you're at. All's I'm sayin' is, just hold tight and see what's waiting for you, baby. Don't sell yourself short." She pats my back. "We'll talk to your daddy, tell him what worries you. But right now, we got us a supper to cook. Why don't you flip on the record player?"

"It's a CD player, Nan," I sigh. We've covered this before. She shrugs as I reach for the power button and press Play. "Mamma Mia," by Nanny's favorite band of all time, ABBA, blasts across the kitchen. She starts disco dancing, chopping board in one hand and a chunk of salt pork in the other.

I laugh, but as I peel potatoes for dinner, my worries pile up like the skins that fall into the sink.

It's six o'clock and Dad isn't here. I call his cell when we sit down to dinner. Leave a message. Text him twice. No answer.

Where is he? Maybe sitting around telling Extreme Cuisine stories to his adoring staff; maybe off with that giggly new waitress. Who knows?

Nanny and I sit down to eat. Only I'm not hungry at all. We're in the small dining room, and the light from above catches the edges of the crystal glasses that Nanny has set out for this celebration. We're even using the fine china that belonged to my great-grandmother.

Nanny is concerned. I can tell. She puts her hand on

mine, talks to me like I'm four. "Remember what I said, baby doll. Maybe you can't see it now, but there's so much in store for you." She puts a hand on her heart, like she's saying the Pledge.

I don't have the energy to argue, so I stand up. I was going to talk to him, to tell him my worries. But the truth is he doesn't care. "I'd better get going. I've got homework."

"All right, but let's have a piece of that ridiculous cake first."

"No thanks. I'll pass."

"Oh, honey."

I pick up my plate and walk away.

"Darlin', I'm so sorry."

I clear the dishes in silence and give Nanny a good-night kiss. As I walk down the back stairs now covered in snow, I glance up and see her at the balcony, peering down at me.

"Love you, sugar," she calls down. I hope she gets on the phone after I'm gone and leaves Dad a nasty voice mail.

"You, too," I say, trudging across the alley.

Back at the house, the message light on the phone is blinking like a Christmas tree. I listen to the first three: Jake Trotter from the *St. Mary Courier* wants to set up an interview; Christopher something-or-other from the *Grand Rapids Times* does, too; and Catherine Dupree, anchorwoman from the local TV station where Dad's done a few cooking segments in the past, reminds him that she's responsible, in part, for his success and asks if she can have an exclusive interview.

There are ten more messages, but I hang up and walk away. Upstairs, I throw on an old T-shirt and worn-out flannel pajama pants. I try to study, but Algebra II has never seemed so useless and my laptop is calling me.

I scour the Internet for *mackinac island bakery* and get a bunch of hits, but nothing seems like a clue. I type in *maggie taylor mackinac island* and I find the photo that Jack showed me. It's on the hotel's Web site, but it says to call or e-mail for information. I want to e-mail them right away. But then I remember Jack's words, and how I've been disappointed—and, okay, almost arrested—in the past. I don't want to be let down this time. This time, it's *got* to be *her.*

I do some research on Mackinac. Print out the driving directions. A little more than five hours. Maybe I could get Jack to drive me up there, if it comes to that.

Around midnight, the phone rings. It's Nanny.

"Is that dummy son of mine home yet?"

"No."

She lets out a breath. "Doggone it. I'm gonna skin him alive."

"Yeah. I guess he decided to celebrate his dream coming true in his own special way." I sigh. "No big surprise."

"You wanna sleep over here?" Nanny asks.

I look around my room. Over the years, I've spent a million nights at Nanny's, when Dad worked late at the restaurant or was traveling or working as a guest chef some-where. He's been gone a lot of nights, but I always knew he would come back. But tonight feels weird, like he's already there in New York City and he's left St. Mary behind, like an old piece of furniture that wasn't worth moving.

"No," I say, knowing I am too old to run to Nanny. "That's okay. Got homework."

"All right. Well, lock the doors. I'll be here if you need me."

"Yeah, I know."

At one o'clock, I can't focus my eyes on the computer screen anymore. I want to throw the stupid thing across the room because I've been through so many Margaret Taylors, Margaret Wellses, and even Margaret Kirbys, though she never used that name on the cards.

The cards. I grab the box out of my closet and pick up the one with the oldest postmark. She left a few months before I turned eight. There was a decorating contest in Dallas, and she'd been practicing for weeks. It was all she talked about; she was so excited. On the morning she left, she packed me a lunch, took me to school, hugged me tight, and told me to say a prayer so that she'd win.

But she didn't win, and when her plane back to Michigan left Dallas that Monday, she wasn't on it. She'd met a man named Frank Kirby and had fallen for him hard.

I was so little Nanny told me Mom was taking a vacation. Dad told me nothing. But I figured that if she was on vacation, she'd certainly send me a postcard or something. I checked the mailbox every day. And one day, just before my birthday, it was there. An envelope, with my name scrawled on the front in her handwriting.

I'm holding the card in my hand now. It is cut in the shape of a big number 8 and covered with glitter and stars. I have the message inside memorized, but I read it anyway.

I'm sorry I'm not there for your birthday. I miss you so much and will send you something from Scotland. Would you like a kilt? I'll see you soon, I promise, Cupcake. Love you, Mommy.

I close the card, put it back into the box, crawl into bed. I flip onto my side, stare out the window, and imagine her love. I can feel it, just as real as the blanket on top of me. I'm fifteen years old, but right now it's like no time has passed. I'm still eight, waiting for my kilt to show up in the mail, waiting for her to come home.

I know she hasn't been an ideal mother. I'm not stupid. But I also know that she loves me. She'll come back. Maybe so much time has passed she's feeling awkward and just needs to be asked. And Dad will stay in St. Mary when I explain how I feel. I mean, they are my parents; they'll want what's best for me, right?

I try to concentrate on the snow outside my window, falling harder now. The wet flakes sparkle in the glow of the front porch light, which Dad will turn off when he gets home. I watch and wait, but finally my eyelids give in and close like shades pulled tight.

Chapter 4

LET THEM EAT CAKE

I wake up with the perfect plan to find Mom. I'll e-mail the hotel in Mackinac and tell them that I absolutely love the monarch butterfly cake and must have the number of Maggie Taylor. Then I'll call Maggie Taylor, tell her I want her to make my wedding cake, and ask when I can come in for a consult.

We'll make small talk, and I'll ask her some questions. Like, does she have any kids? And she'll say, "Yes, I have one daughter," and then she'll start crying. And I'll tell her to stop, and that she doesn't need to cry; I'm here, waiting.

My cell phone buzzes on the nightstand. I pick it up and see a text from Jack.

Don't e-mail the hotel yet.

I throw back the covers. It's disturbing to have a mind reader for a best friend.

There's another text, from Dad, sent at two a.m.

Got caught up here.

No "sorry for missing dinner" or "we need to talk" or "I'm not gonna do that show after all." Nothing.

I don't text him back.

My thoughts turn to school and how badly I don't want to go, especially with the week I've got coming up. On Sunday, Sheridan and Irving's will host their annual Easter brunch, and I am expected to help. Plus, the Bailey wedding cake is due on Saturday morning.

I walk past Dad's room on the way to the shower and see that his bed is still made. Did he even come home? Was it the giggly waitress? Yuck.

I hop in the shower, tromp downstairs, shove spoonfuls of instant oatmeal in my mouth, and work my way through the rest of the Algebra II homework. We don't see eye to eye on many things, Dad and I, but we have one very clear understanding: if I screw up in school, drink, or do drugs, I am off cake duty. Oh, and also I am not supposed to get knocked up. As if that was even a possibility.

Dad and I used to have dinner in his office every now and then so he could check up on me and recite the rules, just so I didn't forget them. But we haven't done that in a long time, not since he's been so focused on getting this show.

I throw an apple and a bag of chips into my bag and notice my dog-eared art class sketch pad—still waiting for me to start my last big assignment of the year. So far, I've got nothing. I asked Mrs. Ely if I could sketch cakes. She looked at me funny, pulled me aside, and told me she wanted to see what else I could do.

Whatever, Mrs. Ely.

I shove on my boots, put on my coat, and sling my bag over my shoulder. When I open the back door, I see that the alley and the parking lot are covered with a thick layer of pure white snow. It's pretty, but positively arctic. I hurry across to the bakery, where Lori waits by the back door.

"Morning," she says, a mischievous glint in her eyes. "So . . . any naughty dreams about Ethan?" She laughs.

"Funny. I'm so glad you're around to crack yourself up."

"Somebody has to."

We walk through the door and are greeted by the most wonderful smells. Sugar, spice, chocolate, and fruit whirl around us like a scented dust storm. Mr. Rasic (aka Mr. Roz), Nanny's baker since forever, is pulling a sheet of cookies out of the oven.

"Ah, vat'll it be this morning, ladies?" he asks in a thick Kosovar accent, his paper hat askew on his white hair.

Lori smiles sweetly. "OMG, if you have any raspberry cream cheese, I will marry you."

"Ha!" He walks to a rack stacked with trays of baked goods. "You marry a nice young man, and Mr. Roz bake you wedding cake, okay?" He tosses a muffin into a small white paper bag.

"And for the star?" He looks at me and winks.

"Star?"

"Well, daughter of star?"

I smile politely. I love Mr. Roz like he's my own grandfather. But this is not how I want my day to start.

"No. There's not going to be a show."

He and Lori stare at me like I'm crazy. I change the subject. "Any lemon poppy seed?"

The Mr. Roz smile returns instantly. "Aha! Today you want the sweet with the tart, eh?" He bags my muffin and Nanny walks in.

"Good morning, girls. Now don't hold up Mr. Rasic; please just get your muffins and go." She looks at me. "Goodness, child, where are your mittens and scarf?" She reaches over and pulls my coat zipper up to my chin.

"I'm fine," I say, shooing her away.

"It's colder than an ice cube in Alaska out there. Don't tell me you're fine." She tries to push up my hood, but I squirm out of her grasp.

"Girl, put that hood up! And both y'all get out. I don't have time for tomfoolery today."

I am pretty sure that Nanny is the last person on earth who uses the word *tomfoolery*. She shoves us out the back door.

"Confounded teenagers!" she hollers to Mr. Roz. Lori

47

and I laugh as we head down the alley toward school.

We're behind schedule, so we speed-walk until we're up the front steps and through the double doors of St. Mary High. We part ways in the main hall, and I head to chemistry.

Whoever had the brilliant idea of forcing adolescents to mess with covalent bonds first thing in the morning definitely wasn't playing with a full deck. But here we are anyway.

Mr. Wasserman looks up over his reading glasses as I slide onto my stool next to Matthew Dunhill, my good-for-nothing lab partner. Wasserman lets out a psychotic chuckle; he's the original mad scientist.

"Ah, nice of you to join us, Mizzz Wells," he says, waddling his enormous belly over to our station. "Lab report done, I imagine?" He holds out a waiting hand.

"Oh. Yes." I grab my bag, riffle through my folders, pull out the report, and give it to him. "All done," I say, waiting for him to walk away.

Instead, he leans his head toward me and in a very loud whisper says, "I understand we have a celebrity in our midst?" His bulging eyes are rolling around in his head, and his hair is sticking out in every direction.

"What?" He's caught me off guard.

"Well," he announces as he walks to the front of the room, "we're all pretty pleased for you and your father. I have a feeling he's gonna turn St. Mary into a real hot spot."

And then leave us all behind, I think as twenty-four pairs of eyes sear into me like lit Bunsen burners. I hear low laughter from the back row. Haley is in this class, along with a few of her pals. Now I've got goose bumps.

I can't believe we were ever friends—until eighth grade, when I overheard her talking to our group of friends, calling my mom a slut, and calling me stupid for believing she'd ever come back. I was so mad I told her I never wanted to speak to her again. But she wasn't sorry; she just got meaner. Now we are pretty much sworn enemies.

I can imagine what she's saying about me now. The witch.

"Open your books to page ninety-two." Wasserman finally decides to get off the topic of my dad's impending stardom and do his job.

Matthew sits next to me, notebook open, doodling. He's drawing a caricature of Mr. W with Albert Einstein hair; big, bloodshot eyes; and a brain in his hand. It's funny, but I'm in no mood to laugh. The whole school knows: Donovan Wells has hit the big time, and he's dragging his daughter along for the ride.

By the time I get to last period, or Art Hell, as I like to call it, I have experienced firsthand the power of the St. Mary telegraph. From what I can gather, sous-chef Danny told his daughter, Lucy, who told Dora McBride, who told Payge Nelson, who relayed the information to Sydney Mann, who everyone knows has the biggest mouth at St. Mary High. Once she got wind of the news, that was it; she ran it up the flagpole, and now there isn't a living soul in a twenty-five-mile radius who doesn't know.

I slip into my chair next to Jack. "Hi."

"Hey. I just heard you're playing yourself in the made-for-TV movie of your dad's life." He is mocking me. But the rumors have really gotten that weird.

"Not now," I warn.

The bell rings and Mrs. Ely stands in front of the class. She's practically glowing; that's how excited she gets about art. Today, we're studying van Gogh, the crazy guy who sliced off his own ear.

"Take out your assignments, please, and pass them to your left," Mrs. Ely says, impossibly frumpy in her black artist's smock and Sears clearance-rack comfortable shoes.

I pull out the homework, a time line of Vincent's life, which was kind of short, thank goodness.

I gotta hand it to Mrs. Ely. She doesn't mention my father or the show or anything related to cheesy cable TV stations. We just slip into a nice discussion about art and insanity. Yes, it's depressing, but at least no one brings up ExtremeCuisine TV.

As we wait for the bell to ring, Ely sidles up to our table.

"Hey, Sheridan." Here it comes. "How are your nature sketches coming?"

"Um . . . okay," I lie. I'm a terrible liar.

"Listen." She taps the table with a chipped fuchsia finger-nail. "There's this art camp for incoming juniors and seniors.

It's in Upstate New York. I thought you might want to apply. I think you'd have a good chance of getting in."

Me? At an art camp?

"Oh. Thanks." I glance at Jack. "I've got so much going on, though." Is she for real? I imagine myself sitting around a campfire with a bunch of smock-wearing, one-eared losers.

Ely taps the table again. "Just think about it, okay?" She waits for me to look up and acknowledge her.

"Okay. I'll think about it." She's always writing gushy comments on my assignments, like *You have natural talent, Sheridan*, or *This is amazing, Sheridan*. But what does she know? A small-town art teacher with questionable taste in footwear?

At last the final bell rings and this horrible day is over. I can't escape fast enough.

"You know," Jack says as we walk to our lockers, "she doesn't suggest that camp to everyone. It's really tough to get in." I turn my lock, open the door, and stare into the jam-packed space. Then I switch out a few books and slam it shut.

"So? I don't want to go to art camp."

Jack closes his locker two rows down and looks disgusted. "What is wrong with you?"

"Nothing," I sigh. "I just wish people could talk about something other than this stupid show."

Mike, the Math Club geek with the locker next to mine, walks up. "Hey, Sheridan. Heard about your dad. Pretty cool."

"Yeah," I say between clenched teeth.

Jack tugs on my arm as we walk away. "Come on, don't worry so much. Your dad won't make you move. Don't you think he'll let you stay here? And then he can go and get famous. Make some serious dough. Maybe you really will get a nice car for your birthday. You know, like with the big red bow on it."

I turn to him. "Stop it, okay? I don't care about a car. It's just . . ." I don't want to go. I don't want my dad to go. I've almost found Mom. Maybe I could have a real family again. At least have both parents in the same place. Why doesn't he understand that? "Never mind. He can't go to New York City. I'm gonna talk him out of it."

We stop at the water fountain. "You wanna know what I think?"

"No, but I'm sure you're gonna tell me anyway."

He bends over and takes a drink, then stands up and smiles at a waving freshman girl who clearly has a humongous crush on him.

"I think you fear change."

"I do not fear change."

"No, you're wrong. You are most definitely afraid of change. But you must remember, Grasshopper," he says in his best kung fu accent, "sometimes change is good."

I have to laugh. "Oh, right. I haven't had enough change in my life? Huh, Grasshopper?"

He nudges my side. "Maybe it's time for the good kind of change."

I laugh again. But as we pass the glassed-in administration office on the right, all talk of grasshoppers and change vacates my brain. Ethan is exiting the office, and he steps right into my path.

"Oh, sorry," I say, attempting to move out of his way. As I do, I stumble on a crack in the linoleum. I start to fall and prepare for extreme embarrassment. But I don't make it to the floor, because Ethan reaches down and rescues me. He's holding my arm.

My eyes travel from his feet all the way up to his blue blue blue eyes. I am a powerless dust mite being sucked in by one of those fancy British vacuum cleaners. No hope for me.

"Hey, Cake Girl," he says, like we talk every day.

"Hi . . . um, hey," I say in a voice that's somewhere between a croak and a squeak.

"You okay?" he asks, still holding my arm.

No, I am not okay. I'm going to die right now. "Yeah, thanks. I'm good."

"Good." He lets go and winks at me. I watch him walk away, and when he turns back around and smiles, I snap my head in the opposite direction. Real smooth.

Jack blows through the front door of the school so hard it slams into the wall. "If you were going for cool, you blew it big-time," he says as I catch up with him on the front steps.

I smack his arm. "Thanks a lot. Real supportive."

He smirks. "You want me to support your liking that guy? Sorry, but that ain't happening."

"Jack?" I smile. "I thought you wanted me to change. A date would be a change!"

"Date? Do you ever listen to me? That guy will date you, get what he wants, and then move on to the next available sucker."

I'm not smiling anymore. "Oh, so now I'm a sucker?"

We stare at each other.

"I didn't say that."

"It was implied." I hoist my bag up on my shoulder. "God, Jack," I say, and walk away. "I'm going to work."

"I saw the way he looked at you, Sheridan. You're on his radar. Just be careful," he shouts to my back.

I wave him off and wind my way down salty, wet sidewalks. Pretty odd for the middle of April. But "pretty odd" fits perfectly with the rest of this bizarre day.

I turn down our alley and all of a sudden the day gets infinitely weirder. Blocking the whole road is a line of shiny black limos. My feet do an about-face. I'll head back around to Main Street and just go to the bakery. Home can wait.

"Sheridan!" It's my father. "Sheridan!"

I keep walking in the opposite direction, trying to control myself. I can hear him running through the crusty snow.

"Hey, stop!" He catches up and touches my shoulder. He's wearing jeans and a University of Chicago T-shirt.

Almost looks like a normal dad; not like a soon-to-be celebrity.

"Hey, what's up?" I say, but don't give him a chance to answer. I point backward with my thumb and swallow. "Gotta get to work."

"I talked to Nan. You'll be late. There are some people I want you to meet."

"No." I shake my head. "Dad. I've got a lot of work to do and tons of homework." I pat my messenger bag to drive the point home.

But he talks over me like I haven't said a word. "I'd like for you to come in and meet the people from the network. They really want to get to know you."

"Oh," I say. "No thanks." I turn and walk away.

"Sheridan. Come back here." I do what he says, cock my eyebrows, and wait. "This isn't really a request. . . ." He tilts his head and chuckles. "Look, come in. It's cold out here. Come on, do this for me. I'll make it up to you."

"Don't bother, I'll just be swamped." I shrug. "I did have time to talk last night, but apparently, you had more impor- tant things to do." I pass him and walk toward what I feel is my certain doom. With every footstep toward the house I can see my entire world crumbling.

I think of Dad, a long time ago, lifting me gently into our sailboat, strapping on my life jacket, reciting his long list of water safety rules. Holding me in his arms when the wind picked up and I got scared. Where did *that* guy go?

That guy would do anything for me. *This* guy is throwing me to the sharks.

"Here they are!" A gray-haired man in a suit and tie pokes his head through the back door and scares away the memory. The smiling stranger ushers me into the kitchen. There are others here, too. An impossibly tall amazon woman with one of those edgy New York haircuts and superchic brainiac glasses. A young guy who is totally wired, looks like a surfer, and probably uses "Dude!" as a greeting.

They look me up and down and grin. Gray Hair leads me to the long dining table in our kitchen and pulls out a chair for me. They stare at me as I fix my gaze to a spot on the far wall. We recently studied Marie Antoinette in world history. She was the famously clueless and eventually head-less queen of France. I feel like her, on the chopping block.

What was it she said? Yeah. "Let them eat cake."

God, if only it was that easy.

Chapter 5

YOU CATCH MORE FLIES WITH HONEY THAN VINEGAR

So I sit at the head of the table and wait. A group of three men walk in from the front of the house, one of them carrying a big camera. Our roomy kitchen suddenly seems very small, almost claustrophobic.

"Well," Gray Hair says, "let me introduce myself. I'm Randall Beaumont. I'll be producing your father's show for ExtremeCuisine TV. It's very nice to meet you, Sheridan."

"Nice to meet you," I say quietly, now feeling like the frog in ninth-grade biology, laid out and ready for dissection.

"This is Jacqueline," he says, pointing to Amazon. She nods in my direction, all business. "And this is Ricky." Surfer flashes me the peace sign. "And here's Dylan, Luke, and Will, our camera crew. They're here scouting locations for the shoot."

Dad is leaning against the counter, looking nervous.

"So." Gray Hair takes the chair next to me, sits back, crosses a leg, and folds his hands in his lap, real casual. "As you know, your dad's show is called *The Single Dad Cooks*. The network has ordered ten episodes, but we're planning tons of merchandising tie-ins. Cookbooks, aprons, coffee mugs—the whole nine yards. We have every reason to believe it's going to be a big success." He smiles, clearly proud of his newest star. "But of course, since being *your* dad is central to the show, we have a proposition for you. What we'd really like is for you to be in the pilot episode."

Say what?

"Me? Oh, no no no," I say without pause, smiling but emphatically shaking my head. No way. Dad stares at me, his eyes steady. *Don't blow this, Sheridan,* those eyes are saying. *Don't you dare.*

"Well now, hear me out"—Gray Hair laughs—"before you say no. You don't need any experience, so there's no need to be nervous. It's reality TV, so you'll just be yourself."

He thinks this is about me being nervous? My eyebrows crinkle. I'm not nervous at all.

"We understand you're celebrating your sixteenth birthday soon?" he says.

"Not soon. In July."

Amazon crosses the room. Her perfect black suit looks

out of place. She belongs in an office somewhere, not here in my kitchen.

"Sharon," she says. "We have a fantastic idea. But we need you on board if it's going to happen." Her big eyes, surrounded by those nerdy glasses, bore into mine.

"It's Sheridan," I half whisper. "My name is Sheridan."

"Yes," she says, like *I'm* the one being annoying. "Listen. We want to film your birthday celebration for the first episode. What better way to showcase the Single Dad at his best?" She motions toward Dad like he's the grand prize on a game show.

There's a knock on the back door, and I turn to see Jack through the glass. Surfer hops across the room like someone put a firecracker down his pants. He opens the door and Jack comes in with a drink tray full of insulated cups.

"Dude, finally. Java!"

Jack stares at Surfer like he's an alien from Mars. He glances in my direction, and I mouth the word *help*. I can tell by his contrite look that he realizes how wrong he was earlier, lecturing me about Ethan. This is good because right now he is my only ally.

The whole room swarms over Jack, trying to figure out whose double soy latte no-foam is whose. All except for Gray Hair, who doesn't take his eyes off me. He does look like a nice guy, with a genuine smile and kind eyes. So I almost feel bad that I'm about to give him a big fat "NO WAY." But he doesn't give me the chance.

"What we propose, Sheridan, is a party. For you. Filmed right here in St. Mary. But obviously, we need you to agree to this. You can even make the cake. I hear you're pretty well known for that."

I rub my neck. My fingers are itching for a pastry bag, or a big clump of fondant to knead. Anything. Of course I'm going to say no.

But "um . . ." is all that comes out. I can feel my heart racing. I stare across the table, at where Mom used to sit. I imagine what would happen if she was here right now. She'd breeze into the room, lace her arm through Dad's, and gently pat his bicep.

"Donovan," she'd say. "Tell these people to get lost."

"Sheridan?" Dad's voice shatters my little fantasy. He squats down next to me, his face close to mine. "What do you say?" He shrugs. "I think this could be fun."

"Fun?" Only he catches my snarky tone.

"Yes. Fun," he says, his voice full of warning.

My mind is twisting, turning inside out. These Suits have taken over our kitchen and are trying to take over our lives. They've convinced my father that he's better off in New York; that *I'm* better off in New York.

I wonder, if I say no to this birthday party, will they cancel the show? Could it really be that simple? Or maybe, if I say no, they'll just move on to another idea and want us in New York even sooner. On the other hand, maybe saying yes will buy me some time to talk Dad out of this craziness. My mind is whirling with all of the possibilities.

"Sheridan?" Dad asks again through the uncomfortable silence. Everyone in the room is waiting for my answer.

"My birthday isn't until July," I say, trying to stall, trying to think this through.

Surfer springs across the room and lands right in front of me. "That's the magic of television, girl; you can have a party now and another one in July, right, Don?"

Okay, no one calls my dad "Don," but he doesn't seem to mind.

"Maybe your dad'll even buy you a sweet ride for your birthday," Surfer offers with a wink.

I clasp my hands on the table, try to remain calm, and meet this weirdo's gaze. "Oh, but I don't really need a car," I say. He looks at me like I'm nuts. "Really, I don't. You can walk across St. Mary in ten minutes."

"Well." Gray Hair gently pushes Surfer aside while giving him a definite dirty look. "Don't get ahead of yourself, Ricky. Where we'd like to start, Sheridan, is to set a date, come up with a production schedule, and shoot the episode in time for the summer season. Which means soon."

Soon? I can feel beads of sweat popping up on my upper lip like dandelions in the summer grass.

"Maybe you two need a moment to talk?" Gray Hair nods to Dad.

Then, by some miracle, a plan starts coming together in my head. I look around the room; my eyes fall on Dad, then move away.

The cake. *That's it.* I find Mom and ask her to come

back and help me make the cake for this fake party. She'd love to have one of her creations on TV, except that this would be better. This would be *our* creation.

If we actually found her, I can call and invite her down. She won't say no. Dad will be totally furious but he'll have to be civil to her with the cameras on him. Maybe this is the excuse she's been waiting for to come back to me. Oh my God, it's perfect.

"Yeah, maybe we need a minute," Dad says quietly as I figure out the details of this plan.

"No!" I push back my chair and stand, smiling. "I'll do it!"

A tentative grin slides across Dad's mouth. "Really?" he says.

I nod eagerly. This is going to work.

"That's wonderful," Gray Hair says.

"Awesome!" Surfer chimes in.

"Great," Amazon says. "But are you sure you can handle the cake?" She *so* doesn't know me. "No offense, Sherry, but it's got to be spectacular."

Dad leans back against the counter again. "Don't worry. Her cakes are better than my food."

I stand up a little straighter. That's the nicest thing my father has said about me since, well, forever. I look at Jack, who is waiting by the back door, his eyes doubtful. He points to his watch—he's got to get back to Geronimo's—then raises a hand to his ear in the "call me" signal.

"This is brilliant." Gray Hair laughs. "Completely fresh concept. Genius. Single Dad throws his daughter a party, and she's following in his culinary footsteps. I love it!"

The Suits spin around the room, throwing out ideas like balls at the batting cages. (Jack made me go with him once; my left eye was black for two weeks.)

"We need a theme!" Amazon says, staring at the ceiling as if she'll find one up there.

Surfer stops in his tracks. "An Extreme Sweet Sixteen Luau!"

That's the lamest idea I've ever heard.

"Yes. That's perfect," Amazon says. "And if we can get some teenage girls in bikinis, we might even pull in the eighteen- to twenty-four-year-old male demographic."

"We'd need an indoor pool. Blue chicks aren't sexy," Surfer says. He is so right, but if he thinks I'm getting into a bikini with my winter-white skin and total lack of boobs, he's got another thing coming.

"Maybe not a pool. How about the restaurant, Donovan?" Gray Hair suggests. Dad smiles.

"Can you do luau food, Don?" Surfer asks.

Dad laughs. "I'll think of something."

"Well, Sheridan, Donovan, I predict this is going to be the hit of the summer." Gray Hair grabs Dad's hand and shakes it. "We'll get back to the hotel and hammer out a production schedule."

He holds his hand out for me to shake, too. I have an

overwhelming feeling that this handshake will seal my fate. Here's hoping that fate is on *my* side.

The Suits gather up their briefcases and drain their coffee cups. Amazon gives some orders to the camera crew, and then they talk among themselves. I hear Surfer: "This is gonna be the show to beat." I hear Amazon: "We're going to bury Food TV during sweeps."

Dad touches my arm. "Can I have a word with you?"

I narrow my eyes and follow him to the kitchen island. "Sure," I say.

Dad takes a glass from the cabinet and fills it with water from the sink. He takes a swig, swallows hard.

"You really okay with this? You sure changed your mind fast."

That's when Nanny's voice pops into my head. One of those phrases she's always saying: *You catch more flies with honey than vinegar.* Be nice to these people, cooperate with them, and maybe I'll get what I want.

"Yes." I gulp, thinking of honey, lots and lots of honey. "I just thought this might be a good way to spend time together, since we hardly even talk anymore."

If I was Pinocchio, my nose would be about a mile long by now.

He eyes me suspiciously. "Just promise, no funny stuff, okay?"

Who, me? I'll be nice to the Suits; I'll slay them with my charm, stun them with my reality TV presence. Maybe they'll

64

realize that St. Mary is the best place to film this show. Why not? This is where my reality is, after all. It's worth a try.

"Right." I nod. "No funny stuff. Promise."

Dad's eyes suddenly get wide, weird-looking. He focuses on my face, and in that split second, I see something come over him. He softens, like butter left out on the counter.

"Good. I'm so glad you're on board. Thanks, sweetheart."

Sweetheart? He reaches up, smooths my hair, leans over, and kisses my forehead. Okay. He hasn't called me that or kissed my head in years.

I smile even though I'm so not on board, and I have no intention of moving to New York City. The honey worked. This fly is mine.

The Suits are at the back door, bundled up and ready to hop into their limos.

"We'll get back to you later tonight, Donovan," Gray Hair calls.

"Great. Just great," Dad says, and walks to the door to see them out.

I let out a deep, deep sigh. I've got a lot of work to do.

Later that night, after finishing a few birthday cakes at the bakery, I walk into an empty house. Dad is at the restaurant, and from the looks of the parking lot, they are booked solid.

The front room is warm and cozy tonight. I sit on the big old leather sofa, drop my bag, and flick on the lamp beside me.

Reaching for my chemistry book, I see my art sketch-book, still neglected and sad. I may just flunk that class.

Instead, I pull out my laptop and start drafting an e-mail. I've started a lot of e-mails like this, trying to contact my mother, and I've been wrong about the person every time. But Mackinac Maggie, she's the one. I know it.

Jack wants me to wait until we find more evidence.

But what does he know, anyway? I need to find her now if this plan is going to work.

So I write.

To Whom It May Concern: I am planning a summer wedding and am wondering if you can give me the contact information for Maggie Taylor, who decorated the butterfly cake on your Web site. Thank you.

I mean, that's a pretty innocent e-mail. No restraining orders could possibly come from this.

I close my eyes and hit Send, then sit back, inhaling the scent of old wood and leather. I do realize that to most people, the idea of an intelligent, cake-decorating high schooler sending fraudulent e-mails to a stranger hundreds of miles away might sound crazy. They might think I'm a fool, searching for a woman who left me, who I haven't seen in eight years.

But I really don't care. *I'm* the one who remembers her hand in mine, the weight of it, the sureness of its squeeze.

That kind of love does not just vanish. My mom didn't stop sending birthday cards for no good reason.

I will find her, she'll come back, and we'll make the cake for this luau together. And maybe when Dad sees how happy this makes me, *maybe* he'll forgive her, at least a little. That's the best-case scenario, of course, but it could happen.

I should start the next lab report, but instead, I take out my cake notebook, flip open to the first empty page, and start to draw the birthday masterpiece. A luau theme? That would, of course, mean gum paste hibiscus flowers. Painted to look like the real thing. And by the real thing, I don't mean a cartoon version of the real thing. I mean people will inquire if hibiscuses are poisonous flowers before they take a bite. That real.

My cell phone buzzes. It's a text from Jack.

U dsign cake yet?

Yep, I reply.

In my mind, I can already see it: pink hibiscus flowers cascading down the side of four tiers covered in cerulean blue fondant. And a butterfly on top, courtesy of Mom.

Chapter 6

THE CREAM OF THE CROP

The week before Easter Sunday flies by like the snow-flakes that fall daily. It's officially the whitest April in St. Mary's history. The weather is affecting everyone's mood, even Mr. Roz, who is normally perpetually happy.

As for me, I'm more than a little worried. The Suits went back to their shiny New York offices after deciding that my fake birthday will be on May 7, less than three weeks away. That gives me almost no time to get Mom here. And I've gotten no reply to my e-mail from the hotel in Mackinac. I even called and left a message with their catering depart-ment. But no one has called back.

Worse, the Suits left the camera crew here, and they're following us around, getting "candid" footage for the hour-long pilot. I understand this is part of the agreement, but that doesn't make it less annoying.

Today is Good Friday, there's no school, and I'm in the back of Sweetie's finishing up the lilacs for the Bailey cake, which is nearly done and beyond perfect. When I'm not working on the sugar blossoms, I'm helping Nanny and Mr. Roz prepare baked goods for the Easter brunch at Sheridan & Irving's. This includes making four lamb cakes (three white lambs and one black sheep, because Nanny says every family needs one), ten assorted cakes, plus strudel and Danish, all while keeping up with the regular inventory. I've been here every day after school. No time for anything else. Not Lori or Jack, not a good long run, and not the project for art class, which I still have not started.

And to top it all off? A few days ago I got a text from the amazon woman asking for a guest list. As soon as possible. So I sat down and, aside from Jack and Lori, could not figure out who to invite. The sad truth is I make the cakes, but I don't get invited to the parties. Not anymore.

My life is cake. For example, today there's no school, and while most kids my age won't be up until noon at least, I was here at five a.m., adding curls of buttercream wool to a French vanilla lamb.

Not that I'm complaining. I'd much rather decorate a cake than sleep in or go to a random high school party.

Now it's seven o'clock, and the bakery is open, so Nanny shoves me out front with Mr. Roz. I don't have to help customers often, except during very busy times, like today. Really, it's not so bad. Mr. Roz and I work like a well-oiled machine, bobbing and weaving around each other, handing out baked goods that are like little pieces of heaven.

Dr. Putnam walks in. This is the worst part of the job: bagging pastries for the one guy in town who has seen me naked.

"Hello, Sheridan," he says in that don't-worry-I'm-not-picturing-you-in-your-birthday-suit voice. Yeah, right.

I swallow and get over it. There are too many customers behind him to worry. "Hey," I say like we're best buds. "What can I get you?"

I fill his order, then prepare a dozen-muffin assortment for Mrs. Beach, the grade school librarian. Behind her are two old couples who have *tourist* written all over them. They start coming to St. Mary this time of year, and my dad's restaurant is a big attraction.

"So," a tall man barks in my direction as I bag up four muffins and a scone, "is the famous brunch really as good as they say?"

The Easter brunch at Sheridan & Irving's has been written up in foodie magazines all over the country. It really is famous.

"Yeah, it's pretty good." I smile and pour them four coffees, black.

"I just can't wait to meet Chef Wells," says the tall man's white-haired wife. "I clipped the article in *Food and Wine*, and I'm going to ask him to sign it. He's a doll."

She smiles goofily and blushes. *Great, lady. Go for it.*

"Mr. Wells, his food very good." Mr. Roz feels the need to add to the conversation. He looks at me and winks. "Nice guy, too."

"Oh, do you know him?" the other old lady asks. Good Lord. *Get a life, people.* Mr. Roz laughs and nods, winks at me again. He won't tell them that they are in the presence of the great Chef Wells's daughter. That would send them into a tizzy.

The women giggle obnoxiously while their husbands talk Michigan football. Some tourists should come with a warning: MAY INDUCE VOMITING.

I give them their change as the front bell rings. A glance toward the door reveals Ethan Murphy standing inside, the sun shining behind his wavy blond hair. He looks like a rock star onstage. Everyone who turns to look at him does a double take. He's the kind of guy who can do that—get everyone's attention. There are four people ahead of him, and I can barely focus on their orders.

When he's the second person in line, we make eye contact. I try to look natural, but a tingle is spreading from my neck up to my ears.

"Hey." He lifts his hand real cool-like.

I raise mine back and try to concentrate on Mrs. Douglas, who was my piano teacher for a short, miserable period of time.

"I'm sorry, we're out of lemon poppy seed," I say to her.

"But can't you look in the back, Sheridan? You probably have some back there, don't you?" Yes, she's that annoying.

"I go look." Mr. Roz thankfully steps in, and Mrs. Douglas moves to the side. And so there he is, Ethan, in front of me. My knees wobble behind the case. *Get a grip, Sheridan.*

"Hi," I say. "Ethan, right?" Oh, that was smooth.

"Yeah." One second of eye contact and my face goes nuclear. "Cake Girl, right?"

I scrunch up my nose and laugh.

"You ready for the French test?" he asks. I didn't think he knew I was in that class. He sits in the back with a few other upperclassmen.

"Oui," I reply, trying to be clever. And failing miserably.

"Yeah. Good." He scratches his head. "That's funny."

I am frantically trying to think of something to top the *oui*, but really don't want to make things worse. I'd settle for one cool-ish word, preferably in English.

"You want something?" That's the best I can do.

"Um, yeah." He's eyeing the case and rubbing his chin. "How are those dark-chocolate raspberry muffins? Those are new."

"They're amazing."

"Good." He smiles. "I'll take eight."

"Eight?" I ask, lost in his perfect chin, cheeks, eyes, face.

"Yeah. Eight." His eyes are sparkling, and his mouth opens in a huge grin. "You do sell them by eights?"

"Yes. Of course. You can have as many as you want." Oh God, he's so cute.

"Well, okay then, eight will work."

There's something wrong with me. I can't think of one intelligent thing to say to him. I can usually hold my own in a social situation. But this is ridiculous. He leans in toward the counter. "All right, then. I'll take eight."

"Right." I snap back into action. "Eight. Got it."

I bend awkwardly into the glass cabinet, my face throbbing with embarrassment.

The best muffins are at the front of the case, and he is getting the best muffins, so I twist my body like an Olympic gymnast to reach them. Also, from here I can see his midsection. It's right in front of me. His coat is open, he has one hand in the pocket of his loose, tattered jeans, and I can see a sliver of finely toned ab under his shirt.

I take a deep breath, throw eight muffins into a bag (he did say eight, right?), and extract myself from the case. But as I emerge, my head smacks the top. A dull thud resounds through the bakery.

Ow.

"Are you okay?" Ethan asks from over the counter. Honestly, things are looking a little fuzzy.

Mr. Roz runs over. "My God, what you do?" he asks, taking the bag of muffins out of my hand and passing them to Ethan. Mr. Roz revolves around me like he's trying to pinpoint a location on a globe.

"I'm fine, I'm fine." I glance at Ethan, his mouth set in a concerned frown.

"Go, go, sit down for a minute," Mr. Roz insists. "Go, sit with your friend."

Friend? That may be a bit optimistic. But suddenly, here I am, taking a seat across from Ethan Murphy. He is one arm's length away, with only a lemon-yellow vinyl tablecloth, a tiny pitcher of cream, and a plastic container stuffed with sugar and sugar-substitute packets between us. I rub the bump on my head.

"That sounded like it hurt."

I flash a coy smile. "Kind of."

I notice that the line of customers is shrinking. "You don't have to sit with me," I say apologetically.

"No, it's okay with me. If it's okay with you." He pushes the bag of muffins to the side.

I tear my eyes off the tablecloth and meet his. They are brilliant. He is a god. And I am a . . . muffin bagger. No makeup, old blue jeans, big old pink polka-dotted apron, hairnet. Oh no—the hairnet!

Like he's inside of my brain listening in on my thoughts, Ethan Murphy reaches across the table, pulls off the hairnet, and drops it in the center of the table. I feel my ponytail slither down my back; a shiver trickles down my spine.

My brain is telling me to buck up. I am a confident, talented person who can talk to anyone, anytime. Except this time. I am floating outside of my body, unable to act normal.

Then Ethan's hand reaches up, and he touches the top of my head. Oh God, why is he touching me?

"You might want to get some ice on that."

Oh right, that's why.

"I'm okay." My eyes drop again. I am mad at myself for acting all shy when I am not shy at all. I am Cake Girl. Fearless. Confident. Capable.

"You're probably gonna have a nice goose egg there."

I shake my head. Grab my hairnet. Nanny doesn't like us to have them off, ever, in case the health inspector drops by. I scan the bakery. Nanny's nowhere in sight.

Roz is working on the last of the customers. I sit up in my chair and open my mouth once or twice, hoping something comes out. Nothing does.

"Hey." Ethan speaks first. "What are you doing this weekend?"

I stare at him.

"Um . . . why?"

"I thought maybe if you weren't busy we could hang out."

So I'm being punk'd. That's it. This is some kind of ExtremeCuisine TV joke. I look around for a camera. The Surfer Suit did mention that they would be shooting some footage of us later today.

"Hang out?" I ask.

"Yeah. You know, like, you and me?"

I swallow. "Do you even know my name?" I say softly, totally serious.

"Yes, I know your name." His voice is so smooth; not

shaky and squeaky like most of the boys at school.

"Well?" I smile. "What is it?"

He lowers his gaze and his lips curl up. "Suzy? No. Savannah? Sybil?"

Is he kidding? He doesn't look like he's kidding. I can't tell.

After a long pause, he rolls his eyes. "Your name is Sheridan Wells." Another killer grin. "There, do I pass?"

But I don't buy this quite yet. "You just want to hang out?"

"Yeah." His body shifts; he's uncomfortable now. "You could call it hanging out. Or you could call it a date. . . ."

I laugh and instantly regret it. He looks surprised.

"So is that a no?"

I clasp my hands on the table in front of me. "You have a girlfriend." Who happens to hate me.

He sits back, looks out the window. "Nope. Broke up with me."

"She did?" *Really?* I saw them making out in front of her locker yesterday at school.

"Yep. We broke up. Last night."

I pick out a sugar packet, flip it back and forth. *What do I say?*

"But it's not like we were serious or anything." He reaches over, puts his hand on top of my flapping sugar packet, and leans in close. "So whaddya say?"

"Well . . ." I am so going to say YES! But I don't have a chance, because Nanny hollers, "Sheridan!" I jump, then look up and see, standing next to the case, one of the

ExtremeCuisine TV camera guys with a huge lens pointed right at me. I knew it.

"Where in tarnation is your hairnet, girl? You tryin' to put me out of business?" When she's done with me, she turns to the cameraman. "And you've got it on film?" She swats at him with a kitchen towel in hand. "Turn that camera off, fool. You want me out on the street?"

She swoops around the case and glares at Ethan. She's got a very effective glare. "And you are?"

"This is Ethan," I say, slipping my hairnet back on, dying as Nanny sizes him up.

"Hi," Ethan says confidently. "Nice to meet you." He holds out his hand, but Nanny doesn't take it.

"I've seen you here before."

"Yeah, well, you've got good . . . stuff," he replies.

"Well. That's mighty nice of you to say. But my granddaughter is on the clock, so if you don't mind . . ."

Ethan stands, the bag of muffins in his hand. "Oh, sorry." He forces my eyes up with his gaze; then he glances sideways at Nanny. "You have your cell?"

Nanny's arms cross as I reach into my pocket and give him my phone. She shifts her weight and harrumphs.

He enters his number and hands it back to me, then looks at Nanny and winks. Oh God, he did not just do that. "Text you?" he asks. I smile and nod.

I peek at Nanny, half of me mad that she ruined a real moment, the other half relieved that she interrupted before I said anything really stupid. On camera. She gives me her you-better-watch-it eye as she walks around the cameraman and back into the kitchen.

Ethan's opening the front door when Surfer swings around from behind the counter. Oh crap. He's here, too?

"Wait, wait, wait," Surfer says, grabbing Ethan's arm. "Ethan, is it?" Surfer doesn't give him time to answer. "Hey, I don't know if you've heard, but we're filming a TV show in a few weeks. May seventh, a Saturday. It's a Sweet Sixteen, for Sheridan here." He nudges Ethan and winks. "Hot chicks in bikinis."

Surfer looks at me. "He should come, don't you think?"

"Uh. If he wants to . . . I guess." I am beyond mortified.

"Awesome. We need the cream of the crop at this luau. Okay, dude, consider yourself invited. Clear the whole day; we'll need it."

Ethan stares at me, and his eyebrows arch like he's asking me if this is okay. The corners of my mouth turn up. His eyes move over my face, and he hits me once more with that smile.

"Yeah, great. I can do that," Ethan says to Surfer.

Then he opens the door and says, "See ya," and he's gone.

The front doorbell rings its familiar, happy sound. I am in shock. I think I just got asked out on TV. By Ethan Murphy?

There's a grin on my face as I get back to work. I make a mental note to slip ten dollars into the register, since my date forgot to pay for his muffins.

Chapter 7

BREAD OF LIFE

It's the night before Easter, and I am a total insomniac. Not because I have to be at the bakery at five in the morning to prepare for the big brunch, or because my fake birthday–slash–TV debut is only two weeks away. It isn't even because the single hottest guy in the Midwest (and possibly the universe) has kind of asked me out.

No. Last night I got an e-mail from the hotel on Mackinac Island. It said that Ms. Taylor's business was in Sault Sainte Marie, on the Michigan-Canada border, but that they hadn't used her services in a few years. On the other hand, if I booked their hotel for my wedding reception, they'd be happy to refer a bakery of equal or better quality.

What? I wanted to scream at the computer. *I'm not really getting married, you idiots. I'm looking for my mother!*

So, what now? That's what I'm trying to figure out.

As soon as I got the e-mail, I texted Jack and alerted him to the situation before I remembered that he told me not to e-mail them in the first place. He was annoyed.

I didn't care. I just told him to keep looking. I haven't shared my plan with him, to get Mom here in time for the party, but we really need to work fast. So far I can't find any online listings for her in Sault Sainte Marie, only a few old-lady obituaries. The last card came from Ottawa, so this makes sense. But Margaret Taylor is a very common name. The search is exhausting.

Lying in my bed, I hear Dad's car start up and drive away. It's four o'clock in the morning. He's going to the market in Grand Rapids to buy fresh meat and produce for brunch. This is a big day for him. Everyone in the world has heard about the show. Of course, the marquee at City Hall says CONGRATS, CHEF WELLS. WELCOME, ECTV! Things like that don't help.

A thought occurs to me. If they insist Dad move to New York, there might not be a Sheridan & Irving's this time next year. The restaurant could be closed. I owe it to the people of St. Mary to keep my father here where he belongs, cooking in his restaurant.

I get out of bed and creak my way through the house to the kitchen. There's a note on the counter.

Be at S&I no later than 7 answer your phone if I call.

That's Dad lately: no time for *Dear Sheridan* or *Happy Easter* or even basic punctuation. I drop the note on the counter and peek out the back kitchen window. Nanny's apartment light is off. She's already downstairs, working.

Restless, I pick up my cell phone, wishing I could just dial my mother. Wondering what it would be like to pick up the phone and call her.

Then I see a text from Jack, left after I went to bed last night.

We have 2 talk possible clue.

Instantly, my heart is a jackhammer. Maybe he found her. I call him; I don't care how early it is.

"Hello?" Jack says in a groggy voice.

"Hey. So tell me! What clue?"

"Huh? What time is it?"

"Um . . . like four something. What clue?"

"Oh." He's silent. I'll give him a second to wake up a little. But only a second.

"Jack!"

"What? All right. Calm down. Last night. Found a bakery in Sault Sainte . . . whatever. In Canada. It doesn't have a Web site—it's just a listing in an online directory."

"Yeah? And?"

"And it's called Sweetie's."

A lump forms in my throat. "Really?"

"Yes." He pauses. "And there's a phone number."

"Yeah?"

"But, Sheridan, we have no idea if it's her. There's no owner listed. Only the name of the bakery. It could be a coincidence."

"No. It's her."

"You don't know that."

He's wrong. "Jack, I have a feeling."

He gives me the number only after I promise not to do anything with it. He makes me swear. We don't know enough yet, he says. But as soon as we hang up, I start to dial. He doesn't understand. I can't wait. I need to find her. The lump in my throat is enormous now. What if she picks up? What do I say?

The phone rings over and over. Finally, voice mail picks up. "Welcome to Sweetie's of Sault Sainte Marie. Leave a message and we'll get back to you."

It's a woman on the recording. It has to be Mom. I savor every syrup-smooth word. I can see her, with her golden hair back in a hairnet, smiling on the other end of that telephone. I don't leave a message. Not yet. Mostly because I have no idea what to say. But as I hang up, my insides bubble over with hope.

I run upstairs and throw on some jeans, an old T-shirt, and my ratty gym shoes. It doesn't matter what I look like, considering I'll be stuck in a hot kitchen for most of the day. My hair goes back in a ponytail, and I take the time to stuff Mom's heart-shaped note into my front pocket. My whole body buzzes with excitement. I have a good feeling about Sweetie's of Sault Sainte Marie.

Before I leave, I go to my closet and reach for a random birthday card.

Twelve years old? How is that possible? I wish I could be there, but we are in Brazil. I'll send you something South American. I bet you are planning a big party with all of your friends. Have fun, sweetheart. Sorry I'm so far away.

God, I miss her. But I realize that I have to figure out what to say before I call her again. We have a lot of catching up to do; I'm just not sure where to start.

It's only four thirty, but I'm restless, so I decide to head to the bakery early. I grab my coat, lock the back door, and run toward the alley. It's still dark and freezing cold, but the piled-up snow is reflecting the moon like a night-light. I push on the bakery door, find it open, and slip into the warmth of the kitchen.

"Hey, sugar. Aren't you a sight for sore eyes?" Nanny keeps a baker's hours and will be napping by noon. But right now she's standing in front of a tray full of diamond-shaped brownies, giving each one a generous coat of chocolate fudge frosting. She stands up and stretches as I grab an apron.

"Well, you look happier than a clam at high tide. What's going on with you, darlin'?"

I shrug but the grin on my face is huge. "Nothin'."

She laughs. "Seem pretty smiley about nothin'."

Mr. Roz walks in from the front of the store.

"Hey, Mr. Roz!" I say as he slides a tray of donuts out of

a rack. He looks surprised, and I know why—usually I am a total grump this early in the morning.

"Hello, Sheridan!" He beams. "And Happy Easter to you!"

"Bunny left you a little something." Nanny nods toward the back counter. I turn and see an Easter basket stuffed with candy: jelly beans, marshmallow chicks, and even one of those cheesy hollow chocolate bunnies with Day-Glo sugar eyeballs.

"Nan. Don't you think that I'm a little old for an Easter basket?" I pop a red jelly bean in my mouth.

"Fine," she says. "Doc says I should watch my sugar, but I'll go ahead and take it off your hands."

"No, no, that's okay." I laugh. "I wouldn't want to give you diabetes or anything."

"Oh, what a sweetheart—always thinking of your old Nanny."

I add a yellow jelly bean to the red one.

"Always."

She chuckles from deep down. Gosh, I love her. I want so badly to tell her that I've found Mom. I think she'll be happy; she knows how much I miss her.

But there's a knock on the back door. "Who's that?" I wonder out loud.

Nanny walks over, wipes her hands on her apron, and lets in a rush of frigid air. I see Growly's bald head sticking up above hers. Great.

"Mornin', Father Crowley." Nanny smiles and gives him a hug. Even though Nanny left the Catholic Church when my grandfather died, she stayed close with Growly, who didn't mind that she went back to her roots at First Baptist of Grand Rapids.

This might make him sound like a nice guy. But he's not. I watch him, suspicious. Maybe he's come to try to save my hopeless soul. I don't have time for that this morning.

"How are you doing this fine Easter Day, Lilian?" he says to Nanny.

"Fine as frog hair; finer, maybe."

He looks at me, his lips drawn across his face in a straight line. "Miss Wells." He nods. "You are a hard worker. Not many individuals your age would be willing to sacrifice so much time for a family business."

"Thank you." I think that was a compliment. But I feel my good mood spoiling. Why is he here?

"She has a servant's heart," Nanny says. "That, and I pay well." They laugh.

Roz walks into the kitchen. "Father!" He gives Growly a hearty two-handed handshake and disappears up front again. In another minute, he returns with a cup of coffee and a slice of Michigan cherry strudel.

"Ah." Growly grins and takes the strudel, then sits on a stool. "One of the perks."

Nanny waves me over and hands me a bag filled with buttercream. "Let's top them with flowers," she says, directing me to a tray of frosted brownies. "What do you think? Roses? Lilies of the valley? Lilacs?"

"Yeah, I don't care if I make another lilac for the rest of my life." I think of the Bailey wedding cake, picked up yesterday. They *loved* it. Another satisfied customer.

"Yes, I suppose that we did OD on lilacs just a bit, didn't we?" Nanny laughs.

"Lilian," Growly, watching me, says between bites of pastry. "Your granddaughter is looking more and more like you did when we first met."

"Yes." Nanny watches me as I squeeze the icing to the top of the bag. "I suppose we favor each other here and there. But I swear this girl is positively shining this morning."

I can't hold back my smile. I don't even try.

I've always been relatively open with Nanny when it comes to Mom. And I don't think I can keep this latest development to myself any longer.

"Well. It's because I've got some good news. Really good news."

I have their attention. Nanny puts down a bowl of buttercream frosting. "Don't leave us hanging. What is it, girl?"

Now that they're waiting, I'm having second thoughts. Nanny knows I've had no luck trying to find my mom in the last few years. And that it's gotten me into some trouble.

But everyone likes good news. Like Jesus and the whole rising-from-the-dead thing, right? It's Easter, a time for good news.

"I think I've found Mom." I just say it, spit it out. They

are staring at me, their mouths hanging open. No one looks happy. I suddenly wish I could take back the words, keep them safe inside.

"What?" My smile disappears. "What's wrong?"

"Oh, really?" Nanny's big soft voice has gone hollow.

"Yes. Jack and I found her," I say, sticking my chin out.

"How?" Nanny looks at me like I've robbed a bank or something. Which makes me very angry.

"It's called the World Wide Web." I squeeze the pastry bag harder than necessary. The frosting squirts across the room. "Ever heard of it?"

I expect Nanny to tell me to watch my mouth. To clean up that frosting blob on the floor. But she doesn't say a word.

I bend over and make a mutant rose on top of a brownie.

"Does your father know?" Nanny asks.

"No. And you can't tell him." I make another rose, this one a little better. "Seriously. None of you can say anything." I should have kept my big mouth shut.

They are dead silent, and I am very uncomfortable. So much for spreading the joy.

Growly breaks the silence, pulls a small brown paper bag out of his coat pocket. "Well, let's get on with it, shall we?" He sighs. "Will you all be receiving?"

"Yes." Nanny walks over to me and yanks my arm over to where the priest stands waiting. "Come on, you're taking Communion."

The old broad can be so pushy. Even about things like taking Communion, though she's not a Catholic anymore.

I'm pretty sure that's against the rules. I yank my arm out of her grip. But I still follow.

Mr. Roz, Nanny, and I make a semicircle as Growly begins to pray. "On this holy day . . . ," he says, or something like that. I'm not really listening. I am thinking of Sweetie's, the Canadian version, and my mother. I glance up and catch Nanny looking at me, her eyebrows knit together in the middle. I glare at her.

"Receive this bread of life and this cup of blessing . . . that you may be strengthened through our communion," Growly says. Bread of life. A cup of blessing. Sounds like God is a bit of a baker. I kinda like that idea.

I mumble the Our Father with them, and before I know it, Growly is in front of me, holding up a wafer.

"Body of Christ." He's searching my eyes, looking less mean and more worried than usual.

"Amen," I say, taking the round, flat cracker, shoving it into my mouth, and turning back to the brownies. I cross myself and grab the sleeve of icing. I wonder about that stale cracker actually being the body of Christ. Seems pretty unlikely. Although I do understand the concept of believing in something that might seem impossible. Like my mother coming back. I can tell that no one—not Nanny, not Roz, and certainly not Growly—believes that it will happen.

But that's what faith is, right? Trusting that no matter how things look, everything's going to work out according to plan.

Chapter 8

WHEN LIFE GIVES YOU
LEMONS, MAKE LEMONADE

My father calls my cell phone a few hours later and tells me that Danny, the sous-chef, is puking and that a few of the staff are also sick. It's a disaster. He orders me to finish up at the bakery and come immediately to the restaurant. They need all the extra hands they can get.

He's not at all nice about it; doesn't say please or thank you. But that's all right. I am still floating on a fluffy cloud of goodness. I don't care what I have to do today. I found Mom. She can come home.

For now, I'm still at the bakery, boxing up pastries for Pedro and Paul, two busboys from Sheridan & Irving's. Nanny is on the phone. She catches me peeking at her and squints her eyes like she's completely annoyed. I am mad, too. Madder than a pig in a poke, which is one of Nanny's sayings. I have no earthly idea what it means, but it seems to fit this situation.

My phone rings. Dad again.

"Yes?" I ask, arranging a layer of lemon tarts in a pink cardboard box.

"I told you to get over here. I need you. Now!" Click. Okay. Love you, too.

I shove the phone in my pocket and growl. "Jerk," I mumble.

Paul is standing next to me. He tries not to laugh, but his shaking stomach gives him away.

"That's enough, young lady," Nanny says, her ears like a bat's. I shoot her a rude look, but she doesn't catch it.

We finish up, all the boxes closed now and tied with white string. "Mrs. Wells?" Pedro asks. "You got anything else?"

Nanny looks to Mr. Roz. "Jakup?"

"Datz all for now. I got more strudel in the oven. I call when they ready." Pedro heads out.

I reach around to untie my apron. "Yeah, I'm going, too. Dad wants me there now."

Nanny takes a deep breath. I know she was expecting to have me for the morning rush. "Fine," she says, and walks up front.

"Fine," I say to the empty kitchen.

I walk out the back door with a pile of bakery boxes. The sun is coming up, its rays creeping across the snow like a cat on the prowl. I replay Mom's voice mail greeting in my head and want to kick myself for spilling the beans. If Nanny tells Dad, I'm screwed.

But I couldn't help myself. I am so happy. Mom is out there, and so close.

I walk through the back door of the restaurant. The kitchen is buzzing; everywhere I look there is someone working. My pastries need to go to the buffet tables in the dining room, so I make my way through the kitchen.

"Morning, Sheridan," I hear from my father's employees, most of whom I've known forever. I smile and say hi, but there's no time for chitchat today. So much electric energy flows through the place that I get goose bumps. Dining tables are being set; buffet tables are going up.

"Good morning, Sheridan." The voice comes from the bar to my right, and I turn. It's Amazon, with two cameramen behind her.

"Hi," I say, looking around for my father. "You guys are here?"

I can't imagine what kind of footage she'll get today. Maybe they'll catch my father having an aneurysm. Now that would make for some interesting ExtremeCuisine TV.

"SHERIDAN!" I quick-hop around and see my dad's red face sticking out of the kitchen's swinging door. *Aim your cameras, boys; here comes your aneurysm.* But he sees Amazon and his look instantly softens, his face fading to a nice pale pink.

"Sheridan, I need you in the kitchen. Please."

Oh, *now* he's going to say *please?* Nice.

"I better go," I say to Amazon.

I step through the door. Dad points to me. "Help Raoul. Now!"

"Yes, master," I mumble all Igor-like, thinking of how fun it would be to tell him right now that I've found Mom. Yeah. Aneurysm City.

I watch him stalk back into his office.

"Señorita." Raoul nods. He's a good guy who knows I'll do the job right. He hands me a big knife and slides away from his spot. I take over, coarsely chopping an enormous clump of flat-leaf parsley. Across the kitchen, Amazon pushes through the door and walks into my father's office.

I wonder if she's into him. So many women are. He's always going out with someone new. Frankly, I don't see the appeal. Luckily, the shelf life for his girlfriends is so short I don't even get a chance to meet them. Which is fine with me.

I scrape the bright green pile of herb into a plastic bin, and a fat bunch of basil magically appears.

"Please . . . chiffonade," begs Raoul. It occurs to me that most fifteen-year-olds probably don't even know how to pronounce *chiffonade*, much less make it happen.

As I finish up, Amazon walks out of Dad's office and leaves the kitchen with a smug grin on her face. She returns in a minute with one of the camera goons and points to me. Hmm . . . this doesn't look good at all.

"Sheridan!" At least she got my name right. "Sweetheart, this is Dylan. He's going to film you for a little while." She grimaces. "So just act natural, all right?"

No way. My hair is once again in a tragically unhip hairnet, and I don't have one bit of makeup on. I think of the zit I saw percolating on my chin this morning.

Amazon stares. Then she runs out to the dining room without a word and comes back with a Prada bag that I'm sure is *not* a knockoff. She pulls out a small pouch, unzips it, and reveals a small tube.

"Come closer," she orders. "You have a little something right here that needs to be covered." She hits the zit with concealer and then pulls out an eyeliner pencil. I put down the huge chopping knife and cross my arms.

"Now stay real still," she says. She proceeds to line my eyes, dab a little makeup underneath them, swipe on some mascara, and touch my lips with a dab of gloss from a pot. Then she stands back to survey her work.

"God, I hope you appreciate how utterly perfect your skin is now." I guess that means I'm camera-ready.

"Okay. So act natural, do your thing, go about your business, and Dylan will film you. Remember, just act natural."

It's weird how she keeps saying that, especially when there's nothing natural about any of this. A fifteen-year-old with a missing mother and a fame-obsessed father, forced into a phony Sweet Sixteen party—could this be any more *un*natural?

Dylan hoists the camera onto his shoulder and I finish up the basil. I try to go into cake mode. When I'm working on a cake, I can totally block out the rest of the world; focus entirely on the process and how good it feels to create something beautiful. Of course, I know the destiny of every cake I make: total destruction, digestion, excretion. Doesn't bother me, though. Cakes make me happy; they make people happy. And that makes me feel good. I'm just like Mom in that way.

I move from station to station. Whenever I hear "Sheridan!" I scurry over to the person in need and finish whatever he or she was doing. Stirring creamy, melting chocolate over a double boiler; separating dozens of eggs; peeling carrots, cucumbers, and potatoes; slicing paper-thin lemons for the restaurant's signature lemonade-and-champagne mimosas.

My mother invented this drink, one of the few things that Dad didn't get rid of that was hers. He couldn't; people loved it too much. With each slice, I feel her standing next to me. I daydream about us slicing lemons together, or making the cake for the luau; maybe even sailing again. Maybe soon.

I glance at the clock. It's seven thirty, and you wouldn't think it possible, but the energy in the kitchen is increasing. The first seating isn't until ten, and everyone around me is in total panic mode. But I love this.

As I chop the leaves off a celery stalk, my mind wanders to Sault Sainte Marie. I've never been there, but I can imagine the bakery where my mother is probably greeting customers right now. This makes me smile. I wonder if her Sweetie's has lemon-yellow vinyl tablecloths, too. And pink polka-dotted aprons.

And just the fact that she named it Sweetie's—it's like she wanted me to find her.

Standing here dicing celery, I make plans to call her again. If I can't get in touch with her, Jack can drive me up there. If my father finds out about any of this, he will blow his top. But I don't care. I just need to get her here.

I wake up from this daydream and notice cameraman Dylan looking totally bored. Amazon is gone, but she'll probably eat him alive if he doesn't get some good film. Feeling plucky, I pick up a slice of lemon and suck on it, making a sourpuss face at the camera. He laughs.

"Man, this stuff is going to be really exciting," I say.

He rolls his eyes and smiles. "Just do what the lady says and act normal."

I pick up my arms and do a funky-monkey walk around my station, then stop and laugh until I hear a woman shout from the dining room. "Sheridan!" I hurry out of the kitchen to see what's up and I am instantly dazzled. The stage has been set: the restaurant has been transformed into a springtime dream. Floor-to-ceiling vases stand in every corner, exploding with brightly colored flowers, and each round table is covered with a crisp white cloth and a short, fat glass vase packed with tulips, daffodils, and greenery.

Three long carved wooden tables, covered with flowers

and smooth green tablecloths, stand at angles along the back of the dining room. Rows of shining silver chafing dishes lie at the ready, tiny blue Sterno flames glowing beneath them.

And this is only the main room. There are private rooms upstairs that are probably even more spectacular.

"Sheridan! Help!" Dominique, Dad's pastry chef, is hunched over something, with her back to me. I slide up next to her and see the black lamb cake—decapitated!

Dominique's eyes are desperate. "First seating in less than an hour, and I don't have time to fix it!"

"Don't worry. I'll be back in two minutes." Cake Girl is on the job. I run through the kitchen, dodging busboys, avoiding pots of boiling water, and steering clear of chefs who wield knives bigger than my head. Just as I reach the back door, I hear him.

"Sheridan Wells, where the hell do you think you are going?"

It's my father. I snap around, fed up with his temper, with everything about him. "Oh, I'm *so* sorry!" The words erupt, loud and sharp. "I am going to save your stupid lamb cake—if that's okay with *the star*!" I fan my fingers out around my face and make my eyes real big. I must sound and look like a complete psycho. Even I am surprised by my anger.

All the people in the kitchen have stopped what they were doing and are looking from Dad to me and back again. No one talks to Donovan Wells like that. But that's okay; these days I am no one to him, just a character in his TV show.

He's frozen in shock, and I don't stick around for a response. I run out the door and into the cold, then sprint through the parking lot, across the alley, and into the back of the bakery. I am desperately trying to hold on to my good mood from this morning. It's a losing battle.

Sweetie's is flooded with customers. Nanny and Roz are out front with Mrs. Bartley and Ms. Pringle, residents of Lake Bluff Retirement Home who come to help out in a pinch.

I poke my head in and see my grandmother, all smiles as she helps her customers.

"Hey, Nan . . . black sheep lost its head!" I say, friendly, even though I'm still irritated by her behavior this morning.

"Oh, no!"

"Oh, yeah."

"Well, take what you need, darlin'. We're busier than a moth in a mitten in here!"

I survey the kitchen, deciding what supplies I'll need. A bamboo skewer. A sleeve of black buttercream. The tub of stainless-steel tips. I'll do better than bandage that lamb; I'll make it look better than it did before.

Shoving everything into a pink box, I think of ribbons. I'll need some, in case I can't disguise the wound. I push my way into Nanny's messy office and stretch for the ribbon dispenser on the credenza behind her desk. I can't quite reach it, so I squeeze between the chair and desk, grabbing a length of pastel plaid wired ribbon. Totally Eastery.

I paw around for the scissors, but there are so many papers that I can't find them. This desk is a catastrophe. I push back the chair and sit, picking through the piles, opening the top drawer.

Hello? Scissors?

As I hunt, my hand nudges the computer mouse. The screen saver flicks off, and there on the monitor is a Google search results screen.

I keep feeling for the scissors, but out of the corner of my eye, I notice the words that are highlighted on the Web page. Not just words. A name. *Margaret Taylor Kirby*.

There are ninety-nine thousand results. I can hear Nanny's booming voice up front, so I click the back arrow to see what else she's been searching for. *Margaret Taylor Wells. Margaret Taylor Canada*.

So, Nanny's been hunting, too.

I gather my supplies and take the whole spool of ribbon. I can't think about this now; I've got a lamb to save. I put my hand on the mouse and hit the back arrow one more time.

Margaret Taylor Sault Sainte Marie.

The back of my throat closes, and there's an acidic taste in my mouth. I scroll down the results, my eyes foggy. How did she know?

Save the lamb, Sheridan. So what if your grandmother has been keeping secrets from you? Do your job.

I slip out the back door, run over to the restaurant, and force myself to calm down. When I enter the kitchen, Dylan, who has been waiting for me, smiles.

"Thought I lost you," he says.

I try to shake off this horrible feeling. Nanny knows I want to find Mom. But did she know all along that Mom was in Sault Sainte Marie? I am so calling that bakery as soon as humanly possible.

Back at the restaurant, I go to work on the lamb. I force my mouth into a slight arc for the camera, but it's hardly sincere. Ignoring Dylan as he hovers over me like a bee above a flower, I fix the stupid cake.

At nine forty-five, Dad does a final inspection of the dining room. There are hungry customers waiting outside in a heated reception tent, sipping Mom's lemonade mimosas.

My father scans the room like a ship's captain. I stand near the door to the kitchen, pull off my hairnet, and watch him. This is a tradition, this final inspection, and I've been a part of it since I was a kid. He motions for one of the waiters to straighten his tie, for a waitress to smooth her apron. And then his eyes land on me. Dad looks me up and down. My once-white apron is now smeared with all the colors of the gastronomic rainbow. He clears his throat, surveys my worn-out running shoes and my hair—which is probably sticking out in every direction—and raises his eyebrows. I turn around and leave.

Although I'm stuck in the kitchen for the rest of the day, I'm sure every guest leaves fat and happy, full of incredible food made by the man who put St. Mary on the map. The famous Donovan Wells.

As I work, a new worry weighs me down. Nanny knows Mom is in Sault Sainte Marie. Is my own grandmother really a traitor?

I try to concentrate on my plan instead: bringing Mom home and convincing Dad to stay put. It's a simple plan, really. But as I dice onions for the frittata station, I obsess about what else Nanny knows, and what I don't. It's all sort of overwhelming. I stop what I'm doing and take a deep breath.

Dylan is keeping busy in the kitchen with his camera, but he doesn't film me anymore. Maybe he's had enough of me for the day, or maybe he can tell that the tears in my eyes aren't just from the onions.

Chapter 9

THE GREATEST THING
SINCE SLICED BREAD

I finally slump into the house, totally beat, at nine thirty. Brunch was served until four, but then there was a cocktail party for VIP customers, including the Suits. It's still going on, but they don't need me anymore.

I stumble up the stairs, take a long shower, throw on my comfy sweats, and flip open my laptop. I go to the Sweetie's listing and stare at the phone number. It's ten o'clock now, so they're closed. But I dial again anyway, listen to the greeting. I know I have to figure out what I'm going to say to her, but right now I'm so tired my brain hurts.

My eyes are drooping and I'm almost asleep when Jack's ringtone blares across the room.

"Hey?" I answer.

"Hey. You home?"

"Yeah. I think so."

"Tired?"

"Oh, yeah."

"Do the chem lab?"

"Oh. Crap," I mutter as my head drops to my chest. "Forget it. I'll just take the zero."

"No, you won't. I'll be over in twenty."

Before I can protest, he hangs up. When the doorbell rings in exactly twenty minutes, I am yanked out of a deep sleep in which I am making six-foot-tall gum paste lilac blossoms, dicing onions, and poring over endless pages of Internet search results—miraculously all at the same time. Weird.

The doorbell rings again.

I trudge downstairs, open the door just a crack. "Is that what I think it is?" I point to the steaming travel mug in Jack's left hand. He raises his eyebrows.

"Thought you might need some."

I fling open the door and throw my arms around him. "I love you!"

He stumbles backward a little. "Here, just take it. No need for public displays of affection."

I take the warm cup of coffee into my eager hands. We walk to the kitchen and sit as I take a sip.

"Mmm . . . you make this?"

He nods, picks up his backpack, and pulls out his chem book.

"Ick. Do we hafta?" I'm just miserable at this stuff, although Jack tells me I use chemistry every time I mix icing colors. I don't even argue back that that is so not the same thing.

"Yes, we hafta." He opens the book and flips back and forth, looking for the right page. "So . . ." His eyes peer up at me warily. "How long did you wait to call the number?"

I sit up a little. I can't lie to Jack, but this is going to piss him off.

"Jack. It's a bakery. Not like a private residence or anything."

He smacks his forehead with his palm. "Why can't you just be patient?"

"I don't have to be patient; I know it's her." I take another long sip of coffee. "I was in Nanny's office, and I saw on her computer that she'd been searching for Mom in Sault Sainte Marie. And I hadn't even told her."

Jack sighs. "Then why don't you ask Nanny first, before you make a fool out of yourself with some complete stranger?"

"Because . . ." I put the mug down on the table. "She'll try to talk me out of it. And I don't have time. I need to get Mom back here fast."

He stares at me suspiciously. "Wait. I thought you just wanted to contact her. Why do you need her here fast?"

Something about Jack makes me blurt things out to him that I should just keep to myself.

"Nothing. Never mind. I just want to find her, okay?

Before my dad tries to drag me to some foreign country."

"Sheridan. New York City is not a foreign country."

"Might as well be." I stare at my coffee, pick it up, take a long swallow.

"No." Jack opens his notebook and clicks his pen. "It's 779.58 miles away. Twelve hours and forty-five minutes by car. I Mapquested it."

I smile up at him. "You honestly think the Beast could make it that far?" I'm speaking of his ancient Corolla.

"That car does whatever I tell it to do."

"Well, that's debatable. But I am still not going."

"No, no, of course not. Why would you want to go live in the most incredible city in the world?"

I sit back. "Okay. Can we just not talk about this right now?"

"Fine."

"And you'll still help me with Mom?"

He nods. "Just promise me we've seen the last of the restraining orders?"

"Ha-ha," I say sarcastically, noticing his face. All his zits are gone, thanks to Dr. Holliday, the magical dermatologist. The baby fat around his cheeks has disappeared, setting off his dark eyes. It's not so hard to see why girls at school think he's cute. And why they get annoyed at me because I'm his best friend.

There's a moment of silence before Jack picks up a pencil and opens his notebook.

"You writing the lab on your hand or something?" he asks.

"Oh. You're gonna make me walk back upstairs?" I stand up. "My bed's up there; no promises I'll come back down."

He steadies his gaze at me. "Don't worry," he says. "I'll come after you."

Our eyes meet and lock, for just a second longer than normal. A tiny spark zaps me. He flinches like it zapped him, too. What was that? Besides weird, I mean. I turn away quickly, laugh, and run upstairs, trying to ignore whatever just happened.

I do come back down, with paper and pencil, and by ten thirty we're done. I send him on his way with a "See you tomorrow" and try not to think about how it made me feel when he said he'd come after me. It wasn't a big deal—not like when I see Ethan. Still, it was something. And that's a complication I do not need.

I wake to a room flooded with light. My head twitches toward the alarm clock. Seven thirty? Oh God! I forgot to set it. I have exactly thirty minutes to get to school. I jump out of bed onto the cold wood floor and hightail it to the shower.

In the bathroom mirror I see major damage from Easter Sunday. Puffy, red eyes, and hair like Medusa's. There's a lot of work to do here and not a lot of time to do it. I hear Dad snoring down the hall and wonder what time he got home.

I make no effort to be quiet or let him sleep in peace.

The shower wakes me up a little, but not nearly as much as a jumbo latte would—if I had time to grab one. Not likely. I jump soaking wet into my fluffy blue bathrobe and feel various body parts turn to icicles. With a toothbrush, I erase my dragon breath and then take a comb to my hair. I'll never make it. And Mr. Wasserman doesn't just give tardies; he makes an example of you.

I can't stand the thought of being humiliated in front of Haley again.

And what if she's heard about Ethan's strange visit to the bakery? What if she's gotten wind of the fact that her boyfriend—er, ex-boyfriend—has kind of maybe asked me out? I'll be dead before lunch. Killed.

I shimmy into my jeans and pull a long-sleeved button-down over a lace-topped white cami. I dry my hair for exactly two minutes, which accomplishes exactly nothing. So I sweep it up into a clip and apply three swipes of mascara and a smudge of lipstick. No time to work miracles. This will have to do.

Seven forty-five. I grab my bag and my coat and hop down the stairs while pulling on my boots. Dad is still sawing logs, but I give the door a good hard slam just so he knows I'm gone.

Oh my God! It's got to be below freezing outside. I quickly stick my arms into my coat and pull up the hood. No cakes for me if I get pneumonia. Then I run—I mean, *run*—down the alley and up onto Main Street.

Seven fifty, by my watch. I can do this. I push through the door of Geronimo's and wave to Mrs. Davis, who then points to the gigantic wall clock behind her.

"I know, I know," I say. "But I won't make it to second period without some coffee." There's a line, but in under a minute, she passes me a cup from around the side of the counter.

"Now get to school," she whispers.

"Thank you, thank you, thank you." I whisk the coffee out of her hand and head for the door. I can feel the warmth of the cup through my mittens and can't wait to take a sip.

I round the corner. Only one more block. By the time I can see the building, the front steps are deserted. I must have missed the first bell.

I'm trying to stabilize my coffee and walk as fast as humanly possible when I hear footsteps in the snow behind me. Apparently, I'm not the only delinquent this morning.

"Mornin'." As soon as I hear the voice, I know who it is. I turn my head and see Ethan closing in on me.

"Hi . . . ," I say through an awkward smile, trying to act cool and totally not succeeding. "I'm so late. *We* are so late. Come on."

But he's slowed down. His long legs could beat mine by a mile, but they stall and stop.

"You coming?" I ask.

He smiles, a cat-that-ate-the-canary grin on his face. That's what Nanny would call it.

When he doesn't answer, I assume he's staying put.

"All right . . . ," I say, totally rejected. "Bye."

"You wanna skip?" He kicks a pile of snow next to him.

"Skip?" I try to keep moving toward the steps, but I am caught in his tractor-beam smile. "For real?" He's kidding. He's got to be kidding.

"Come on, you probably worked all day yesterday. I'll call in for you." He looks at me from under lowered lids. "No one will ever know."

I laugh. No way can I do this. "Really? I mean, I can't." I am on the first step. "I've never . . . Are you serious?"

"Yeah. Come on, let's do it." He looks up at the front doors. "I mean, look at that rat hole. I can't even stand the thought of going in there today."

I follow his eyes up to the school, all prison-like and stone-faced. It *is* a total rat hole. But still. "If I get caught . . ." I finish that thought in my head. No cakes.

Ethan turns and walks away. He seems to have made a decision. "You are not going to get caught." He motions for me to follow. "But the first rule of skipping and *not* getting caught is to put as much distance between yourself and the actual school as possible."

The final bell rings. He motions for me again. One foot moves away from the steps. The other one follows. Oh God. I'm ditching with Ethan Murphy. And no matter how many times I repeat that sentence in my head, I can't believe it's true.

* * *

Once we're off school grounds, he slows down. I am a step behind him, glancing sideways. What now?

"I can't believe I'm doing this," I say, more to myself than to him.

"You'll get over it." He grabs my hand like it's the most natural action in the world. My mittens are still on, but I can feel the heat coming off his bare skin.

I peek over my shoulder like an escaped felon holding the hand of an accomplice. And the fact that I'm trying so hard to steady my latte so it doesn't slosh around strikes me as completely ridiculous. I mean, what kind of fugitive cares if her coffee spills?

"So what do you wanna do, Sheridan Wells?" he asks, and squeezes my hand.

Three options come to mind: (1) kiss him—hard, (2) figure out how not to be a spaz around him, or (3) run away, go get my tardy, and pretend this never happened. Number three is my most likely choice.

"Wanna go for a drive?" he says.

"Um . . . sure. Where to?"

"Anywhere that isn't here." He laughs.

"Okay." I'm sure this sounds utterly uncool, but I say it anyway: "For how long?"

We turn another corner, and then we're standing in front of his house. Well, his mansion, really. The tall wrought-iron fence casts shadows on the sidewalk as we reach the gate.

"I don't know." He shrugs. "As long as you want."

He grips my hand again and pulls me along like I'm completely brain-dead. Before Ethan lived here, Nanny was a member of the Historical Society and worked to make this house a landmark. It was built by some cereal baron a long time ago and is undoubtedly the biggest, most ornate house in St. Mary. When we reach the door, Ethan unlocks it, pushes it open, and walks in. "Here we are."

I step inside and gasp. Marble floors in the entrance lead to a sweeping grand staircase. An enormous chandelier hangs above us. I am in awe. He laughs when he sees my face.

"I know, it's ridiculous, isn't it?"

When I stop gawking, my wide eyes land on his.

"You're funny," he says.

What? Was that a compliment? "I'm funny?"

"Yeah. Funny. Different."

"Thanks." I do a 360 in the huge foyer. "I think."

He walks away, through a giant dining room. "Come on, let's pick a car." We move through a short hallway into a kitchen that would fit my entire chemistry class and then some.

"Wow!" Now I'm in complete shock.

"What?"

"This is the nicest kitchen I've ever seen."

"Oh, come on." He rolls his eyes. "Whatever. Donovan Wells is your dad. You've seen kitchens nicer than this."

I don't know what he thinks it means to be related to Donovan Wells, but he's got the wrong idea.

"No. This is definitely the nicest kitchen I've ever seen. Is your mom a cook or something?"

I clamp my mouth shut. If I ask him about his family, he might ask me about mine. And that's the last topic I want to discuss.

"That's the joke," he says. "No. She hates to cook. I'm the one who loves it."

"Oh, right," I say, sure that he's kidding.

"I'm serious. I'm actually pretty good. I'll prove it to you one of these days." He leans against a counter. "But my mother really just got the kitchen to piss off Rod."

"Rod?"

"My dad." Ethan walks to the fridge, a beautiful Sub-Zero that could hold a side of beef or two. "She's determined to make him pay."

My fingers slide across the cold white quartz countertops, probably worth more than most of the houses in St. Mary.

"He must be paying big-time."

"Yep." He shrugs. "You want a Coke?"

"No thanks." I have yet to take a sip of my latte, which is sitting on a corner of the kitchen island.

"That's what happens when you take off: you pay," he says, reaching in and grabbing a can for himself.

My eyes skip around the room. I am not sure how to

respond to that comment. I wonder if he knows about Mom. I wonder what price she's paid for leaving us.

I glance at a clock on the wall, figuring that by now I have been marked absent by Wasserman. Funny—I'm feeling nervous but also exhilarated. Not just to be here, with the hottest guy in St. Mary, but also to be breaking the rules. I am not a rule breaker.

I finally take a sip of my latte, which is now cold. This will all be fine—as long as I don't get caught. If I do . . . I don't want to think about it. I have a lot of cakes on the books for the next few months. Who will make them if I'm locked away?

I watch Ethan walk to the phone and start dialing. "This is Donovan Wells calling in for Sheridan." His voice is so manly he doesn't even have to deepen it to sound like my father. "She's got a fever and will be staying home."

He hangs up like he pretends to be someone else's dad every day.

I guess it's official: I am skipping school.

"Thanks?" I try not to look terrified.

"Sure." He is so cute I can't stand it. And his stare makes me blush from forehead to feet.

"Are you gonna call for yourself?"

Ethan stops, smiles. "No one cares if I skip school. My mom's in Gatlinburg with her latest boy toy. Doesn't care."

"But . . . don't you need an excuse?"

He shuffles over to where I'm standing and leans on the

counter, his face a foot away from mine. So close we are sharing the same oxygen. The little hairs on my arms are standing at attention; my whole body is trapped in this electric field that seems to surround him. His blue eyes are shining.

"If it makes you feel better, I'll forge a note from my mother and bring it in tomorrow."

"Yes, I think that's a good idea." He touches my arm and I quiver, even under my thick coat. My body is one big fat nerve ending.

I try to act confident, like I'm in on some joke, but I am a total fraud, an imposter. He's still looking at me. I think his face has moved closer. Just a millimeter. But still. I have no idea what to do.

"Um . . . is there a bathroom?"

He stands straight up and turns around. "Right through there." I wasn't trying to kill the mood, I swear. But I have. Completely.

I walk into the most beautiful powder room ever, with scarlet walls and a fancy gilded mirror. A light fixture drips with crystals above the toilet, and on the wall is a painting. Not a framed print but a real painting. He has fine art in the bathroom.

The golden mirror mocks me as I wash my hands.

What are you doing, Sheridan? You've never even kissed a boy. Not really. And Ethan is used to a different kind of girl. You are so far out of your league, they're gonna have to send up a flare so you can find your way back.

I switch off the light and the mirror stops talking. I lean on the wall in the dark and think. Or try to. This is not a good idea. I know that.

But in my defense, I have had it rough. My mother, gone all these years. My father with his own big plans. I work hard. I put up with a lot. I think I deserve to ignore the rules once in a while. To spend one day with someone like Ethan Murphy.

I push the door open before I change my mind. "Okay," I say. He's waiting for me, just outside the door.

"You sure?"

"Yes."

"Good. Let's go." He leads me down a hall and through a door to the garage. A light comes on. Okay, so not only is his *house* bigger than my house, his *garage* is bigger than my house . . . and it is filled with sparkling cars. There's a black BMW SUV, a blue Volvo sedan, and a cherry-red convertible Corvette with racing stripes. At the far end, a speedboat.

"Which one do you like?" he asks.

"I have no idea." I turn to him and give him a flirty smile. "You choose."

"Okay then." He looks at me as he moves down the row. "Definitely not a Volvo girl." He keeps walking. "The SUV?" He shakes his head. "Too expected." He makes it to the Corvette and opens the passenger door. "You may not be a Corvette girl, either, but I think I can convert you."

I take a step forward. "What if I don't want to be a Corvette girl?"

He smiles. "Don't worry. Give me ten minutes, and you'll be begging me to let you drive. Come on. Get in."

I hesitate, still back by the BMW.

"You know I'm a very trustworthy individual," he says in a mock serious tone.

My feet walk me over to the open car door. "Hmm . . . that's not the story I've been told." I slide into the car, and he leans in, grabs my seat belt, pulls it across my lap.

"Don't believe everything you hear, okay?" He's so close I can smell his shampoo. I attempt a cool smile. If I leaned forward, our lips would touch.

He closes my door, crosses over to the driver's side, and slips behind the wheel. The garage door inches open as he sticks the key in the ignition and revs the engine. We pull out with a loud *vroom*, announcing to the entire town that I, Sheridan Wells, am skipping school and going who knows where in a bright red sports car with a boy that I really just met.

Ethan turns the car around in the circular drive and peels out onto the street. School, the restaurant, my mother, the TV show, even my cakes—they're all dropping away behind us. This is a scary, out-of-control sensation, like jumping from an airplane. I might be petrified that the chute won't open, but the free fall is awesome.

Ethan shifts gears like a race car driver as we climb uphill, still-dormant trees passing by in a blur.

"You're not worried, are you?" Ethan asks.

"No." That's a lie, but I am trying to relax. I may never get an opportunity like this again, and I don't want to waste it. "I'm not worried at all."

His profile is so handsome that it's all I can do not to reach out and trace it with my finger. Mr. Roz, who doesn't speak English very well, likes to use the phrase *the greatest thing since sliced bread.* He usually uses it in the wrong context. But those are the words that come to mind as I fix Ethan in my peripheral vision.

And it's so true, really. I mean, where would we be as a society without sliced bread? It makes life so easy. No matter how crazy things get, you can always slap two slices of bread together, make a sandwich, and go.

Yep. Sliced bread. Best thing ever.

Chapter 10

HAPPY AS A CLAM

Ethan drives and talks, a lot, which gives me some time to pull myself together. I remind myself that I am not shy. Ethan is just a boy (though an incredibly hot one), and I am not afraid of boys. I can do this!

"You have any brothers or sisters?" he asks.

"Nope. Just me," I say. "You?"

He tells me about his half sister, who lives in Paris, down the street from the Cordon Bleu. After he graduates, he wants to go to school there and learn how to cook. "Yeah, I've got half siblings all over, but I pretty much function as an only child." He revs the engine as we climb a steep hill.

"When did you start cooking?" I ask, relieved that I am no longer mute around him.

"I was eleven when my dad left, and my mom was always working. When I got home from school, she wouldn't let me go anywhere or do anything. She thought he'd abduct me or something. So I stayed home and watched cooking shows. After a while, I started trying some of the recipes on my own."

I picture him as a kid, all alone in a fancy kitchen, cooking for just himself. Kind of sad.

"What about you? When did you become Cake Girl?"

I laugh at the way he says "Cake Girl," all loud and echoey like it's a superhero name.

"My mom started teaching me when I was little." I smile, remembering. "She could make anything out of cake. She got me into it. And my grandmother, too. Then when I was like twelve, I started doing it on my own."

"You love it?"

I look out my window; I've lost track of where we are. "Yeah, I do." If I knew him better, I might tell him more. Like how sometimes when I'm decorating cakes, I can almost feel Mom there with me. And how I worry that if I ever stop, I lose her forever. But I keep that to myself, for now.

He rounds a corner fast. I hold on to the door handle.

"What kind of food do you cook?" I ask, trying not to watch as he zooms around blind corners.

"Just about anything. No cakes, though." He winks at me. "But French, Southwestern, Italian. I make a mean clam linguini." He suddenly shifts the car into a lower gear and turns onto a small one-lane road. "What about you? What do you wanna be when you grow up?"

"I guess I'll run the bakery, eventually."

"No college?"

"No, my father will make me go. But I can go to Grand Valley State and still live at home."

Ethan's head flips toward me. "You serious? I thought your dad was gonna have a show. Aren't you gonna move to New York or L.A. or something?"

"Not me. I like it here," I say, desperately searching for a change of subject.

"Really?" He sneers. "What's to like? Just a bunch of nosy freaks and pain-in-the-ass tourists."

I pick at the edge of my seat, like a little kid. Then I realize that this is not cheap fake leather, so I stop. "It's not so bad here."

"No, not if you like hick towns."

Most of the kids I know feel the same way about St. Mary, like it's the most boring place on the face of the earth. But to me it's perfect.

"Seriously, the only thing this town has going for it is your dad," Ethan continues.

"My dad?" I can't help but laugh.

"Yeah. Your dad. He is an awesome chef. Last week, I had his veal marsala. Oh my God, best I've ever eaten. And I've eaten everywhere—in Paris, Rome . . . Your dad is phenomenal."

"All right, all right. Jeez, why don't you marry him?" I laugh and roll my eyes.

"You know, if he looked like you, I might consider it."

He reaches over and puts his hand on my thigh. I peek down at it, just resting there, on my leg. I'm not believing this is happening. He moves it off to shift gears, but I can feel its imprint.

"You don't know how good you've got it, Cake Girl. And a TV show? Man, that's crazy."

My fingers twine together and I shrug. "I'm actually pretty happy the way things are."

"Come on. You don't really think that."

Actually, I do. Or I will, once I talk to Mom and convince Dad to say no to New York City. I twist my hips in the seat to face Ethan. "Can we not talk about this anymore?"

He smiles and makes another turn, this time onto a narrow gravel road. At the entrance is a sign that says CREEKWOOD in fancy letters, and below that, NO TRESPASSING, PRIVATE PROPERTY.

My eyes follow the sign as we pass, and I silently pray that I won't end up in jail by nightfall. "Where are we?"

"This is my dad's place. Don't worry, he's in Milan." He stops the car and points to the snowy hillside, thick with bare trees. "Look at that."

I follow his finger to a family of deer in the woods. "They're hungry . . . probably sicker of this weather than we are."

That's when he turns to me, our faces so close now that I wonder if he might kiss me. And then he tilts his head to one side and wrinkles an eyebrow. "Why haven't we met before?" He moves closer and I smile.

There's a sudden thunderstorm in my head. Nanny's been lecturing me about this for years, ever since I was twelve and Lori was caught French-kissing a boy under the bleachers at school. I asked Nan what French kissing was, and man, she gave me the Baptist "boys are evil" lecture of a lifetime. Her exact final words: "It's simple. Your body is a temple, youngin. Don't go lettin' any boy deface your temple. You will regret it." I was twelve and had absolutely no idea what she was talking about.

But it's clearer now. With Ethan. Does he want to deface me? Do I want to be defaced? Okay, this is the weirdest train of thought ever. He's close, moving closer. There is nothing simple about this. Nothing simple at all.

"What are you thinking about? Cakes?" I can almost taste his words. He lifts a hand, touches my cheek, brushes my hair back.

"No." A little giggle escapes. "Not exactly."

Then his lips come closer, and I know it's going to happen. Those lips touch mine, light and sweet. No big deal. Only it's a hugely big deal. It's my first real kiss, and I can't even believe it's coming from the mouth of Ethan Murphy.

He pauses, then pulls away, leaving my smiling face hanging in midair. "I've been wanting to do that for a long time," he says. Then he faces forward and guns the engine, moving us up the hill.

Really? I wonder how long he could have possibly been wanting to do that. Before the day he came into the bakery, I'd thought I was invisible to him.

I tell myself to stop it. Just be happy. My first kiss is under my belt, and from the most gorgeous guy on the planet. I let out a big internal *whee!* and try not to worry about what will happen next.

He doesn't speak as the steep hill evens out into a circular driveway in front of another huge house, built onto a bluff. Ethan puts the car in park, gets out. "Let me go shut off the alarm."

I emerge from the passenger seat, still feeling the kiss, the weight of those lips. I walk to the edge of the driveway and glimpse, far below me, Lake Michigan. I've never seen it like this, from so high up, surrounded by tall, dense forest, the lake churning and reaching beyond the horizon. It's beautiful. I have this crazy thought that maybe we took one of those turns too fast and collided with a truck or something, and now I'm dead. I think this would make a pretty good heaven.

Ethan comes back, stands at my side.

"This is so beautiful." I can't think of anything more profound to say.

"Yeah. It's my favorite place."

I choose to ignore the fact that I'm probably not the first girl he's brought here. In fact, Haley may have been the last.

"Let me cook for you?"

That sounds relatively innocent. I nod. "Sounds good. Clam linguini?"

"Of course."

I stare out at the lake. I've got this insane feeling that I might cry. I am so happy. But I concentrate really hard and push that feeling back. Crying right now would maybe be the dumbest thing ever.

Ethan leans toward me and grabs my hand, and I turn to him. Before I know what's happening, our lips are touching again, and all I can think is *Am I doing this right?* I want to savor the moment, but I'm so unprepared. Two kisses in ten minutes is a lot to handle. I think of big movie love scenes and try hard to pretend I'm one of those stars who make it look so easy. His lips are soft and his mouth tastes toothpaste-y. But I'm not keeping up with him. He pulls away first. Not a good sign.

"Come on." As he gently leads me toward the giant house in front of us, my cell rings in my pocket.

"It's Lori."

"Who?" he asks. Of course he doesn't know my friends.

I pull the phone out, hit Ignore. But a few seconds pass and I'm hearing her ringtone again.

"What's up with her?" he says, opening the front door.

I press the phone to my ear. "Hey." I try to sound

irritated. But by now she knows I didn't come to school. I've got some explaining to do.

"Hey yourself, nerd. You'd better get your butt back here. They let us out of school. The Monster finally croaked."

"What?" I say, in shock.

"You heard me."

The Monster, the legendary ancient furnace at the high school, is dead?

"They let us out early, Sher. And if your dad or Nanny catches wind of it, they'll wonder where you are. By the way, where are you?"

"Um. Sick?"

"Don't even. I was right inside the front doors waiting for you with a muffin. Saw the whole thing. So did Jack. We were late. Got detention."

So much for being sneaky. I suck at it. Ethan walks inside the house, but I haven't made it over the threshold.

"Not that I have anything against you getting a little action," Lori continues. "But consider yourself warned."

"I can't come back now," I say, even though I know that I have to.

Ethan returns and leans on the door. "Come in," he mouths, and disappears inside.

I shake my head. Lori's right; the St. Mary telegraph will get me in the end. My father will find out. *What was I thinking?*

"Hello?" Lori says, then laughs. "You do anything you regret yet?"

"Good-bye." I flip my phone down, and Ethan is back in the doorway, holding a saucepan. My mouth contorts into an embarrassed grin. "I've got to get back. The furnace died. School's out."

His arm drops to his side. "Why? You're not skipping if there's no school, right?"

I scrunch my eyes up, and I hope, hope, hope that he'll understand. "I'm sorry. But I'll be in so much trouble if I get caught. I can't get in trouble now . . ."

Before I can finish my sentence, he turns around and walks away. "Fine," he says over his shoulder.

"Sorry."

He carries the pan into the depths of the house, which I still haven't entered, and comes back empty-handed. He moves to the alarm pad on the wall and resets it, then comes outside without a word. As he descends the porch steps and gets into the car, he won't even look at me. I follow, arms crossed.

I slip into the passenger side. He doesn't help me with my seat belt this time; just waits for me to close the door. The engine roars and he backs up, turns around, and speeds off down the hill, kicking up dead leaves like a tornado.

He doesn't talk, and I feel this dream going bad really fast. "Look, I'm sorry," I say. "I've never done anything like this. There's something really important I'm trying to do, and if I'm grounded for eternity, it won't happen."

He twitches his head toward me. Maybe he can tell this is important, because his eyes soften, and I feel like maybe we're okay again.

"Sounds pretty mysterious." He laughs. If he asks me now, I will tell him about bringing my mom back and convincing a major TV network that we don't need to live in New York City. But he doesn't ask. "Whatever. I was just looking forward to spending some time with you."

He reaches for my hand and pulls it to the gearshift.

"You ready to drive?" I've never driven a stick; I can't even drive an automatic, really.

"No! I have no clue what I'm doing!" I say, smiling, relieved that he doesn't seem to be mad anymore.

His hand stays on top of mine, shifts to a different gear. I have no clue how to have a boyfriend, either, but for Ethan Murphy I'd be willing to learn.

We slip back into town, talking and laughing the whole way. He's funny and real, and I'm really starting to feel like myself with him. Before we can step out of the car and into the dark garage, he leans over and kisses me again. I need to relax and focus because my lips are not cooperating. But I can't concentrate. I feel his hand messing with the bottom of my shirt and there's a voice in my head that is telling me very unromantic things. Like *Slow down, sister.* And the voices sounds just like Nanny, which is definitely a mood killer.

He's getting pretty into this. *Slow. Down.* I stop first this time.

He sits back in his seat. "Wow," he says.

Wow what? Wow, that sucked, or wow, that was the best kiss ever? He doesn't explain.

"We better get you back to town. Don't want you to get a reputation." He climbs out of the car, and I let that comment sink in. Like my mother? Is that what people will think when they see me with Ethan?

I swing open the door and he's there, waiting. "Want to go for coffee?"

It's almost lunchtime, and all I've put in my stomach today is a latte. The last thing I need is coffee. But I also don't want this to end. He grabs my hand again. If the kisses are a little awkward, at least there's this: his hand feels perfect in mine.

"I would love a coffee," I say.

We walk out of the garage, through the gate, and down the hill from his house.

"You wanna give this a try again? I mean, legally, next time?"

"Legally?" I ask.

"Like, a real live date?"

I know that if I go on a date with Ethan, Jack will hate me, Haley will kill me, and Lori will never give me a moment's peace, wanting to know all the details.

But as Ethan and I are walking together, his hair

blowing back in the freezing wind, I don't care. He catches me watching him, and he delivers that smile. The one that makes me all wiggly inside. "Legally would be good," I say.

Ethan pushes open the door of Geronimo's, and I'm feeling so blissed out that it takes me a minute to register all the faces that have turned to stare. I look down and realize that we are still holding hands, like we're going out. Like Ethan Murphy is my boyfriend.

My eyes travel to our regular table. Lori's there, with Tuba Dude Jim, her boyfriend of the minute. I look from her to the next table, then to the next, where my eyes land on Haley, live and in person, surrounded by her groupies. She glares at me like I just threw up on her.

Ethan shouts to one of his buddies waiting in line. He hasn't let go of my hand yet. I look back to Lori and then see Jack coming out of the back room with a gallon of milk in each hand. Geronimo's is busy with school letting out early, and Mrs. Davis probably asked him if he could work. Of course he said yes.

When Jack sees me, his entire face turns to stone. And then, as he passes a table full of jocks, one of the long-legged basketball morons sticks out a foot, and Jack drops like a sack of potatoes. He falls flat, saving one gallon, but all he can do is watch as the other hurtles out of reach and bursts open on the floor. I let go of Ethan's hand and rush to my best friend, the room filling up with laughter.

Mrs. Davis hurries around the counter. "What happened?" But Jack won't tell.

"Accident. Sorry. I'll clean it up."

He's still on the floor when I hold out a hand to help him up. "You okay?"

But his eyes are fierce, and he gets up on his own. I go from worried to scared in less than a second.

"You get that chem lab turned in okay?" he says in a cold voice. My heart plummets like a boulder in my chest.

The room applauds as he stands up. And being Jack, he bows to the audience. A few ninth-grade girls are circling, checking to see that he's all right.

"Jack?" I say.

Mrs. Davis brings a few dish towels to throw on the spill.

"Jack?" He's not looking at me.

"I don't want to talk to you." He turns away and smiles at one especially perky freshman.

Ethan, done talking to his friend now, steps over the milk puddle, oblivious to what happened. He puts his hand on the small of my back. It's a nice, new sensation, Ethan's touch. But I can't enjoy it. "Come on, let's sit," he says.

"Okay. Just a minute," I say, and watch Jack go to the back room.

I stand paralyzed on the edge of this river of milk, wondering what to do. The sounds of the espresso machine and teenage gibberish echo in my ears as Jack returns with the mop and bucket. He stares at that mop as he moves it back and forth, back and forth. Finally, he glances up and our eyes meet.

And that's when I know. It's as clear as the sky on this frigid April day.

I've broken his heart.

Chapter 11

MAKE LIKE A BANANA AND SPLIT

It's like my life has taken a 180-degree turn since Palm Sunday, only a week and a half ago. It's Wednesday now. Ethan meets me in the hallways, greets me with kisses. I think I'm getting better at the kissing, but I've got a lot to learn. It seems like the most natural thing in the world to him. I, however, am a total amateur.

Everyone knows about me and Ethan, and the buzz about the TV show has reached a fever pitch. Now all these kids who I haven't spoken to since grade school come up to me and act like we're best friends. Except for Haley, of course. She passes me between classes, always with the same smug grin plastered across her face. Like she's up to something.

The worst part is that Jack isn't talking to me at all. And I have no idea what to say to him to make things better. Whatever it was I saw in his eyes at the coffee shop on Monday has spooked me. Sadness? Anger? Love, maybe? At the very least, I think he likes me. Scratch that. He *liked* me. Now he can't even look at me.

Art class is especially uncomfortable, since he sits right next to me. I want so badly to update him about Mom. Tell him that I called the bakery again and got the machine. Called again, got a woman, and hung up on her like a big chicken.

I still have no idea what to say.

But the party is a week from Saturday, and preproduction is in full swing. I need to talk to her if this plan is going to work. Like today.

The Suits have the cake sketch, but they want the guest list, too. I've been stalling on that one. Amazon sends me text messages fifty times a day about it; I can't hold her off much longer.

I'm in my room now, and due at the bakery in a half hour. The guest list is up on the laptop, but my cell phone is in my hand. Mom's number is selected and my thumb is hovering over the Send button. I can do this.

In an attempt to calm my nerves, I pull out the box of cards. I pick one out and read the note inside.

One decade old already! I just won first place in a huge contest here in London and thought of you and your birthday cake. I wonder what it will look like. My winner was covered in silver butterflies. You would have loved it. Hope you have a happy day. Love you, Cupcake. Mom.

I smile. Why am I so afraid of talking to my own mother? Ridiculous. I hit Send and the number dials. It's late in the afternoon and most bakeries close early. But I've got to take a chance.

One ring. My heart is beating faster. *Don't freak out. Just relax.* Two rings. Then another.

Click. "Hello?"

Oh no, it's a woman's voice. My palms are sweaty, and I almost panic and hit End.

But I stop myself. "Hello?" I say, my voice a shaky mess.

"Yeah, hello?" She sounds harsh, not at all like my mother.

"Hi. Um, I'm interested in ordering a cake by Maggie Taylor. Does she work there?"

The person on the other side laughs. "Not really. Owns the place. But she's never around. Always off at some contest or other."

"Oh."

"You wanna leave a message?" Clearly this woman has no real grasp of customer service.

"Um. My wedding is coming up soon; I really need to get in touch with her."

"Well, she's gonna be in Chicago this weekend, and she doesn't like me giving out her private number."

"No. I understand." My heart is beating even faster now. "But she's going to be in Chicago?"

"Yeah, some cake contest. Big surprise."

"Oh, that's where I live. Maybe I can go and see her?" I ask, trying hard to sound casual.

"Look, lady, see her, don't see her. Whatever. I got work to do."

"Wait—"

She hangs up without another word.

But I don't care because this is the break I needed. Mom's going to be in Chicago, only a few hours from here. I *can* go to see her. And maybe Jack will drive me; maybe that will smooth over his weirdness about me and Ethan.

He can't say no. At least I hope not. Still, I know better than to ask him over the phone or in a text. It has to be face-to-face.

I get back to the guest list. They want me to give fifteen names. So far I've got Lori, who will bring Tuba Dude Jim if they are still dating when the party rolls around. That's two. Ethan, of course, unless he wakes up and realizes that I'm no superhot cheerleader. Three. Jack, because he's been to every birthday party I've ever had.

That's just four, and Lori is the only sure thing, really.

On the desk my phone starts to wiggle. It's a text from Ethan.

WU? he writes.

I wish I could tell him what was up. I found my mom,

and now I'm going to Chicago to see her. But how do you explain that in a text?

Going to work, I type.

It's true. I've got to get to the bakery. Growly's eightieth birthday party is Friday, and I'm making the cake. Growly's a real pain, but this cake is going to be fantastic. There's also a basket weave wedding cake due on Saturday.

I need to go to work for other reasons, too. Anytime I'm stressed or worried, it's the only place where I can totally relax. And feel close to Mom. I know who I am when I'm at the bakery.

That sux, he texts back.

Yeah sorry.

Date fri night?

I don't have the heart to tell him I've got to work at Father Crowley's birthday party. But we can meet up after.

Yeah sounds good. Delete, delete, delete, delete.

I change *good* to *great.*

I'm crossing the alley on my way to the bakery when I notice something. I've been so preoccupied with everything else, I hadn't realized: most of the snow is gone, and there's a smell in the air. Spring.

This puts a smile on my face, and I decide to go to Jack's after I'm done at the bakery. Maybe he'll run down to the beach with me. Then I can ask him about Chicago. And we can put this ridiculous fight, or whatever it is, behind us.

I push my way through the screen door to the bakery kitchen. The inside door is propped open, to let in the fresh air. Mr. Roz is standing there, waiting with the next item on my to-do list, an enormous round banana layer cake. This is for Growly. Banana is his favorite.

I came up with the idea to replicate the rectory garden, which Growly probably loves more than Jesus Himself, on the top of the cake. The garden is a pretty spectacular place during the summer, with about a million flowers in bloom. We used to go there for church picnics when I was a kid, but it's been a long time since I've visited.

Nanny brought out one of her photo albums to inspire me. There're a few pages of pictures that were taken in the garden. I'm in them, too, all smiles. I must have been eight or so. Anyway, it was after Mom left. I'm surprised that I don't look sadder, considering my mother had disappeared.

But I guess I've always had hope. Never stopped believing she'd come back one day. Even if I had to drag her back myself.

"Where's Nanny?" I ask Roz, who flashes me a ready smile.

"Senior Movie Madness Night," he says.

"Ah." Nanny and the rest of the St. Mary widows never miss it. But that woman's been avoiding me since Easter. It's like she knows that I found out she's a big liar.

"You okay? You look not so happy."

"No. I'm fine. Better than fine, actually. Just busy. Too

much going on up here, you know?" I point to my head.

He laughs. "Yes, I do know how dat is." He's making meringues for a tea party at the mayor's house tomorrow morning. "You needing someone to talk to?"

I guess I could tell him a little. "Off the record?"

"What is dat, 'off the record'?"

"Like, just between you and me."

"Ah, sure, sure. Of course. You and me."

I smooth frosting around Growly's cake. This is called the crumb coat, and it'll form a base for the fondant I'll add later. I pause, wondering how much I should reveal to Mr. Roz.

"You ever lost a good friend?"

I level the thick buttercream until it's perfectly even, pick up the cake, and place it in the cooler to firm up. In the meantime, I pull out some white fondant and work some red food coloring into it for the roses. Roz finishes a tray of the teardrop-shaped treats and puts them in the oven to bake. I wonder if he heard me.

I'm about to ask again when he speaks. "I have. I have lost many friend."

Nice, Sheridan. Mr. Roz is from Kosovo. He came to America during their war, with nothing, lost everyone and everything. Nanny says he barely escaped with his life, but that's all she knows. He doesn't talk about it very much.

Now I feel like an idiot for even bringing it up.

"I'm sorry."

"No, don't be sorry. What you want to know?"

"Well, did you ever lose a friend because they were maybe a little jealous?" I ask.

"Ah, now you must be talking about love. That can be a fast way to lose a friend, no?"

I grab a rolling pin and begin to flatten the fondant on the counter. "Yeah, I guess."

"Can be a difficult thing, love." He picks up a clipboard and flips through orders. "But you want my advice? You listen to your heart; it will tell you right way to go. Believe me."

If that's true, I think my heart must be gagged. It's not talking.

After a few hours, I have a nice collection of fondant flowers and a rotund figure of Growly in his black priest outfit with a sun hat on, a rake in his hand, and a big, uncharacteristic smile on his face. Sometimes Cake Girl has to alter the way things really are in order to make them more appetizing.

I work until Roz shoos me out the door at six, muttering something about me spending too much time at the bakery. The warmish air reminds me of my plans for a run with Jack.

At home, I eat a cup of yogurt and run upstairs to change. My hands shake a little as I tie up my Nikes. I am worried about seeing him. We've never been in this situation before. And I'm not sure what my heart wants me to do. He can't have a crush on me. He's Jack. I'm me. We go too far back to risk ruining things with romance, don't we? Yes. We do. I need his friendship too much to let love potentially ruin everything. *Plus, you* have *a boyfriend,* I remind myself.

I brush my hair back into a ponytail and sail out the door, zipping through the dusk-filled square toward the other side of town, where Jack lives.

Ten minutes later, I ring the doorbell. His mom answers, with one of Jack's little brothers hanging off her leg. "Hi, sweetheart!" Jack ambles up behind her, looking disappointed. I have a terrible feeling this isn't going to go well.

Jack nudges his mother out of the way. "I've got it, Mom. Thanks."

He stands in the doorway with his arms crossed, waiting for me to talk. Of course, there are two little brothers poking their heads out on either side of his legs. One of them passes gas. Charming.

I clear my throat. "Hi."

"You want something?" He looks over my head, his voice flat.

"Jeez, Jack. What did I do?"

He rolls his eyes.

"I came by to see if you want to go for a run." He pushes his brothers back, steps outside, and closes the door behind him. I notice how tall he's gotten over the last year. He's positively towering. His hair has gotten long, too. I think back to middle school, when he refused to wear it in anything but a buzz cut.

"Well?" I say when he doesn't answer. "You want to run or not?"

"No. Not really."

I furrow my eyebrows and shove my hands into my pockets. "Fine. Whatever."

"But I will," he says as I turn around to leave. "Give me a minute." He goes inside without inviting me in, and even though I'm having serious second thoughts about this, I wait for him.

When he comes back out, he's got on a hat and gloves.

"You won't need those," I say. "It's really warm out."

"Yeah, well, there's another cold front coming through, so I'll wear them if you don't mind."

I am tempted to remind him that it's not cool to be a know-it-all. But I think now is probably not the time. I want to be friends again. And I need him to drive me to Chicago.

We run in silence. Sure enough, within ten minutes I can feel the temperature dropping. When we turn down the road that leads to the beach, he speeds up.

"You'll never make it at that pace," I shout after him. He doesn't listen, so I speed up. "Hey!" I'm already out of breath. "Okay!" I swat at his back. "Hey! I get it, you're mad at me! And now you're gonna kill us both. Would you slow down?"

He stops, then turns, puts his hands on his waist, and bends over, breathing hard. I almost run into him as I try to stop my forward progress down the hill. We are both out of breath.

Jack straightens up. "Look . . ." He's avoiding my eyes, looking anywhere but at me. "Maybe this was a bad idea."

I take a few deep gulps of air. "Why? Why is us being together a bad idea?"

He finally looks at me, but doesn't answer.

"Why are you so mad?" I ask, my voice quiet, trying to calm us both down. "Just because of Ethan?"

Jack visibly flinches when I say the name. "Oh, come on," he says, his voice just below a roar. "You're not one of those brainless girls. He's a player, Sher!" I can hear his anger; he's seething. "And he totally has your number. You're all 'he's so sweet, he's so hot,' but he's one of them— one of those jocks who trip people for no reason and then laugh about it. Can't you see that? He's dated every hot girl in school. You're just the next available target. That's all!" He throws his hands up. "I don't know. I just don't get it." He's stepping backward, away from me.

But now I am mad. No. I am furious. "So is it impossible to believe that he's interested because he actually likes me? You know what, Jack, that's just mean. I thought we were best friends, no matter what. Now I can't even count on that?"

I shake myself. I need to calm down. I need Jack this

weekend. There's no way I can make the Chicago trip without him. He's the only one who knows; he's the only one who understands.

"Listen," I say, forcing my voice to a lower volume. "I don't want to talk about Ethan. I called the bakery. In Sault Sainte Marie. It's her. She owns the place. And"—his eyes are wide; this is going to work—"she's going to be in Chicago this weekend, at a cake competition. There's a big one there, at McCormick Place. I want to go. I want you to come, too." I look at him, hopeful, and wait for his reaction.

"You did *what*?" His reaction is not good. "What is wrong with you? You are totally certifiable, you know that?"

I am in shock, and I swear I can feel the blood bubbling in my veins. "Excuse me?"

Jack steps back again, shaking his head. "Sheridan, when are you gonna take the hint? If that's her bakery, she's *five* hours away." He's shouting at me, exasperated. "Haven't you asked yourself why she's never come back? Why she can't send you a freaking birthday card, or even an e-mail? When are you going to . . . ?" He hangs his head, then lifts it again, staring directly into my eyes.

"Going to what?" Tears are building. I can't believe this is my best friend.

"When are you going to grow up?"

I feel like he's slapped me, so I swing back my arm and push him hard. "What do you mean? I thought you . . ."

My voice breaks. "I thought you wanted to help me. . . . I thought you understood." Tears begin to drip steadily from my eyes. "You aren't my friend. A friend wouldn't say those things."

I shove him again, harder, then turn and run away as fast as I can. It's almost dark and I'm not supposed to run at night alone. He's coming after me, but I turn around and yell, "Go away! Don't you dare follow me!"

He stops, but I keep running. With each footstep I feel doubt chasing me. Mom lives five hours away. She's only been five hours away, all this time.

I'm at a full sprint now, and I'm almost to the beach. I usually love to run along the packed sand, but tonight my legs and lungs burn in the cold. When I get to the deserted shore, I let go, run faster than I ever have before. My lungs chug like a freight train. I feel like if I stop, the entire world will crash down on top of me.

There's a branch in the sand that I don't notice until it's too late. I stumble forward, fall flat on my face. Sand is in my mouth, on my eyelashes. I spit, flip over onto my back, and scream. Loud.

I try to catch my breath, but I can't. A deep moan escapes my throat, and tears start to flow from my eyes as if out of a gushing faucet.

I lie like this for a long, long time. Thinking of my mother, wherever she is; hoping she still loves me. Please, God, let her love me.

My cell phone vibrates in my pocket. It's another text from Amazon.

Need the guest list asap.

Ha! I drop the phone on the sand. Maybe this is God's idea of a joke. Maybe it makes him laugh, watching my life crumble. I wipe my eyes with the backs of my freezing bare hands. Then I wrench my body up off the ground and grab the cell.

My feet start moving across the sand. With each step I become more determined to get to Chicago. No, she's not the ideal mother. But she does love me. I remember. And if I have to get down on my hands and knees and beg her, she's coming to St. Mary.

Chapter 12

WITH A GRAIN OF SALT

I'm back home and pacing like a tiger I once saw at the zoo. He looked like he wanted to rip something apart. That's kind of how I feel right now. Restless, angry, caged. I have this mad desire to see Ethan, but I'm not so sure I want him to see me like this, so on edge.

Amazon has texted me again and called twice asking for the guest list, but instead I go to the kitchen and pull out my tub of decorating supplies. I need to start on the gum paste hibiscus blossoms for my birthday cake. This will calm me down. I sit on one of the stools at the island and lay out my work area like I'm prepping for surgery.

My mind spins like a pinwheel. Jack's ugly words float around in there, taunting me, making me want to cry. How could he hurt me like that? And why has he been helping me look for her if he thought I was such a nutcase?

My first hibiscus petal looks more like week-old roadkill than a beautiful flower. My cell phone vibrates and I pick it up, hoping to see Ethan's name. But it's another text from Amazon. The guest list is due, they have to get the names to legal so the forms can be signed, blah, blah, blah.

I'm starting to regret agreeing to this party, but I know that it's all I've got. If Mom needs a reason to come back, this is the best I can do.

I fold up the roadkill gum paste and put away my tools for now. I have to do something to get Amazon off my back.

I sit down with my laptop, try to think of names. Who do I invite? Lori. Tuba Dude Jim. Ethan. I backspace over Jack's name, add three girls who were on the cross-country team with me last year, then backspace over them because we hardly know each other. Depressing. I have no friends. Acquaintances, plenty. Friends, practically zero.

Underneath the three names, I add Nanny, Mr. Roz, Mrs. Davis, and, out of utter desperation, Father Crowley. So much for them wanting to show girls in bikinis.

I type Amazon a quick e-mail.

Here's my list. Sorry so short.

My stomach is rumbling. But as usual, we have no food. We never have any food. So I decide to go to the restaurant and forage. I pull on a pair of jeans and change into a T-shirt and a hoodie.

It's Wednesday, not the busiest night at Sheridan & Irving's. Still, the parking lot is full. The local news has covered the story of Dad's show, and the people of St. Mary are thrilled. The mayor has even proclaimed May 7, the day the pilot episode will be filmed, as Donovan Wells Day. For real.

Before I leave the house, I catch a glimpse of my face in the mirror in our entryway.

My eyes look tired. My hair is a limp mess. I brush leftover sand off my cheek. Am I crazy to think that my mother will come back? I watch my reflection. I do look a little crazy. Maybe I have gone off the deep end.

I make my way across the parking lot, walk through the door and into the kitchen. Someone is humming the theme from *Star Wars*. It's Raoul.

"Hey, Miss Sheridan!" he greets me.

"You here to work, kid?" Dominique says from the pastry station.

"Nah. Here to eat."

"Well, well," sous-chef Danny calls, "do I have a plate for you. Give me just a minute."

I smile. Here I am in my father's restaurant, wrapped up in the warmth and cheer of the people who work for him. They are our friends, our extended family. I don't understand how Dad can even think about leaving them.

I chat with a few of the busboys, and in ten minutes Danny passes me a plate: clam linguini. I stare at it and wonder if Ethan will date me long enough to make me his version.

"Thanks, Danny."

Just as I sit down on a stool to eat, Dad pokes his head out of his office.

"Sheridan. Can you come in here?"

Crap. I thought he was up front talking to customers.

He doesn't wait for an answer, so I take up my plate and fork and the glass of Coke that Raoul has given me and make my way across the kitchen.

The door is open, and Dad's behind his desk with his reading glasses on. In the light of the small lamp, he looks older and softer somehow. But when he raises his head, gives me a look like I am somehow disappointing him, the softness is gone.

"Come in. Sit. Eat," he orders.

I do what he says, though I have no idea what we'll talk about. He keeps his eyes on the papers in front of him.

"How's Father Crowley's cake coming along?" he asks in a monotone.

I nod and suck down a long string of linguini. "Gauuw," I say through the stringy mass in my mouth. Oh wow, it's delicious.

"Good. And you got the guest list in to Jacqueline?"

I had forgotten Amazon's real name. I nod, even though I know the guest list was not even close to what she wanted.

"And you're clear to work here tomorrow night, right? We've got a full house."

"Yes," I say, my mouth temporarily empty. "I got your message."

He flips the paper in his hand, barely paying attention to me.

"And school? All's well there?"

Well, yeah. Except for a certain art project. I nod my head anyway. I'll get the thing done, eventually.

"Good. Now is there anything else we need to talk about?" He checks his watch. "I've got plans."

"With who?"

For the record, my dad's plans usually don't interest me, but I'm curious who it is that could distract him from the show.

"Oh. I'm taking Jacqueline to a jazz club in Grand Rapids."

My eyes open wide. That Amazon freak better not screw this up for me. If they start something, she'll sink her claws in him and drag him back to New York for sure.

"Is that all right with you?" Dad asks. He looks serious.

"Well, honestly, I don't really like her. She's kind of . . ." I search my vocabulary bank. "Don't you think she's kind of brash?"

Dad's gaze shifts. He's looking beyond me, thinking of something, someone. Maybe my mother?

He shakes himself out of his own thoughts. "Well, brash

is okay, within reason. You've kind of got to take her with a grain of salt. She's not so bad."

I have never met any of his dates. Not one. But I've met Amazon. "What, you like her or something?" A panicky feeling is crouching in the back of my brain, ready to pounce.

"Sheridan, I don't know. We're just going to listen to some jazz. It's not like I'm gonna run off with her . . ." He glances up at me. Oops. *That's right, Dad. Wrong thing to say.*

"Right, why would you run off with her? You're the perfect father." My heart rate increases and I stand, ready to leave.

"Sit down, Sheridan. I'm too tired to fight tonight."

I plop down into the chair, twist another forkful of linguini into submission, consider flinging it at him.

"How's your grandmother feeling?" he asks.

"Fine. I guess. Why?"

"She was sick the other day. I asked Roz to make her take a day off."

"Well, she didn't."

"No, of course not."

I take another bite of pasta, a sip of Coke. This is the most I've talked to my father in months.

My eyes wander to the painting on the wall above him. It's of the beach, where I was sobbing earlier.

I glance at Dad as I swallow the last bite. "Why don't we sail anymore?"

Dad keeps his head down, signing papers, acting busy. Danny sticks his head in the door.

"Hey, boss, you want anything to eat?"

"We slowing down out there?"

"Yep. Everything's under control."

"Yeah, I'll have some linguini if you didn't give it all to my kid."

Danny laughs and walks away, calling out behind him, "Not all of it, boss. Not all of it."

His kid? I feel so separate from him right now, like we barely even belong to each other anymore. In his mind, he's already a big ExtremeCuisine TV star, a resident of New York City.

But I'm here to remind him that he's a lifelong citizen of St. Mary, Michigan. He can't just leave it. He can't leave me.

"Well, why don't we?"

He flips a page, stares at it intently. "What?"

"Why don't you ever want to go sailing? We used to do it all the time, before . . ."

"I don't know." He sounds annoyed and scribbles his pen on some scratch paper. Apparently, it's out of ink. "Look"—he rubs his temple—"I've got a lot of work to do."

I nod again and watch as he grabs another pen out of the pencil cup I made in second grade. Just after Mom left. It's wrapped with pink, red, and white yarn. Each kid in class had to make one for a Mother's Day gift. Dad said he'd keep it for her, until she got back. He is not going to answer me.

"Fine." I stand up, empty plate in hand, and grab my glass. "Well, then, have fun with Amazon."

"Who?"

I turn toward the door. "Never mind."

On my way back to the house, I can see Nanny's apartment light above the trees. I didn't know she wasn't feeling well. It's time we had a chat, anyway, about what I saw on her computer screen.

I go to the house, let myself in, and plop down on the leather sofa in the front room with a massive *whoompf.*

My eyes travel across the dark expanse of the room; it's always quiet now, always empty. Not like when we were a family. Back then, we played Chinese checkers at the table in the corner or watched movies on the little TV. God, I'd just love to have a little bit of that again.

I lift myself off of the sofa. I'm tired, but I go into the kitchen, nuke a cup of water for tea, and dial Nanny.

"Hello?" she says, groggy.

"Hey. You want a cup of tea?"

"Oh, Sheridan, sugar . . . that sounds mighty nice, but let me have a rain check. I'm whupped. Tomorrow, okay?"

"Sure." I hang up.

I sit in the darkness of the kitchen. Dad's out, having fun with a giantess. Lori's at home with her mom and stepfather. Jack's at home, despising me, surrounded by his gaseous brothers. Ethan is not calling. So I head up to my bedroom, turn on the television, and pull out Mom's cards. I choose thirteen.

This is it—you're a teenager now! Happy Birthday! Hey, we're in Canada, but still kind of far from you, in Ottawa. It's beautiful here. I wish you could come and visit. I'll try to call your father and set something up—maybe for the summer, if we're still here. I miss you, Sheridan. Don't ever doubt that. And I'll love you forever, Cupcake. Love, Mom.

Needless to say, I never went to see her. Things happen. I get that. But I have to believe that she loves me, forever. I've got to hold on to that. I put the card back and flop onto my bed.

I flip through a few channels and just happen to land on ExtremeCuisine TV. This network is ridiculous; it shows everything from gazillion-dollar celebrity weddings to this crazy survivalist show that's on now, *Extreme Campout with Jeff "Flamethrower" Reynolds.* At the moment, he's roasting a squirrel that, yup, he killed himself. Yuck.

And now my family is supposed to be part of this madness? No thanks.

I pull out my cell phone and start texting.

Top secret road trip? Chicago this weekend. U in? Also can u drive?

I have no idea if Lori will be able to escape with her mom's car for the weekend, but this is a matter of survival. I could maybe learn a lesson from Flamethrower Reynolds, but I turn the channel quickly as he takes a juicy bite of roasted squirrel.

Chapter 13

NOT MY CUP OF TEA

It's Thursday afternoon, and Amazon hasn't texted me back ordering me to redo my sad guest list, which is a relief. Jack ignored me in school, and I returned the favor. Ethan and I got caught making out in the band hall. He wanted to see me tonight. But I've got a cake to make. As soon as I get home, I pound out the next chem lab (on my own) and then make a beeline for the bakery to forget my troubles.

When I enter the kitchen, Roz is waiting with Father Crowley's cake. He knows I'm busy this week, so he mixed up the green fondant that will cover the cake for me. It's a little too Day-Glo for my taste, but there's nothing I can do about it now. I've finished all of my flowers and a flagstone path made of fondant. There's even a spun sugar trellis for the roses to climb on.

In an hour, the cake is assembled. It's colorful, bright (thankfully the green isn't as bad as I first thought), and absolutely perfect. But now it's almost five and I need to get to the restaurant.

My weekend plans are working out nicely. Lori's sister is a sophomore at Notre Dame, which is on the way to Chicago. So Lori told her mom that we were going to spend the weekend in the dorms. And we will drive through, just to say hello, so we're not complete liars. But then we'll head to the big convention center on the other side of Lake Michigan, to find Mom.

When I get to Sheridan & Irving's, the dining room is full, but Dad is upstairs filming interview segments for the show. This show seems to have taken over everything. All he thinks about is May 7 and maybe Amazon, too, since he didn't come home until four last night. "Just jazz" my butt.

I spend the night bussing tables and working prep and don't say a word to my father. When I finally creep up to our front porch at ten o'clock, Ethan is waiting on the top step. I'm so tired that for a second I imagine he's a ghost.

But as I come closer he stands up, and I know he's the real thing. I can smell his strong boy smell—like soap and sweat mixed together, in a good way. The butterflies that do cartwheels in my stomach whenever he's around are fluttering like gangbusters now.

"Hi," he says. He's slightly hunched over, with his hands in his pockets. He doesn't look like the most popular guy in the junior class right now. He looks like a mortal, and this helps me relax.

"Hey," I say. He comes down one step, then another, and I can see his face in the glow of the parking lot lights. The way he looks at me makes me feel beautiful.

"Whatcha doin'?" I ask, meeting him on the middle step.

"Looking at the stars," he says. We are definitely within kissing distance. I wouldn't mind the practice. But instead, he points to the sky. "Look at 'em tonight."

There they are. Millions of them, twinkling brilliantly. I suddenly feel positively microscopic. He sits down on the step, pats the spot next to him.

"Tired?"

"Yes."

I sit and lay my head against his shoulder. He lifts an arm and wraps it around me. This is nice.

The cold front lingers. I am freezing. Ethan moves a little closer so that our thick winter coats mush up against each other. I worry about my breath. Danny fixed me shrimp scampi for dinner. Lots of garlic.

Ethan turns his face toward mine. If I taste like scampi, it's way too late to do anything about it now. His lips lean in and touch mine, and this time I don't worry about whether I'm doing it right or am a total hack. I just let it happen. A definite improvement.

He smiles when he kisses me. I can feel his lips curl.

I pull away slowly. "Why do you like me? You do know I'm not popular?" I whisper into his ear while he kisses my neck.

He laughs quietly.

"I'm serious. I really have no life outside of this triangle." I spread my arms to indicate the bakery, my house, and the restaurant.

"That's totally not true," he says between pecks on my cheek. "I have seen you at school once or twice."

"Well, yeah, that doesn't count."

"And we met at Geronimo's."

"That's true."

He's slowly inching back toward my mouth. "I don't care about popular. I want different. You're different. Not like any of the other girls here."

Now my lips curve. "Is it my superhuman ability to make anything out of cake?"

He pulls back. I'm amazed how his bright blue eyes shine, even in the dark. "That is pretty cool, you know. You've got a passion for something. I think that's . . . I don't know . . . uncommon. Plus"—he leans in again—"you're hot."

I almost laugh in his face, because no one has ever used the word *hot* to describe me, unless I had a fever. But right at this moment Ethan seems so sincere and sweet that I don't even try to argue with him.

His hand wraps around my waist, and he pulls me even closer. "Can we go inside?"

Uh-oh. I was afraid of that. Part of me would very much

like to go inside the house with him. But I also know it could be the most dangerous thing I've ever done. EVER.

That's when I hear a voice floating down through the ice-cold air. "Sheridan!" I jolt upright, pulling away from him.

It's Nanny, screeching from her balcony like a barn owl.

"Who is that?" He looks behind us.

"My grandmother."

"Where is she?"

"She lives above the bakery."

"How can she see us? We're on the front porch."

"She's psychic. And a little psychotic. Both, really." I swing my head around the porch railing. I can't make out the details of her face, but I glare in her general direction. I see the silhouette of her rounded body, her hands perched on her hips. I'm hoping she can see the daggers that I am shooting at her on this starry night.

"That's enough of that now!" she calls, loud and clear.

"Man, it's like living next to the warden," Ethan says, and stands up. I'm so embarrassed. "I guess that's my cue," he says. I watch as his long legs stretch themselves out. I have this crazy desire to hop on his shoulders and ask him to piggyback me away from here. He walks down the stairs, grabs my hand, pulls me to him. "Maybe it's time you had a life outside of the triangle?"

Our fingers weave together. I am wrapped up in his scent and the richness of his voice and those impossibly blue eyes. Every time I see him I am more at ease, and I think, *This could really work.*

As much as I love my cakes, and as much as I want Mom back to fix things, at this moment I'd give it all up to spend one more minute in this cocoon with Ethan.

And then I have a terrible thought. This is what happened to my mother. She got wrapped up in her feelings for that man and she walked away from Dad, and from me. She couldn't say no.

Would I be able to give up everything I love for a guy?

"So, we on for tomorrow night?" He snaps me back from the past.

"Oh. I have to help at Father Crowley's birthday party," I say. "You can come, though. The whole town is invited. And I made the cake."

"Course you did." He grins. "Nah." He lets go of my hand, takes a few steps away. "I'm not really the church type."

"Well, it's not church; it's a birthday party." But I can see in his eyes that he's not going for it. "But I can get away after that." I hear the desperation in my voice.

"You ever go down to the lighthouse?"

"Yeah." Which is a lie. I run by sometimes, but I don't go there for the same reason other kids do, which is to party.

"There's a bonfire tomorrow night."

"Oh. Okay." I bob my head.

"Meet me there? At nine?" he says, so confident, like there's no chance I'll turn him down. He's right. I won't.

"I can do that."

"Sheridan!"

I whip my head around the side of the house again. "Okay!" I yell, not even trying to disguise the anger in my voice.

Ethan looks amused. "You'd better go. I'll see you at school."

When he leaves, I go inside and close the door, then flip on the foyer light, still tasting him. I strip out of my clothes, which reek of garlic, and take a long, hot shower. Dad's not home, and maybe he doesn't plan on coming home. That's fine with me. If I can't be with Ethan, I'd rather be by myself.

As I pull up my flannel pj pants, my cell rings. Guess who?

"Hi?" I say, totally irritated.

"Sheridan," Nanny says.

"What?"

"Are you and that boy dating?"

Could she be more old-fashioned? "Yeah. Maybe."

"Oh." She sounds a little panicked. "Well, I don't think he should be over at the house so late."

"I didn't invite him. He showed up."

"Well, tell him there's a proper way for courtin' and that ain't it."

You have got to be kidding me.

"Nanny. I have to go."

"Wait a minute. You promised me a cup of tea. I've been feeling pretty lousy and wouldn't mind one now."

"I'm tired, Nan."

"Oh, come on, get over here. I've got some chamomile that'll make you sleep like a baby."

"All right. Just one cup." I know better than to talk Nanny out of this one. She'll want to have a good look at me and make sure I haven't been defaced.

I slip on my Uggs and throw my coat over my T-shirt. Nanny is waiting for me on her balcony. "Hey, girl."

"Hey." I kiss her on the cheek and follow her inside. Once we're in the kitchen, I notice that her face is very pale. I grab the teapot from her as she's filling it under the faucet.

"Sit down. You look awful."

"Told you."

She settles in the blue velvet love seat on the far end of the room. Nanny likes it better than sitting at the kitchen table. Calls it her tea-drinkin' and thinkin' spot.

I put the kettle on the fire and join her, curling my legs up beneath me.

"You feeling better at all?"

"Yep. Much. Just a cold. I'll be all bright-eyed and bushy-tailed for the party tomorrow night."

Nanny may be all holy and stuff, but she never misses a good party.

"So what is happening with that boy? What's his name?" she asks, feet propped up, eyes squinting.

"Ethan."

"Ethan. Hmm. He go to church?"

I roll my eyes. "No."

"Ah. Well, you just remember what I taught you. Your body is a tem—"

"Yes, I know. My body is a temple, whatever that means."

"What?" She sits straight up and smacks my arm. "You better know what that means."

"Nanny." Our eyes meet, her imposing gaze met by an imposing gaze of my own. "Maybe someone should teach that particular Bible-ism to Dad." I stand up and walk toward the whistling kettle.

"You better hush. Your daddy is a good and decent man."

"Right. I'm sure every one of his girlfriends will tell you that."

"Don't you dare judge him. He's a very honorable person."

"Mmm-hmm . . ."

"I don't think I care for your sarcasm. Your father has never even introduced you to one of those women. You know why? None of them been good enough."

"Really?" I take out two of her china teacups and pair them with their matching saucers. "But they're still good enough to spend the night with?"

"Girl, you are exasperation personified. Bring me my tea; you're raisin' up my blood pressure."

Now that I've already upped her blood pressure, I decide to push it even higher. I hand her a teacup and sit down again beside her.

"Listen. On Easter, after I told you about finding Mom,

why were you searching for her in Sault Sainte Marie?"

Once again, she sits up. Busted.

"You been snooping on me?"

"No." I put my cup down on the small glass-topped coffee table in front of us. "It was an accident, when I went in your office for ribbon. But if you knew where she was, why didn't you tell me?"

Nanny is silent. She does that—takes her time to think before she speaks. I didn't inherit that particular family gene.

"Well, she had some contact with your father a few years back. He told me that's where she was. I figured she'd moved on by now, but when you dropped that huge bomb on me, I thought I'd check up on the situation." She takes a sip of tea. "Have you talked to her?"

"No, but . . ."

"But what?"

"Nothing."

She shakes her head and tsk-tsks. "Don't do it, Sheridan. Please don't. Let her come to you. She will if and when she's finally ready." Nanny wipes her eyes. I'm surprised to see that she's crying. "I know it stinks to high heaven, but I don't want you getting hurt."

"Nanny, don't worry." I pat her leg. She looks terrible and she's crying harder now. I want so badly to spill my guts. I want to tell her I'm going to Chicago, the day after tomorrow, to bring Mom back.

But she's so upset, I can't. I can't make her understand

that Mom will not hurt me, that she only needs a reason to come back. I'm giving her that reason.

Nanny sniffs. I lean over, into her shoulder. "Don't cry, Nan. It's okay."

"Oh, I don't mean to be wailin' like a newborn, but if I see you get hurt again, I don't know what I'll do." She sits up and wipes her eyes. "You know what? I think we need some cheesecake."

I laugh. Cake cures all in the mind of my grandmother.

"Nah, I better go home. I've got some homework to finish."

"Gracious, girl, I didn't know that." She stands up and groans. "Then go. Shoo, shoo."

I drain my cup. "Thanks for the tea," I say as she walks me to the door. We stand face-to-face as she swings it open.

"You know I love you more than anything else on this great big earth?" she says, her voice breaking.

I make a mental map of the crinkles around her eyes, focus on the sparkle in the deep blue flecked with gold.

"I know you do." And she gives me the hug of my life, tight and tender all at the same time. "I love you, too."

The walk home is quiet and cold. When I get to my room, I throw my schoolbag off the bed. It falls on its side, and out slips the dreaded sketchbook. I pick it up and flip it open. The project is due in one week. I need to finish it. *I need to start it.*

Mrs. Ely doesn't get it. Art is hard for me. With cakes,

I can talk to customers and come up with a design that they'll love. With art, there is no one to consult; it's just me and the paper. Scary.

I pull a charcoal pencil out of my desk drawer, and my hand starts to draw a curved line, a jaw, a loose lock of hair that looks like sunshine. Eyes that curve downward and seem sort of sleepy. My mother.

I rip the page out and crumple it up. Every once in a while I try to draw her, but whenever I do, it's the same story. All wrong; a terrible likeness. Honestly, I barely remember what she looks like anymore. It scares me.

I need to get to her soon, before she disappears forever.

Chapter 14

THAT TAKES THE CAKE

The party for Growly starts in half an hour, but I'm still recovering from the school day. Wasserman is trying to murder us slowly with chemical equations, and Mrs. Ely asked to see our projects so far. I had to lie and tell her I left my sketchbook at home. "Monday, then. I want to see it on Monday," she said as if she knew full well that I hadn't completed even one of the ten drawings we're supposed to sketch and color.

People are already showing up in the parish hall. Lots of people. In fact, it looks like the whole town is here. My beautiful cake is sure to be history in record time.

"Dat is the best one yet," Mr. Roz says, nodding toward the fondant flower garden I've created. "How you say? It 'takes cake'?" He says that about every cake; it's our little joke. And then I say, "It takes *the* cake." And then he says, "Where it take the cake?" He laughs and pats my back, then takes a few pictures for the bakery's Web site before it's all gone.

I humor him with a chuckle and adjust a tiny hydrangea bloom. It really is perfect.

As the party progresses, I am called a genius more times than I can count by the guests. A steady stream of thank-yous comes out of my mouth as I help the guys from Sheridan & Irving's get set up. They are handling the bar and serving hors d'oeuvres. People are practically drooling over the spread in front of them. There's even a rumor going around that Chef Wells himself will make an appearance. Oh, brother.

I don't think he'll come at all. He made an appearance in my bedroom doorway about an hour ago and handed me a card to give to Growly.

Then he had the nerve to get all "Dad" on me. I had on my favorite jeans and a tightish, lowish-cut shirt that makes the most of whatever minuscule curves I have.

"You wearing that?" Dad asked.

"Yes," I said without a moment's hesitation.

He grunted. "I don't want you wearing something like that in South Bend." He also thinks Lori and I are going to Notre Dame for the weekend. I had told him that I was feeling stressed and needed some time away. He hadn't liked the idea of my being gone right before the show, so I cried a little, and then he said yes. Doesn't suspect a thing.

"Fine," I said as he turned to leave.

Once he was gone, I reached into my jewelry box and picked up my mom's heart-shaped note. I felt like I needed it. For luck or something.

Now at the party, Father Crowley walks up to me with a glass of wine in his hand, his face puckered into its usual scowl. The man is never happy.

"Good evening, Sheridan," he says, oh-so-friendly-like. "I've heard the cake is your creation?" He has me in his death glare.

"Yes, it is."

I'm sure he's going to wag a finger and remind me I'm doomed because I never go to church. But something even freakier happens. He smiles. Then laughs. Then pats my arm. "Well, it's just wonderful. Thank you!"

He is still smiling, and I am more than a little creeped out. I've never seen him this cheerful.

"You're welcome." I look sideways. "No big deal." *Someone get me out of here, please.*

"I mean, the way you captured my roses, and the peonies. And the lilies, in sugar! You are just brilliant. . . . Such a gift. It really is quite an honor to be the subject of one of your masterpieces."

I don't know what to say to him, and then I remember Dad's card. I run over to the chair where I've hung my coat, pull it out, and hand it to him.

"It's from my dad."

He opens it and his smile grows wider. "Ah. Your father . . ." Growly laughs, fanning out four tickets in front of him. "Tickets to *Godspell*! He's a good man. Such a good and thoughtful friend."

A good man who never goes to church? Who walks out in the middle of Mass? My eyes grow wide. Not only is Growly a big grump; he's blind, too.

Growly moves on and Nanny walks over and gives me a squeeze. She is looking better, and I am relieved. Lori is here with her mom and stepdad. No sign of Jack.

Mrs. Klunder, the church secretary, is at the mic, and she calls Growly to the small stage that's been set up. Soon a series of never-ending toasts begins. I walk over to Lori, who said she'd help me work so that I could meet Ethan, but has instead set up residence at the hors d'oeuvres table.

"What up, dawg?" she says, shoving a crab-stuffed mushroom into her mouth. "Mmm, good 'shrooms," she says with her mouth full. She swallows. "You all ready for tomorrow?"

She's the best kind of friend. No questions, no lectures; just always there for me. Here she is, driving me to Chicago, and looking forward to it. Now *that* is a friend. Jack could take lessons from her.

I nod. We are leaving at six in the morning so that we can get to the convention center by nine, when the competition starts. One change of clothes in my duffel, pj's, toothbrush, and iPod—that's all I need.

"More importantly, are you ready for tonight? You better report back to me everything that happens. . . . No detail too small." She picks up another mushroom. "He is so fine. I bet he's a world-class kisser. I bet he tastes yummy."

"Shh!" I warn, staring sideways at the old retired ladies next to us. "You want the whole town to know?"

"So what if they all know? Sheridan, you've got a boyfriend, and he's totally *hot*!"

"Would you hush?" I whisper, moving closer to her. "All right, fine. I'd say he ranks somewhere between tiramisu and a rich ganache . . . tastewise."

She curls her lip. "Oh. Ganache, huh? Real sexy. Sounds like something you dig out of your butt."

"Gross." I laugh, wondering what I'd do without Lori. "He is a good kisser, you know." I lower my voice as a trio of nuns pass nearby. "But I really suck at it."

"Oh God, give me a break. Don't obsess about this, too. You just do it. And enjoy yourself!" She's saying this way too loud when I feel hands on my shoulders.

"You girls having a good time?" It's Nanny. My eyes grow wide.

"Yeah. Great time."

"Good. I know I'm ready for the speechifyin' to be over. I want to boogie."

Lori nearly snorts her third stuffed mushroom out of her nose. I shake my head. Nanny kisses my cheek. "Have fun, girls. I'm gonna go see if I can get this party started."

It's a full house in the Blessed Sacrament parish hall. Everyone seems to be having fun. There are lots of old folks, but also plenty of young people, kids, and babies. Certainly every Catholic in St. Mary is here, and at least one Baptist.

When the music starts, Nanny is the first one on the dance floor. There's a deejay playing Sinatra and other singers who might appeal to someone turning eighty. Lori and I, in the meantime, bus tables, push in chairs, help walk the old people to the dance floor.

I'm watching the clock. Eight. One hour until Ethan.

In another half hour, the food is gone and the cake has been reduced to a mashed-up pile of icing and crumbs, but the deejay is still going strong. He's finally escaped the 1940s, and there are kids all over the dance floor. Even Father Crowley is out there, and I can't believe it, but he's doing the Electric Slide. Frightening. I hope this ends soon; I need to head home and get myself ready.

Lori and I stack chairs to give everyone the hint. That's when I hear the first few notes of "Mamma Mia." Oh God, we're doomed if they start playing ABBA; Nanny will have the deejay play all their greatest hits by the time she's done. As I stack another chair, I turn and witness my grandmother getting funky with Mr. Roz. Oh, that's just wrong.

I turn and pick up another chair, bend over to pick up a crumpled napkin. Someone screams.

"What in the . . . ?" Lori says.

"Lilian!" a man yells. That's Nanny's name, and the world clicks instantly into a weird sort of slow motion. I turn and see a pair of stockinged feet sticking out from the middle of a group of people who are all hunched over and staring at something on the floor. Nanny. She'd taken her shoes off to dance.

"Call 9-1-1!" someone shouts, and through a space in the crowd, I see her. Mr. Roz and Growly are on their knees. A man pushes Roz out of the way and starts to do CPR. He's pushing on her chest so hard.

"Sheridan." Lori is next to me. But I walk away from her and move, zombie-like, to my grandmother.

My heart is beating too fast. I can hear it throbbing inside my head. "What is it?" I ask. People are talking, but I can't understand a word. The man pounds on her chest. There's her face. It's gray. Her eyes are closed.

I don't know how much time passes before two men in dark blue uniforms run into the hall and order everyone to move. One of them listens for a heartbeat and feels for a pulse, and the other gets out those crazy paddles like they use on TV. "Clear!" he yells, and sticks them on her chest. Her body pops in an unnatural way. The paramedic presses on her wrist again.

"I've got it!" he says. In a matter of seconds, there's an oxygen mask on Nanny's face and she's lying on a gurney.

There's a commotion at the stairs, and my father runs in, dressed in his chef whites.

"How long has she been out? Mom! Mom!"

I can't make sense of what they're saying. Roz, Dad, and Growly follow the paramedics as they wheel her out.

But I can't seem to move. "Sheridan." Lori's voice cuts through the sound of my heartbeat. Her parents already went home, but I hear her call them, telling them what's happened.

Lori hangs up and leads me outside. We watch them push Nanny into the back of an ambulance. Dad stands back, hands on his head. He looks completely freaked. Panicked.

We catch sight of each other. He walks up to me with purpose.

"Sheridan. Can you get a ride to the hospital?"

Lori answers for me. "My mom's on her way. We can follow."

I am shaking. He grabs me by the shoulders.

"Calm down, Sheridan. We need to keep it together; Nanny needs us." He hurries into the ambulance, and I watch as they pull away in a blur of lights and sirens.

Soon, Lori's mom drives up, and we get into the car. I hope she drives fast. My eyes close tight.

Don't let her die, God. Don't let her die! Don't you dare let this be part of your plan.

We are in the buttery yellow waiting room of the hospital in Grand Rapids. I was born here. But now I stand at the window and look out at the black night.

There are no stars in the sky. Just clouds. It's nine thirty. And Ethan is waiting for me by the lighthouse. But I can't call him. The hospital has no signal, and I'm afraid to go outside, to leave Nanny. They rolled her in over an hour ago and still no word.

He will be angry. Probably break up with me. Even after I explain, I have a feeling that he won't care. He'll finally understand what I told him. I am a part of this triangle. A part of this family. And when you take away one side of a triangle, it falls. At least for now, I need to be here to hold up my side.

A doctor comes through the swinging doors at one end of the room and walks to my father, who has been sitting in a chair, completely silent, looking down at his lap. They talk. After a few minutes, the doctor leaves, and we all clamber over to Dad, afraid to hear what he has to say. Lori grabs my hand, and I watch the worried faces of Father Crowley, Mr. Roz, and Lori's mom.

"What he say?" asks Mr. Roz. I've never seen him upset about anything. But Nanny is his best friend.

"She's having a bypass. It'll be a while before we know anything for sure." I feel terrible for even thinking about Ethan breaking up with me when my own grandmother is on an operating table, the chest that's caught me in so many squishy hugs cut open, her heart in some random doctor's hands.

Please don't let her die. Please don't let her die.

"Bonnie." Dad turns to Lori's mom. "Why don't you take the girls home?" He looks at me. "You were spending the night, weren't you? So that you could go to South Bend?"

His voice is razor-sharp, and his eyes are strange. Like he knows it's a lie. But there's no way he could have found out.

"I want to stay here," I say. There's no way I can leave Nanny.

Dad's eyes blaze at me. Lori takes a step back. "Sheridan, can I have a word alone with you?" he says.

He walks down the long white hallway and stops by a water fountain, then bends down, gets a drink. When he stands again, I can see clearly that he is fuming mad. And I am afraid.

"Were you really planning on going to Notre Dame this weekend?"

Gulp. "Yes."

"Then why did I get a phone call at the restaurant confirming your registration at the Food Expo?"

I stare at my feet and my stomach sinks. I had to give the name of my employer when I registered. And the phone number. I never thought they'd use it. Who uses the phone anymore? Anyway, it doesn't matter. There's no time to come up with another lie now; I can't think that fast. So I take a deep breath.

"We were also driving up to Chicago."

"And why is that?" Dad says in a creepily calm way while his face turns brilliant shades of red.

"Because . . . Mom is going to be there."

"Excuse me?" His eyes look wild now.

"Yes. I found her. Well, Jack helped. She has a bakery in Sault Sainte Marie." Funny, but I feel myself calming down as the facts pour out of me. "They told me she is going to a cake competition in Chicago. This weekend."

"Sheridan." He shakes his head and smiles, but not in a normal way. More like in a pissed off, what-did-I-do-to-deserve-a-kid-like-you way. "Just what is your plan here?"

Something shifts inside me as I watch his mouth move. For once I am in control, able to see things clearly. My breathing is normal; my heart isn't pounding inside my chest. But I am angry. And the anger is so deep and wide and high that suddenly I can't see anything else.

"You knew where she was all along. You've always known."

He sputters. I've thrown him. "It's my responsibility to know the whereabouts of your mother."

"It's your responsibility to tell me where she is if you know I'm looking for her. You *owe* me that much." I cross my arms. "I don't get it. You don't want her in my life. But you don't want anything to do with me, either." My face is burning hot.

He staggers backward, just a little. His top lip is quivering. I take a teensy step backward, too. He looks like he might blow.

"I *owe* you?" A manic chuckle erupts from his mouth. "I owe you? Really, is that so?" He lifts a finger and points it directly in my face. "When . . . ? How . . . ? You . . . You ungrateful little brat. Everything . . . I mean, everything I have done since the day you were born has been for you. And you pay me back by planning secret trips to find that woman?"

His voice is loud, and I glance to my left to see if anyone in the waiting room heard him. "Look at me when I'm talking to you. You owe *me* that much." I gulp again. "Don't you dare do anything to sabotage this show. I will not have it. And don't you dare tell me I don't want anything to do with you. There isn't a minute that goes by that I don't think about what she put you through and what I can do to make up for it." His voice shakes and his eyes are glassy.

The anger in me is now oozing out of every pore. My chin is up. My eyes are set, my voice even.

"You want me to just forget about her? Like you have?" I take a step closer, propelled by this wave of courage. "Well, I won't. She said she wants to come home; that she misses me. You are wrong about her."

He stands a little taller, sticks his hands in his pockets, takes a deep breath.

"Right." He sneers. "The cards. *When* did that last card come?"

I shake my head and look away. "Fourteen," I mumble.

"When!" He blasts the word into the hallway. Everyone is looking at us now.

"When I turned fourteen!" I yell back at him.

He smirks. "She was ready to come home, right? Two years ago? So where is she, Sheridan?" Now he's looking at me with pity. Like I'm a total loser. "Leave it alone, I'm warning you."

I laugh. He's got to be kidding me, talking to me like this, thinking he can squash my hope like it's an ant on the sidewalk. "You're wrong, Dad. You're wrong. She hurt you—I get that. But that was between you and her. She loves me, and I will always be her daughter. She's coming back. And that'll work out well for you, since it's your turn to leave now." These words slip out of me so easily, and they cut him like a big fat meat cleaver. I can see it.

"Go home," he says over his shoulder, shaking his head and walking toward the stairwell door with a red EXIT sign over it.

I watch him, wondering if he's going to turn around, come back, hug me and tell me he's sorry. Say that he'll never leave me. But he keeps walking, and he flings open the door with so much force that it slams into the wall.

And I am left here in the hallway. Alone.

Chapter 15

NUTTY AS A FRUITCAKE

Lori's mom drives me home so that I can get my duffel bag. It's all packed, sitting on my bed, ready for our trip to go find Mom. I grab it, disgusted, not believing the mess I have made of everything.

We ride to Lori's house in silence. My plan is blown to bits. Dad hates me. And if I lose Nanny now, I might as well curl up and die. Tears build in my eyes, and they drop one by one down my cheeks.

On the big comfy chair in Lori's room, I sniff and wipe my face with the back of my hand. We turn on some music and wait for the phone to ring with an update on Nanny. I text Ethan to tell him what happened, but he doesn't respond. I dial his number and get voice mail. Lori makes a bowl of popcorn and brings in a couple of drinks, but I'm not hungry. My gut is filled with worry.

The doorbell rings, and Lori turns down the CD player. We hear a deep voice from the living room. I close my eyes.

Don't let it be bad news.

In another minute, there's a quick knock on the bedroom door. My palms are damp; I can't breathe.

"Come in," Lori says. Jack peers around the side of the door. He puts his hands up in surrender.

"I come in peace," he says.

"Get in here, idiot." Lori has a way with words. Jack's got on his Geronimo's T-shirt, and the scent of coffee enters the room with him.

"Hey," he says, facing me but looking at the carpet. "I heard." He peeks up quickly, then lowers his eyes again just as fast. "How is she—"

"She's going to be fine," I say, cutting him off.

An uncomfortable silence settles in the room. I never thought it would be like this with Jack.

"Here, I brought you this." He smiles with his jaw clenched and holds out a small, rectangular box wrapped in metallic pink paper and stuck with a pink bow. "I wasn't sure I'd still be invited to the party. Or if you'll even have one. So I thought I'd give it to you now."

"There weren't supposed to be presents." I sound so rude. "But thanks," I add, too late.

He raises his eyes and stares at me full on. "Look, I'm trying to cheer you up." He tosses the box on the bed.

"Chill, dude. No need for drama," Lori interjects, trying to break up this horrible tension. I sit up and reach across the bed to grab the gift.

"You want me to open it now?" And again my words are like sandpaper on skin, rubbing him raw.

He's silent; then he sighs. "Open it, don't open it—whatever. Do whatever the hell you want; you always do anyway."

And before I can process his words, he's gone and the front door slams.

"Jerk!" I shout, as if he can hear me. Though I suspect I am the real jerk here. I can't help myself, though. I feel like an empty bag, crumpled up and thrown away.

"Oh, come on," Lori says. "Stop it."

"What?" I shrug.

"Sheridan." She rolls from her back onto her stomach and faces me. "I love you like a sister, but you can be a real moron."

I settle myself back into the soft chair cushions, way too tired to argue with that statement. "And why am I such a moron? Please enlighten me."

She laughs. "Because you are as blind as a freaking bat. That boy is so in love with you. He'd do anything for you. He *does* do anything for you."

"Right." I pick at the blanket draped over the arm of the chair. "Well, I do stuff for him, too. We're friends."

"Oh, you bring him coffee in the middle of the night and do his chem labs? You spend hours searching the Internet for his AWOL mother? You go for a run whenever he calls, just because you want to be with him—even though you hate to run?"

"He hates to run?"

"See, what did I tell you? Blind as a bat."

"No. I'm not totally blind." I sulk.

"You mean you know?"

"I suspected."

"I mean, really, look at that gift. For my last birthday he gave me a bag of M&M's wrapped up in the Sunday comics."

I moan, hold my head in my hands, feel its weight. Tears start brewing again, getting ready to drop.

"I can't think about this right now."

"Yeah, you need this like a hole in the head. But it's Jack. And he's trying to figure stuff out, too. He hates Ethan for a reason, besides the fact that he is kind of an ass. . . ." My head snaps up. "Well, he is, honey. But that's a whole other conversation. The problem is, Ethan's your boyfriend. This is not just a crush; this is the real deal. Jack's freaking out."

I sniff. Shake my head. Could things get any worse than they are right at this moment? I suppose I could contract the bubonic plague or something. That might make it worse.

"You know," Lori continues, "I'm all for playing the field. I mean, we're only teenagers once. But I think you need to remember who your friends are." She stands up and shoos me out of my chair. It opens up into a sleeper and will be my bed tonight.

"I know you're my friend."

"You'd better." She picks off the cushions and throws them in the corner, then pulls out the bed. "But you know, you can get a bit, um, distracted, with your cakes. And now Ethan."

"I'm sorry." My throat tightens. "I know. I just wish he told me he liked me. I mean, before Ethan happened."

"Right. Sheridan. He's scared. You know, like what happens if your best friend rejects you? Where does that leave you?" She picks a pillow off her bed and fluffs it, then throws it at me. "You may not have to deal with it for long, though. He had a date last night." She stares at me, her eyes bugging out of her head.

"A date?" I try to act casual, but Jack has never asked anyone out. Never even had a crush that he talked about. I guess now I know why. "With who?"

Lori plops down on her bed. I sit on mine. "With whom."

"Whatever. Who was it?"

"You really don't want to know."

"What do you mean? Of course I do."

"Fine." She lies back on her bed and covers her face with a pillow.

A muffled word comes out that sounds a lot like . . . but no, I must have heard wrong.

"*Who?*"

Lori lifts the pillow. She says the name slowly. "Haley Haversham."

"Nuh-uh. That is so not funny."

She sits up. "I am totally not kidding." Her lips form a thin line, and she nods her head. "Yup. He went out with her."

"Why?" I stand up. "There's no way he would go out with her! Why would he do that?"

"Because she asked. And he's a stupid guy. And you were otherwise occupied with Haley's ex. A match made in heaven, eh?" She walks to her bathroom door. "I gotta pee. You gonna open that thing or what?" She points to the shiny gift box on her bed.

"No! No way. I am not opening it."

"Jeez, relax. But just for the record, I think you and Jack would make a perfect couple. You're both a couple of fruit-cakes." She goes into the bathroom, closes the door. I grab the box, tempted to throw it against the wall. But instead, I sit back on the chair and close my eyes.

I see Jack, coming over, bringing me coffee, helping me with homework, helping me find my mom. See his dark hair falling into his dusky brown eyes. Feel that zap of electricity that passed between us the other day.

Wait. I need to *stop*. I have a boyfriend. And what is up with Jack dating Haley? I think of her sideways glance in the hall at school. She did this on purpose. She's got it in for me. And Jack knows how much I can't stand her. Oh, I hate him!

I open my eyes, sit up, and rip off the pink ribbon and tear the lovely paper. Inside is a long midnight blue velvet box. I flip it open. My stomach churns. It's a charm bracelet. I see a bird, small and silver, attached to one of the links. It's beautiful. There's a piece of paper, too, folded to fit inside.

I open it and see Jack's familiar scrawl.

Happy fake birthday to my best friend. I hope you get everything you've ever wanted. Love, Jack.

I pick up the bird charm, see a word etched on its side. *Dream.*

I flip the lid down and stash the box in my bag just as Lori comes out of the bathroom. Can't think about that right now.

"You all right?"

"Just tired."

"Yeah. It's late."

She crawls into bed, but I get up, grabbing my bag. "Why would he go out with her?" I ask.

She shrugs. "Not like they're getting married or anything." She punches her pillow. "Bothers you, huh?"

"No. I just wish he had told me he liked me."

"Yeah. That would have made it easy for you." She laughs. "Not that I'm an expert or anything. I mean, Jim drives me crazy with that stupid tuba practice. But that's the thing about love, or like, or whatever it is; I don't think it's supposed to be easy." She smiles.

"She's only dating him because she hates me."

"Well, then he'll learn a lesson, too."

"Good. Because she's like one of those bugs that eat their mates when they're through with them." Lori laughs and I go into the bathroom, open up my bag. The velvet box sits on a nest of my pajamas.

I stare at my reflection in the mirror above the sink. I know I'm not especially pretty. There are girls at school who are better-looking than me by a mile. I grab my brush, run it through my hair. Mom used to brush my hair, every night before bed. It put me into some sort of trance. Something about the pressure of the bristles on my head and the sound of her voice, so peaceful, like a smile and a hug and an *I love you* all rolled into one. As frustrated as I can sometimes get with her, I can't forget those moments. They are always reminding me that what we had was real.

I pull the brush through my hair again and again, but it's not the same. My eyes tear up. I wonder if I'll ever stop crying. My life feels like an enormous whirlpool; I'm swirling downward, powerless to fight it.

I put down the brush and sit on the toilet lid, my feet sinking into Lori's fluffy red bathroom rug. It looks like Elmo's been skinned.

"Please," I whisper. Then I sink to my knees, lean my elbows on the edge of the bathtub. Assuming Nanny is right, about God watching out for me, about a plan for my life, I squeeze my eyes tight.

"Please." I look up. At what? I don't know. The bathroom ceiling? "Help. Make Nanny better. Make us a family again."

I want my mother. I don't say this out loud, because I can't speak through my tears; the words are coming from my heart. It's the truth. I want what we used to have, all those years ago. Maybe it's impossible. But I can't give up this dream. I just can't.

I sit backward, with my legs crossed, and cry some more. I pull up my knees, hug them with my arms. Tears fall free, run down my thighs and onto poor Elmo beneath me.

And that's when I hear it. Maybe it's the voice in my heart, the one that Nanny tells me never to ignore. It's like a whisper or a breath; it starts in my head but flows through my entire body.

Let go.

I hear the words as clearly as if there's someone else with me in that little bathroom. It's kind of freaky. But then I hear it again, more insistent this time.

Let. Go.

I inhale deeply and breathe out. My muscles relax, and I feel wrapped in warmth, as if I'm in a fluffy robe after a long bath. This is so close to what I used to feel when my mother took me on her lap and brushed my hair. Comfort. Safety. Peace.

But it's fleeting.

I grab the doorknob, walk back into Lori's bedroom. I don't mention the voice to her. There's no reason for me to prove her whole fruitcake theory. She's sitting up in bed, paging through *People*.

I lie down, pull the quilt over me, and turn toward the wall.

"You okay?" she asks.

"I'm good." I wipe at my eyes one last time. "Night, Lori."

"Night."

She flicks off the lamp. I don't know if it's exhaustion or that crazy voice I heard, or just the result of living through the most horrible day ever, but I fall into a deep, dreamless sleep. Maybe the best sleep I've had since she left.

I sit up and gasp when my cell phone rings. Lori's alarm clock across the room reads 3:18.

I don't even look to see who is calling. "Dad?" My voice is stuck somewhere in my throat. I feel numb. I will not let go of Nanny.

"Hello." His voice is hoarse. I can hear how tired he is. "She's out of surgery. Looks like she's going to be okay. She's going to make it."

I can't speak because the voice stuck in my throat unclogs itself and turns into weeping. Lori turns on the light. I look at her and smile through the tears.

"So yeah. It's good news." His voice cracks, and I can tell he is crying, too. "I gotta go. They're moving her to ICU."

"Okay."

"Yeah, the doctor wants to talk to me. Get some rest. I'll call you in the morning."

"Okay."

"Sheridan?"

"Yeah?" I sniffle and wipe my eyes.

"It's *not* my turn. I love you." He hangs up before I can say a word.

When I wake up in the morning, before I can recall that Nanny is in the hospital, that I can't go to Chicago and get my mother, that Jack likes me, and that I said horrible things to my father, I notice the sunlight streaming in through Lori's blinds. A mysterious stillness surrounds me. Makes me feel lighter, somehow.

Then I remember. Nanny is going to make it. My father actually said he loves me. And into my mind has popped a brilliant idea, one more chance to talk to my mother before the show. It's foolproof, really.

So maybe things aren't as bad as they seemed last night. Maybe someone up there is listening to me after all.

Chapter 16

PIE IN THE SKY

$\mathcal{A}$ text comes through from Dad shortly after I get up. Nanny will be in the hospital for a week, if all goes well. That's awesome. But it's Saturday morning, the busiest day for Sweetie's. I jump out of my chair-slash-bed and start folding it up. I am ready, and totally sure that today is the day. I will talk to my mother.

Lori sits up in bed, groggy. "What are you doing?"

"They'll need me at the bakery." I grab the cushions and put the chair back together. "I've got a lot to do today."

She falls backward and moans. "I suppose you want me to get up, too?"

I laugh. "A little coffee would be nice."

"Fine."

I check my cell again. Still no word from Ethan. But that's okay. Today will be a good day.

I go into the bathroom and take a quick shower, dry my hair, pull on the sweater that I packed for Chicago. My optimism flags for a second, but I push all feelings of doom as deep as I possibly can.

By the time I'm done in the bathroom, Lori is waiting for me with a hot cup of coffee.

"Oh, bless you." I take it and sip. "Yummy."

She looks at me funny. "You're acting weird. Like cheerful or something."

"Yeah." I put the coffee down and pack up my bag. "Everything's cool. New plan."

"Uh-oh."

I laugh. "It's all good. Don't worry." I pick up the cup again, take a long swig. "Just come by later, and I'll tell you. I gotta go help Roz."

"Okay." She takes the coffee cup from me. "Sheridan. Don't do anything stupid, promise?"

"Why are people always saying that to me? I'm fine."

"You want me to drive you?"

"Nah. I can walk." I give her a quick hug and say good-bye.

I need the time alone to work out the finer points of my plan. It's only eight o'clock, too early to call Chicago. But I can call information and get the number for the McCormick Place convention center. It's right on the shore of Lake Michigan. Nanny and Dad took me there to see *The Nutcracker* for Christmas when I was ten. I can picture it; I bet Mom's already there, getting ready for the competition. I hope she wins.

But more than that, I hope she takes my phone call.

I dial information and write the number down on my hand. I'll call at nine thirty, which will be eight thirty Chicago time. The competition won't have started yet, so I won't distract her. Well, that's ridiculous; of course I'll distract her. But I hope it will be a good distraction.

As I round the corner to Main Street, I see a crowd of people outside the Sweetie's door. Oh no. I pocket my phone and run.

Mrs. Davis sees me first. "Sheridan! How are you, sweetheart?"

"I'm fine. What's going on?"

"Oh, I'm here to help. But Mr. Rasic sent me away."

"*You're* here to help? What about Geronimo's?"

"Oh, don't worry, we're covered. No, I heard about your grandmother and was so worried. I'm no Lilian Wells, but I can certainly brew coffee."

"Sheridan." Sous-chef Danny walks up and gives me a hug. Lucy, his daughter, stands next to him, and when he's done, she hugs me, too.

"I'm glad she's gonna be okay," Lucy says. I feel kind of guilty. We ate lunch together every day in the sixth grade. What happened to us? We were good friends once. Until the cakes. We were good friends until I got busy with my cakes.

"Thanks," I say.

Everyone I see says something nice to me about Nanny and tells me they're praying that she's okay. When I go inside, I see that the bakery's case is full and that Mr. Roz is smiling behind the counter. I see pastry chef Dominique walk in from the back with a full tray of pies. The part-timers from the retirement home are also buzzing around, waiting on customers.

I see the Suits, crowded around one of the little front tables.

"Sheridan." Gray Hair stops me. "How are you?"

"Fine. Thank you."

He reaches out and pats my arm. "Quite a shock. But I'm so glad to hear the good news."

I nod, then make my way around the case and into the back. Mr. Roz follows me, begins filling another muffin tray with batter.

"What do you need me to do?" I ask.

"Sheridan. You don't need to be here. We taking care of things. Except for we need more room."

He lifts an arm and points to the side counters. I see a lineup of homemade muffins, coffee cakes, pies.

"What is this?"

"That is how much people love your grandmother." Then he leans in close to me. "Don't ask me why they bring bakery food. We already got plenty. Who gonna eat all this?"

There're a pile of cards, a few potted plants, a vase of freshly cut white tulips with a big pink ribbon. Nanny will love those.

My eyes are fogging up. I shake my head. There will be no crying today.

"This is amazing."

"Yes, amazing." He stops, walks over to where I'm reading a small card on a potted hyacinth. "You have good friends here." He pats my back. "They like family."

I look up at him. He's right. St. Mary is where my family is. Except for Mom. And she'll be on her way.

"You go home. We have plenty of help here."

"What about the basket weave cake?"

"You finished. They come pick it up. No worries."

"But I can do something."

"No. You go home and rest. But wait . . . first . . ."

He flicks open a white bag, picks up a lemon poppy seed muffin, and drops it inside.

"For you." He hands me the bag and walks me to the back door. I shrug. I don't think he's going to let me stay. And of course, it would probably be better if I made the call to Chicago at home, all by myself. So I don't argue.

"Sheridan?" Dominique comes into the kitchen. "There's someone up front asking for you."

I step around her, see Ethan's head above the crowd. "Thanks," I say.

He sees me and smiles, and I wave him to the back. Nanny would never let him in here, especially without a hairnet, but I lead him right out the back door and into the alley.

"Hey." He reaches for my hand. I am relieved he's here. That he still wants to see me. He has terrible bedhead. I reach to pat down the sticking-up part. Then I kiss him. Hard. Let myself enjoy the moment and try not to think of the trouble with Jack. Or the fact that I am the world's worst kisser.

"Did you get my messages?" I ask after our lips detach.

"Yeah, I'm sorry. I left my phone at home."

"You were at the beach?"

"Yeah, I was waiting for you. Then everyone showed up and things got kind of crazy. I'm sorry."

"Oh."

"I'm sorry about your grandma."

"Yeah. It was scary."

He puts his arms around my waist and pulls me in closer.

"You think we can get together this week?"

I scrunch up my face. "We can try."

"Do you *want* to get together?"

"Well, yes. But I don't know what's going to happen with Nanny in the hospital. And this show, too." I roll my eyes. "But after this is all over, I'll have more free time. I promise."

"Sometimes you gotta make time, you know. If you want something bad enough."

I wish he hadn't said that. I mean, my grandmother did have a heart attack. But he pulls me in for another kiss and I remember: he just wants to be with me. That's a good thing.

"I'll try."

"You got some free time now? We can go to your house." He looks at me hopefully.

"No. I gotta go back in." This is a lie, of course. But I need to call my mother, and there's no simple way to explain that to him. Plus, I am way too stressed out right now to think about making out with him and what that might lead to.

"Okay." He steps back with a sad, crooked smile. "Well, call when you can fit me in."

"Okay," I say. "Maybe like Wednesday?"

He shrugs. "Sure. Whatever." He holds my hand until both of our arms are stretched out. Then he lets go and walks away, down the alley.

That didn't go well. If we can just get through this week, just get through the rest of school and into the summer, we'll be fine. I hope we can make it that far.

All alone in the alley, I check my cell phone. Still an hour before I can call Chicago. Maybe I should have gone with Ethan, or invited him home. But I couldn't, not with Nanny in the hospital. If she found out we were alone in the house, it would give her another heart attack for sure.

I go back into the bakery, pick up my bag. Everyone is so busy in the front that they don't even notice.

Up in my bedroom, I pull out a notebook, try to

hammer out a script of what I might say to her. She'll be upset. Think it's an emergency. So I'll have to calm her down, tell her everything is okay. It's me, Sheridan.

For the next hour, I try to psych myself up for the phone call. Finally, it's nine thirty. I pick up my cell phone. My chest is so tight I fear *I* might be having a heart attack.

Five minutes pass. I've still got the phone in my hand. Luckily, I copied the number off of my palm, because sweat has made it unreadable.

I dial. And the phone rings. I take a breath so deep I can feel the air in my toes.

"McCormick Place Information."

"Hello." *Don't throw up, Sheridan. This is too important.* "Yes, I am trying to get in touch with a contestant in the cake contest."

"One moment, please." And now I am listening to some ancient Elton John song.

"Hello?" It's a man's voice.

"Yes, hi. I need to get in touch with someone in the cake contest." I gulp. "It's an emergency."

"Well, we can page the person. What is the name?"

"Margaret Taylor." I am sitting on the end of my bed; my leg shakes, up and down, up and down. My blood is pumping fast. This is it. I have to stay in control.

"She's a contestant?"

"Yes, sir. I believe so." I hope so, anyway.

"Oh yes, here she is. I'll page her, put you on hold."

"Thank you," I say, too late, because I'm already hearing Elvis on the hold music. I press my hand to my chest, as if that can calm the beating of my heart. Every muscle in my body is tense. I wait. The Elvis song is over; now we're on to "Across the Universe," by the Beatles, which I know because Nanny loves them too.

After a while, I stop paying attention to the music. She's not coming to the phone. I've been on hold for ten minutes. I haven't breathed in about that long; I might drop dead soon.

Okay, another five minutes and I'll hang up.

Some song I don't recognize at all starts playing. At the end of this song, I'm going to hang up, then try again later.

"Hello?" The woman's out-of-breath voice takes me by surprise.

I stand up, open my mouth. Nothing comes out.

"Hello! Is there anyone there?" the woman shouts. She's upset, as I predicted.

"Yes!" Okay. My mouth works again. That's good.

"Who is this? They said it's an emergency? Who is this?"

"No. Everything is okay. It's me."

"Who?"

"It's me." I swallow. "Sheridan."

"Excuse me?"

"Mom?"

"Oh . . . Oh."

"Yeah, it's me, Mom!" I'm grinning. I can't believe I'm talking to her. "Mom, oh my God, it's been so long!"

"Yes. Yes, it has. Listen. I'm at this contest." She laughs; she's happy. "Can I call you back?"

"Mom, it's taken me so long to find you. It's so good to hear your voice." I'm smiling so wide my face might crack in half. "Mom, Dad got a cable show. We're filming next Saturday. And they need a cake. I'm making it, but it's got to be perfect and I need your help. Can you come?"

The words trip clumsily out of my mouth.

"He got a show, huh?"

"Yeah, he did—can you believe that?"

"Yes, I can," she says in a kind of faraway voice. "But . . . But I've got to go now. Let me call you back."

"All right. Okay. I can't wait to see you."

"Right, I'll call you."

"But you don't have my number. Let me give you my number."

"No. I'll call you back. I've got to go now."

I am silent.

"Okay?" she says. It hits me that her voice is only vaguely familiar. Like something I heard in a dream.

"Okay." I feel impatient suddenly. "Don't forget, Mom."

"No." I can hear in her voice how badly she wants to get off the phone.

"Promise?"

"Yes. Bye."

I don't want her to go. "You said you were coming back. In my card. Remember?"

"Oh." She laughs again. "I did say that. That's right. But, Sheridan, honey, I've really got to go now, really. Things are just getting going here."

"So you'll call me?"

"Right. So . . . okay, good-bye?"

"Okay. Bye."

And that's it. She's gone. I put the phone down. Fall backward onto my bed. That was not what I thought it would be. At all. But she's going to call back. She promised.

I reach into my bag, grab the blue velvet box, and pull out Jack's bracelet. I fasten it around my wrist. Rub the bird between my fingers like a good luck charm.

I will not cry. Will not. She said she'd call back. She promised, didn't she? I play back the conversation in my head. I can't remember. Did she promise?

I roll the velvet box around in my hand, take out Jack's note. *Hope you get what you really want.* I close my eyes, tight, until I see funny shapes and colors behind my eyelids.

She promised to call me. That's what I really want. I want my mother to keep a promise, for once.

Chapter 17

GUM UP THE WORKS

So when is she going to call? It's Tuesday. I can't sit by the phone all day, waiting for her. But when I check the messages at home, check the caller ID, there's nothing. As far as I know, she doesn't have my cell phone number, but I check it constantly anyway, just in case.

The Suits have a full agenda for me this week: they'll film me working on the cake tonight, then I have a wardrobe fitting tomorrow night, and there's more crap on Thursday. Whatever.

And to make matters worse, Ethan hasn't been in school. He texted me to say that he has a cold. Then Mrs. Ely actually called my father yesterday and ratted me out on the art project, telling him that it's 50 percent of my semester grade. Thanks a lot, Mrs. E. And now I have to show him my work every night, like I'm six years old. So I've been going over to Growly's garden, frantically sketching the spring flowers.

Surprisingly, Dad doesn't seem too mad about the project, and he hasn't said a word about our fight in the hospital or even punished me for planning the whole Chicago trip. I figure he's waiting until the show is over, so he can be sure I'll behave, and then he'll slam me.

All of these things are particularly annoying to me today, and I head to the bakery after school in a wonderful mood.

As I finish up the birthday cake for little four-year-old Logan Ellis, Dad walks in the back door. I'm concentrating on some muddy tracks for the monster truck I've already sculpted and covered with fondant. Nothing too complicated.

Roz walks in with a tray of cookies. He's cleaning out the case for the day.

"Jakup." Dad nods at him.

"Ah, Donovan. Good to see you." He walks over to Dad, grabs his hand in both of his, and gives his signature shake and wide smile. "How is Lilian today?"

"Much better. They think she'll be out of the ICU soon. In fact, I'm taking Sheridan to see her now."

I stand up straight. "What? No. I don't have time." This is the truth, but I'm also a little nervous.

It's not that I don't miss Nanny; I just don't want to see her all zoned out with tubes sticking everywhere. "I need to start the gumballs and work on the hibiscus flowers."

"Gumballs?"

"Yeah." I go back to my monster truck. "An engagement party. They met at a gumball machine or something."

"Gumballs? Christ, what will these people think of next? I thought I told you not to take any more cakes this week?"

"It was already on the books. And I gotta have it done on Thursday so I can finish the cake for my fake birthday party." There's a sharp edge to my voice.

"Can you handle it? And your schoolwork?"

I am so not in the mood for this today. "It's not rocket science, Dad. They're gumballs."

"How's the cake for your party coming?"

"The cake is made. I'll cover it on Thursday and finish the flowers between now and then."

"Well, remember, it doesn't have to taste good; it just has to look good."

I glare at him. "Yeah. I got it. But I am not going to the hospital. I don't have time. You said Nanny's out of it, anyway."

Dad absentmindedly picks up a spatula and turns it over like he's flipping imaginary burgers. "She's better today. So come with me now, and I'll help you later."

"Yeah, right."

"Sheridan, I grew up in this bakery. I could make a buttercream rose before I knew how to read."

Mr. Roz chuckles and walks back to the front of the shop. I don't need him chuckling at me.

"I don't need help. I mean, thanks, but I have it all planned out. Tell Nanny I say hi and that I'll see her soon."

"Look, we're going. Finish up," Dad says like the total dictator he is.

Mr. Roz walks back in, comes to my side, pats my back. I flinch. He inspects the cake and grins. The man is always smiling. Drives me nuts.

"Dis girl has the magic touch, no? What a beautiful cake, eh?" he says to Dad, who is busy sending a text.

"It's not done yet," I say. It's not bad. But there's something missing. I stare at it from all angles. No, it's not right. I close my eyes, think of her.

What's missing, Mom?

"Hurry up, Sheridan. We need to get to the hospital," Dad says.

"No. I said I have too much to do."

"You need to visit your grandmother. We won't be long."

The bell on the front door jingles. "Ah, dat would be Mrs. Ellis," Mr. Roz says. "Here—I help you put cake in box." He grabs a piece of flat cardboard and begins to fold it.

"Okay, I'll wait in the car, Sheridan. Get that cake out of here and let's go," Dad says, and walks out the back door.

"Hello?" a woman calls from the front.

"It's not done," I whisper. Mr. Roz is crowding my space, so I nudge him out of the way. "Something's not right."

"Oh, it's perfect!" Mr. Roz glides in front of me, picks up the cake, and places it into the box he's made. "One minute, Mrs. Ellis!" he calls up front.

I slide the box and cake away from him. "It is *not* done."

I pore over every inch of the cake. What will make it perfect? I'm drawing a blank.

He reaches for the box again. "Don't!" I bat at his arm.

"Sheridan." He laughs, like I'm joking, and whisks the cake away from me. Again. "It's just what she ordered. She will love it. Now is time to let go."

Let go? No. I won't! Who is he to tell me when my cakes are done?

But he takes it up front before I can stop him.

I can hear the woman oohing and aahing over it. What does she know? Then I hear the cash register open and close, and hear my client walk out with an imperfect cake. I am furious.

I toss some pastry bags into their storage bins and am throwing metal tips into the sink when Mr. Roz comes back, whistling. Really, whistling? He goes to the sink and acts like nothing happened.

"You got homework tonight?"

"Of course I do," I bark.

He washes the tips, his back to me. "You good girl,

Sheridan. I think you becoming a very fine woman. You have many gifts."

"Yeah. I'm like my mother. Except she never would have let that cake go unfinished." I throw the buttercream into the walk-in cooler. Mr. Roz is quiet for a moment, then turns off the faucet. I look at him; he is staring at me.

"Yes. Your mama was good—good for cakes. Nice with customers. But she did not make good choices. *You* make good choices."

I step back. It's like he's smacked me across the face, insulting her like that. Good choices and bad choices?

"Really?"

He turns back around and picks up a towel to dry the tips; he still hasn't picked up on my tone.

"Who are you to tell me about my mother? You have no idea why she left." The words seep from my mouth like poison. He turns around slowly. Now he knows I'm mad. "You have no clue." I'm finished cleaning up the counter, so I grab my schoolbag, still facing him. "But she loves me. I'll bet she tells everyone about me. Tells everyone how proud she is of me. And she's coming back, too. So don't you dare judge her!"

His large eyes turn downward. "Yes, I think she is very proud of you." Then those eyes meet mine, and they are filled with so much love I can't stand it. "You are wonderful girl. We *all* very proud of you."

I shake my head and push in a stool, banging my toe in

the process. "Ouch!" I shout, much louder than necessary.

Roz runs from the sink and catches my elbow. "What happen? You okay?" I wrench my arm out of his hand and hobble away, my bag on my shoulder.

"I am fine! And don't say another word about my mother. I talked to her, and she's coming here. And stop acting like you're part of my family. You are *not* my family!" I yell that last sentence and regret the words even as they roll off my tongue. But it's too late to take them back.

"Sheridan! Shut up!" My father is standing at the back door. Crap.

"No, Donovan," Mr. Roz says in a kind voice. "It's okay. Really, this is hard time for her."

I wish he'd stop being so nice.

"Get in the car. Now," Dad says.

I know that face, and I know better than to argue.

I walk out the back door and get into the car. Dad doesn't come out right away. Probably apologizing for my horrid behavior.

A chill runs through me. I pull out my cell phone and scroll down to my sent calls. Look at the number for Mom's bakery. I want to hit the number so bad and ask her why she hasn't called back.

Dad slams his way out the back door and looks like he's going to kill me.

He slides into his seat, grabs the phone out of my hand, stares forward in silence for a long minute.

"Are we going?" I barely finish the question when he snaps his head to look at me.

"First of all, if you ever talk to Jakup like that again, you will never drive, never leave the house, never decorate another cake again. Got it? He is the best kind of person, and he's working his ass off right now!"

I look out the side window and don't say a word.

"And second—am I right in hearing that you called your mother?"

I shrug.

He starts the car and peels off down the alley. I still don't answer.

"What did she say to you?"

I shrug again. "Nothing. She said she'd call back."

He snorts.

"What? What's wrong with me talking to my own mother?" I ask.

"You are a real piece of work. Tell me, has she called back, Sheridan?"

"She will."

"Sheridan! Your mother is *not* going to call you back. Trust me. I'm sorry, but she's not. It's just you and me, kid!" He's ranting like a lunatic, and I just want to jump out of the car. "God, I wish you'd stop acting like a four-year-old and accept the fact that you got stuck with a shitty mom."

I gasp. My eyes narrow. I completely hate him. "How can you say that? You know what?" I face him, my voice positively thunderous. "Do your show without me. I quit!

I'm sure they can find someone else to play me; just tell them that I act like a four-year-old and can't handle it!"

He sneers. "Oh, no way. You are not quitting. I don't care if I have to paint a smile on your face; you are not blowing this for us."

"For *us*?" I throw my hands in the air. "What part of this is for us? It's all about you. You just want to get out of here and get famous. So go! Go get famous. Leave me. I'm *not* doing it."

He slams on the brakes when we come to a stop sign. The car jerks backward. He turns to me and sticks a finger in my face. "Stop this, Sheridan. Right now. You aren't going to be like her. I won't allow it. Your mother is selfish. Can't you see that? She was never able to put anyone else over herself. But that's not how I raised you. You are *not going to be like her.*"

"What? I *want* to be like her. She's not selfish. *You* are. All you think about is yourself!" I take a deep, heaving breath, and my upper lip starts to spasm. I squeeze my eyes shut, trying to hold back tears.

But Dad isn't done with me yet. "Oh, you think she's not selfish because she sent you those cards? You have got to be kidding me." A cruel laugh escapes him as we sit at the stop sign. "I'm wondering when you're going to see the pattern in those cards; promising you this or that; sounding like she's missing you, like she thinks about you all the time." His booming voice hurts my ears. "And then another year passes and nothing. When are you going to see? Not only is she selfish, she's a lying bitch."

Oh, that's it. "Don't you ever talk about my mother like that!" I scream across the space that is rapidly closing in on me. "You're the liar—you're selfish one! You're the one who wants to take away everything that I love!"

Hot tears pour like mini-waterfalls down my face. I can't fight them anymore. I grab for the handle and yank the door open. There's a car behind us now. I step out onto the street.

"Get in the car!" he bellows with fury.

"No!" I slam the door shut as the car behind us honks.

And then the greatest dad on the face of the earth hits the gas and squeals off, out of town and away from me. I watch the car until it rounds the corner; then I turn, unable to see through the fog of tears in my eyes.

"You okay, honey?" The honking car's passenger window is rolled down, and I see the tourist lady who was in Sweetie's the other week. The one who wanted my father's autograph and thought he was a doll. I wonder what she'd think of him if she knew he just abandoned his daughter by the side of the road.

I force a smile and nod. "I'm fine." I point to my head. "Allergies."

She gives her boorish husband the go-ahead to drive away, and I trudge up a hill. My father says he loves me, but he does not. He'd be happy to leave me in St. Mary and go to New York alone. I'm sure of it.

I reach the top of the hill and see all of St. Mary below: the high school football field, the town square, the courthouse, and even Lake Michigan. But for the first time in my life, I wish I was someone else, somewhere far away.

In the center of my vision, I see Ethan's mansion. The red brick almost pulses in the pinks and yellows of the setting sun. Like it's alive, calling me over.

Let go? I think of the voice I heard in Lori's bathroom.

Oh, yeah, I'll let go. My feet step one in front of the other, and I know that I have to see him, hold him, kiss him, feel his arms around me. I force everything else from my mind.

I wipe my eyes, sniff, and straighten my back, determined. Ethan thinks I'm different, in a good way. He thinks I'm special. Not just for my cakes, but for everything I am.

By the time I get to the gate, I am practically running. The front door knocker is a giant lion, like the one in *A Christmas Carol* where Marley's face pops out of Ebenezer's door. I half expect a ghostly version of my grandmother to show herself, warning me not to do what I'm about to do. So I bang on the thing hard and then cover it with my hand.

One more knock and I hear the lock unlatch on the other side. The door creaks open, and I am staring into the face of Haley Haversham. I can tell she is surprised to see me, but a wicked grin spreads across her face, like a wound peeling open.

"I got it!" Ethan yells from inside the house. He appears in the foyer, waving some money.

"Sheridan!" he says, and goes all pale.

"It's not the pizza guy," Haley snickers.

I turn and walk away before I start bawling like a pathetic loser in front of her.

"Wait!" Ethan runs up behind me, but now I'm running too.

"It's okay," I call over my shoulder, concentrating every ounce of energy in my body to keep myself together. "I get it; it's no big deal."

I am almost to the gate when he catches the side of my arm and turns me around to face him.

"Come on, Ethan," Haley calls from the front door. "Let her go. I'm sure she's got some cake to make or something." She's laughing.

"Sheridan . . ." He is breathing heavy; his voice is a harsh whisper. "This isn't what you think. She came over. I don't want her here." His voice breaks, like he might cry. "I want *you*."

"Ethan!" Haley again.

I wrench myself out of his grip. "Come on." I step back from him. "This isn't going to work. I don't have the time. So this is fine." And here come the tears. God, I'm turning into a human sprinkler.

"No. Don't say that." He grabs me again. "Don't go away like this. I'm so sorry. She called and wanted to study.

We are not back together." His eyebrows are all scrunched up. He does look sorry.

"Really, Ethan." I pull myself away again. "It's okay." No matter what he says, nothing changes the fact that Haley is standing in his doorway. And I am not.

"No, Sheridan. Listen to me." He's moved so close that I can feel his breath on my face. He puts his arms around my waist. "Don't go away like this. You are the one I want to be with. Not her."

I don't want him to hold me, not in front of her, but then I breathe in that Ethan scent and I am toast. I don't know if I should believe him. God, I love being in his arms.

"When? When are we supposed to be together?" I look up at him with worried eyes.

"We'll find the time." He touches my cheek, wipes away a tear.

"Ethan! Here's the pizza. Finally!" Haley is losing patience.

"When?" I ask.

"Tonight? Can you get out?"

"No. I told you." I shake my head. It's the truth. They're filming us at the bakery later, even though I just quit. But I also know that if I refuse, Dad will make me pay. As in, no cakes. There's no quitting. I'm stuck.

"Okay, tomorrow night. Even just for a walk? Meet me at the harbor. What time?"

"Probably not until late."

"Ten?"

"I'll try."

"Good. That's fine. Just try. Good." He leans in like he's going to kiss me, but I step away. There's no way I'm going to kiss him while she's watching. And certainly not in front of Grant Flickner, the pizza guy, who walks through the gate at that moment.

"Hey, Cake Girl!" Grant says as the pizza box tips precariously in his hands. I made a Fender guitar cake for his bar mitzvah a few years ago. It looked just like the real thing.

"Hey, Grant," I say, avoiding his eyes and walking out of the gate wishing that the ground would open up and swallow Cake Girl whole.

Chapter 18

SOUR GRAPES

The farther I get from Ethan's house, the better I feel. The sobbing stops, and now I am resolved to see my plan through. I will call Mom as soon as I get home. And if she's not there, I'm leaving a message. As for Haley being at Ethan's, I'm still trying to work that one through. If this was happening to Lori, I would tell her to forget him. But now I know firsthand that's easier said than done.

When I turn the corner near the restaurant, I see limos and trucks all over the parking lot. They're swarming in and out of the restaurant: the Suits, cameramen, and crew. No way can I run into one of them now.

I turn around, head back down the alley, and enter the house through the back door. I run upstairs, close my bedroom door, turn on my laptop, and go to my jewelry box. Mom's note floats on top, Jack's bracelet just beneath it. I stuff the heart-shaped piece of paper into my front pocket, then pick up the bracelet, slip it around my wrist, and fasten it tight.

I growl at the computer, which is taking its sweet time booting up. Since Dad took my phone, I need to get the number for Mom's bakery off the Internet. I am going to call her and very simply insist that she come back.

Finally, I get online and search for *Sweetie's in Sault Sainte Marie.* I punch the long Canadian number into the cordless and wait. I am not even a little bit nervous. This is no time to panic. This might be my last chance. Do or die.

The phone rings and rings, and then finally the voice mail picks up, again.

"Hello. This is Sheridan." I pause. Too late to change my mind now. "Um, you said you'd call me back." Okay, so I am a little nervous. "Uh, you need to call me back. You promised, Mom. This is my number." I leave my cell number, but as soon as I hit Off, I realize I just gave the number to the phone that Dad took away.

Oh crap. This day just keeps getting better. I toss the phone onto my bed, grab my bag. Jack's bracelet gets caught on my sweater sleeve. I miss him. It's like there's a big hole where he used to be, like a missing piece to a puzzle. I miss his goofy sense of humor. I miss his just being here. There's no one I can talk to like I can talk to Jack. I want to be friends again.

The doorbell rings, but I grab my coat, tiptoe down the stairs, and sneak out the back door.

I head down the alley and around the corner to Main Street, walking west toward the church rectory. It's five thirty and the sun is starting to go down, but there's enough light to start a few more drawings.

I walk through the open gate and feel instantly protected by the brick walls around me. I can hide here, for a little while. My eyes are swollen from crying, and I could really use a tissue, but I flip open my sketchbook anyway.

I sit on a small concrete bench that's curved like a smile and scan my work from yesterday, when I sketched the tulips. I notice today that they are open just a little bit wider. The daytime temperatures have been warmer the last few days, and the garden shows it.

I glance around and decide to draw the grape hyacinths, which are so low to the ground I have to lie on my stomach to get a good look.

They are beautiful, like clusters of bright indigo bells. I focus on one single bulb and begin. My right hand seems to know exactly what to do, where to shadow, where to lightly trace. My eyes move from the paper to the flower. It's like making music, notes and instrument working together. The flower comes alive, right there in my sketchbook.

It's not the same as making cakes, but still, this picture is coming along. When the sketch is done, I reach for my colored pencils so that I can capture the way the hyacinths look in the fading sunset, the way they rustle ever so slightly in the cool breeze.

As I pull out the green pencil, I hear footsteps on the flagstone path and snap the sketchbook closed.

"Good evening, Sheridan," Growly says, stern, as always.

"Hi, Father," I say, scrambling off my belly. "I was just leaving." His usual scowl is there when I look up at him.

"Oh, don't rush off on my account. It's a lovely flower, don't you think?" He points to the clump of grape hyacinths at my feet.

"Yes. Lovely."

"May I see what you've done?"

No way. "Well, they stink, so . . ."

"Perhaps they do"—he sits on the bench—"but I'll be kind. I promise." He reaches out. I want to turn around and run. But I open the book and give it to him.

He stares at the hyacinths for a long time, turning the paper this way and that. And then he flips the page backward.

"Oh, please, don't." I reach for the book. "Those are worse."

He laughs quietly. "Oh, let an old man appreciate some art." He considers several of the tulip and daffodil sketches from yesterday and then the withering crocuses from the day before.

He closes the book, hands it back to me.

"Yes." He looks straight ahead at the still-sleeping

rosebushes. "There's definitely some talent there."

I look down at my feet. "I told you they weren't good."

He crosses his arms, leans back a few inches. "Well, actually, they are quite remarkable."

"Oh." I shove the sketchbook back into my bag. "Thank you. But it's not really my thing. Art, I mean. I don't like it very much."

"Hmm. Life is full of ironies like that, isn't it?" He straightens his body and chuckles. "The Father hands us what he hands us. A calling. A family. A gift. And yet, we can hate the things we've been given. Or love them. Or sometimes feel both ways at the same time. Odd, don't you think?"

I don't know exactly what he's getting at. But I feel I have to make one thing clear. "I'd rather make cakes. I love making cakes."

"Yes." He nods. "Like your mother before you." He leans to one side, picks a piece of grass, and throws it into the air to see which way the wind is blowing. "Your mother was gifted, certainly. But not like you."

"She is *very* talented," I say. He'd better not insult my mother, too; he'll be sorry.

"No, no, there's no doubt about that." He points a finger at me and smiles again. "But she is not you and vice versa. Your talents are not the same as hers. Thankfully, we don't become exactly what our parents are; we have gifts of our own to develop and explore."

I look hard at the old guy. He's trying to impart some priestly wisdom to me. But he doesn't know me or what my cakes mean to me. He doesn't know what my mother means to me. No one does.

"I think I'll sit out here for a bit and enjoy the evening. Would you care to join me?" he says.

"No. Thank you. They're filming us tonight, or something."

"Ah, the big show." He grins.

"Yeah."

"Well then, good night." He reaches out his hand to me. I consider him for a second and then place my hand in his. He squeezes it, just a little.

"May God bless you and bring you peace, Sheridan."

"Thanks." I let go and walk toward the gate, hoping that maybe God heard him, thinking that a little peace would be a nice change.

Dad's car is back at the house. I don't want to talk to him at all. But I know I need to get my cell phone back before Mom calls. The filming starts in half an hour, and the crew is now streaming in and out of the back of the bakery, setting up.

I take a deep breath and walk quietly inside the house. I don't see Dad, but as I walk upstairs, his voice booms out.

"Sheridan!" He's in his study down the hall. My feet move like they are in quicksand. *Squelch. Squerch.* When I get to the doorway, I see that he's at his desk, leaning on his elbows, tapping his chin with his fingers.

"Where did you go?" he asks.

You mean after you left me by the side of the road?

"Art project," I say, trying to sound like I don't hate him for what he did and said to me earlier. I need that cell phone. It's there on the corner of his desk. If he's still mad, there's no way I'll get it back.

"Come in for a minute. Let me see your progress."

Fine.

I walk in quickly and pull the sketchbook from the bag on my shoulder. Open to the page with the hyacinths. He scans it quickly, closes the book, and hands it back.

"We have to talk." He motions to the chair across from him. I shake my head.

"I'll stand, thanks."

"Sit."

I sit and fling my bag to the ground.

"I saw your grandmother, briefly."

"What?" I sit up. "Is she okay?"

"She's fine. She should be home this weekend." He leans back in his chair, tilts his head. "But she says I was wrong."

"What?"

"She says it was wrong of me to treat you like I did earlier. And I agree. So, I'm sorry for what I said and for leaving you."

The ticking clock echoes through the silence. I see right

through his act. He needs me to be a good girl on his TV show, doesn't want me to blow his big chance.

"And she thinks I owe you some answers." He lifts his eyes to meet mine. "About your mother."

Well, this is not what I expected.

"So, go ahead—what are your questions?"

My mind is like an orchard of questions; I can just reach out and pluck one from the nearest tree. "Why did she leave?" I ask, drained of all emotion. I just want to know the truth.

He nods, leans back in his chair. "She fell in love with that man. Of course, you know that." He looks down at the desk, then up at me again. "But I guess you're old enough to know. He wasn't the first."

"What?"

"There were other men." He pauses. "You sure you want to hear this?"

I'm not sure. I nod anyway.

"She had a problem being faithful. She was always sorry after, and I always took her back." His voice is slow, steady. "I thought you needed her. But after a while, her behavior started to affect you, too. Do you remember the time you went to stay at Nanny's for a while, when you were in kindergarten?"

"No."

"Yeah. I was invited to be the guest chef at the Governor's Mansion. While I was away, she went off to meet some guy.

Left you alone in the house, sleeping. Nanny found you and took you to her place, and she wouldn't give you back until your mother and I figured things out." He shakes his head. "She said she'd call child services if we didn't. Kept you for about a month. And we tried to make it work."

He shifts, uncomfortable now in his chair. "She shaped up after that, for a while. But when she didn't get on the plane after that contest, I knew she was gone."

I am like a statue, barely breathing.

He nods. "I did hope she'd be part of your life. I wanted that for you. But I think as each year went by, staying away was easier than facing you and facing up to what she'd done. I know those ridiculous cards didn't help."

I am listening, trying to sort through his words. But they are jumbling up inside of my head.

"I don't care." I stand up, trying to stay calm. "I don't care if there were other men. I am her daughter, and she loves me. She'll come back if I ask her."

His eyes are closed. "Sheridan. She doesn't want to come back."

"Well, I'll bet I can make her. Give me my cell phone. I'll show you."

"No. Sit down." I sit, too tired to argue. "I'm sorry, but you can't *make* her do anything. And . . . I want you to listen to me."

"No, you're wrong, Dad." How can I convince him? "She's coming back."

"No. She's not."

But I can hear her voice. *Hold my hand, Cupcake. Come and let me brush your hair. Here's how you make a buttercream rose, Sheridan. I love you. I miss you. I will see you soon.*

"Listen to me very carefully, Sheridan. If you keep calling her, you are going to get hurt. I want you to leave this alone, okay? We'll film the show. And when we're done . . . Are you still listening?"

"No." I straighten my spine. "After the show, you'll leave, too."

"I told you it's not going to happen that way. You are coming with me."

I shake my head. He'll never listen. How can I make him understand that leaving here will kill me?

He keeps talking. "You don't have to agree with me, but this show is the chance I've wanted for you. Your chance for a remarkable life. Look at those sketches." He nods his head in the direction of my bag. "You have so much talent. I won't let you waste it."

I stare, confused by his words. "No, Dad." My voice breaks. "This is *your* chance. Not mine. I am happy the way things are." I take a deep breath. "I'll be in the show. But I am *not* going to New York." I stand, pick up my bag. "And if *you* go, if you leave, then I don't want to see you anymore. I'll live with Nanny and you won't have to worry about me."

His broad shoulders sag. "I'm not going to leave you, Sheridan," he says in a whisper. *"I'm not her."*

"Please stop talking about her like that. She *loves* me."

We stare at each other with the same unwavering look.

I can see the pain in his eyes. I've hurt him. I'm getting scary good at hurting people lately. My cell phone is on the corner of his desk. I walk to it and pick it up.

"Since you admitted you were wrong, I assume I can have this back?"

His jaw tenses. My stomach flips. I turn around and walk down the hall with the phone in my hand.

I close my bedroom door. Sit on the edge of my bed. Flip open the sketchbook in my hands. Slowly, I page backward. Bright yellow tulips, tinged with red.

There were other men?

Purple crocuses edged with yellow.

She doesn't want to come back?

Daffodils with delicate ruffled petals.

I stop on the hyacinths. This sketch was the tenth picture. I'm done with the project. I run a finger over the deep purple blossom. I don't wonder what's missing. Don't wonder what my mother would do. I drew what I wanted. And I know that it's right.

Staying away was easier? I can understand that. It's not easy to admit when you're wrong.

I pick up the cell phone, check for messages. Nothing. And then I dial Jack. I can't help myself. I need him. I want him back—Haley or no Haley, Ethan or no Ethan. It's ringing. I hope he will answer.

"Hi." It's him and he doesn't sound thrilled.

"Hi." I stand up, walk to my window, push aside the curtain. What do I say? "Jack." Well, that was profound.

"What?"

"I'm sorry." I take a deep breath, relieved to just say the words. "I am sorry. I'm not doing anything right and I hate it." I am crying again. For the millionth time today. "And I don't want to lose you, too."

He hesitates. "Okay. Calm down."

"Okay, what? Okay, you forgive me? Or okay, you're through with me?"

I hear him sigh. "You know you're not getting rid of me that easy." I sigh, too, so glad to hear those words. "But I still can't stand Ethan. Just so you know."

"Fair enough." I laugh. "And I can't stand Haley. Just so you know."

He's silent for a long second. "Who told you?"

"Does it matter?"

"Look, I was mad at you. And she asked me. It made sense at the time. But there's not much to her, really, other than what we already knew was there."

I sit down, my out-of-whack world a little closer to being back in orbit. "Good."

"How's the mom hunt?"

I pause. "Don't ask." I press my fingers to my temple and my voice breaks. "Not good."

"Okay, change of subject, then?" he says. "How's that art project coming?"

I sniff. "Done."

"For real?"

"Yes, for real," I say, and wipe my eyes. "I'm done."

"I'll believe it when I see it."

"Jack . . . I *am* done."

He laughs. "So can I see it?"

"Yeah."

"What are you doing right now?"

"They're filming us at the bakery tonight. You wanna come?" Having him there might just make it bearable.

"Will I be in the way?"

"No way."

"Ethan going to be there?"

"No." Haley is probably still at his house, doing "homework."

"Good. I'll come over," he says. "And, Sheridan?"

"Yeah?"

"I'm glad you called."

I laugh, so relieved. "Me, too." I hang up, rub the bird charm on my bracelet. Check my cell phone to make sure it's charged and the signal is strong. I'm not giving up on Mom yet.

I need to look on the bright side here. I've just patched things up with Jack. The project is finished. Nanny is on the mend.

Miracles are happening all over the place.

Chapter 19

LET'S TALK TURKEY

The camera crew films me making a gum paste hibiscus flower for the cake; then they ask me to show Dad how to do it.

He's nervous. Thinks I'm a loose cannon, like I might lose it in front of the camera. Well, I won't. I told him: if he goes to New York, we're through. If he thinks I'm gonna change my mind, he's wrong.

I cut out the shape of the petal. Dad tries to copy, but he's miserable at this. It's very funny, and I'm sure this segment will be good for some laughs on ExtremeCuisine TV. At one point, he holds up his awful petal and says, "You have so much more talent than your old man." Then, while they are still filming, he puts his arm around me. "Love you." He sounds so sincere that I almost believe him. But when Amazon yells, "Cut!" he drops his arm and walks over to her.

Jack shows up while we're filming and watches quietly from the back. When we're done, and they whisk Dad into the front of the bakery to watch the footage, I wrap my arms around Jack's neck in the longest, tightest hug ever.

"All right . . . can't breathe." He pulls me off him.

I hold up my arm and rattle my wrist, showing him the bracelet. "Thank you. I love it."

"Yeah, I knew you would. Babes and jewelry and all," he says, his brown eyes all lit up.

"Don't let it go to your head," I say.

It's good to be myself with Jack right now, even though it's strange to know that he's got this crush on me. As we talk, I notice he's acting different—holds my gaze just a little longer than normal, smiles at me for no good reason. The biggest surprise of all, though, is the fact that I'm acting kind of different, too.

Then I remind myself to stop. I have a boyfriend. I think.

"Hey," I say as I settle down to work on another petal. "If you're free tomorrow after school, I thought . . . I was hoping maybe you could take me to see Nanny?"

"Sure, I guess."

"I haven't gone yet."

"Really?"

"Yeah. The thought of seeing her like that freaks me out

a little." I attach the petal to a small metal pin that sticks out of a Styrofoam base. It will take at least a day to dry. "But I've gotta do it."

"Okay, I'll take you."

"I can't stay long. I've got a wardrobe fitting." And plans with Ethan at the harbor, but I keep that to myself.

"All right. We can leave after school, then?"

"Perfect."

He looks at his watch. "Well, I guess I should go." He sticks his hands in his pockets and hovers like he has something more to say.

I put down my work, nod my head. "Cool. I'm about ready to pack it in, too."

"Okay, cool."

I walk with him into the alley, holding open the screen door with my body. He stops. We're standing in the shadows; a light breeze dances between us. But he doesn't make a move to leave.

"What is it?" I nudge his arm and laugh. "Are we okay?"

He doesn't speak; just stares down at me, his eyes cutting through the darkness. Then he takes a step closer. He looks hungry; he looks like he wants me. I let go of the door. Jack lifts a hand and touches my cheek. "I'm sorry if this ruins everything, Sheridan. But if I don't do it now, I have a feeling I'm gonna be sorry." He brings up his other hand and holds my face, all the while looking at me with those starving dark eyes.

"What are you doing?" I whisper, but it's a stupid question, because I already know the answer.

He lowers his head and his lips touch mine. His mouth presses softly, tender but firm, so that I have no doubt it's happened. Then I feel that same electric current, the one I felt that night at my house, only this time multiplied by a thousand. My eyes snap shut, and I am transported like those people on *Star Trek*, blown into a million pieces and floating weightless through outer space. And my brain begins to process what is happening: *Jack is kissing Sheridan.*

Then he stops. He smiles, drops his hands to his sides, and walks away down the alley without a word. A few minutes later, when I hear the crew come back into the kitchen, I force myself to unfreeze and act like nothing happened.

Even though something definitely did. I know this because my legs feel like Jell-O and I can't focus on what the people around me are saying.

I hear footsteps and look up to see Mr. Roz heading down the alley. Instantly, I recall my despicable behavior. He smiles at me and I wonder how I could have been so cruel to him.

"Oh, Mr. Roz, I'm so sorry." My hand goes to my mouth.

He swings an arm around my shoulder and squeezes me to his side.

"No need for feel bad," he says. "I know your heart." He lets go and opens the door. "You get good film for da TV?" And that's it. I'm forgiven.

I shrug and nod. "I think so." We walk inside.

I see Dad and Amazon across the room, talking. He touches her a lot, and he laughs a little too loud when she says something. I can't imagine her saying anything funny ever. My eyes narrow. How dare he tell me all those things about Mom when he flirts with every woman who looks at him?

The crew begins to pack up. Mr. Roz gets to work prepping for the morning, and I start helping him. It's the least I can do.

"Sheridan," Dad says from across the room. "Go home, okay? You've got school in the morning."

And now look at him, being all Dad-like while he hits on his new boss. Nice.

I pat Mr. Roz on the back. "Sorry."

"No sorry. The beauty need her beauty sleep."

"Good night, Sheridan." Amazon waves. Now *she's* trying to suck up to me?

I lift a hand. "Bye."

As I walk out of the bakery, into the cool night, I pass the spot near the door where Jack and I kissed. I touch my lips.

Where did he learn how to do that? It was remarkable. It occurs to me that through that entire kiss, I didn't worry once that I was doing it wrong. That was what I always imagined the perfect kiss would be. I just never thought it would be with Jack.

I step across the alley toward home, and a lightbulb

clicks on inside of my head. Maybe I'm not such a bad kisser after all; maybe I've just been attached to the wrong lips.

The next day, Jack comes up to my locker and grimaces. "Let me just talk first. You wanna forget that whole thing last night, that's fine."

I peer up at him. "Do *you* want to forget it?"

He smiles. "No."

I lock my eyes with his, hoping he can read my mind, and the corners of my mouth curl up ever so slightly.

I'm not quite sure what to say or how to say it. All I know is that I would like to kiss him again. But then Ethan walks up beside me in the hall, in all his godlike glory.

Boyfriend, Sheridan. You have a boyfriend.

"Hey." He captures me in his sweet smile and in his arms like I am the only girl in the whole world. I look at him, all the while watching Jack out of the corner of my eye. Smoke is practically coming out of his ears.

"Hi," I say.

"You ready for the French test?" Ethan asks, and kisses me. Like yesterday with Haley never even happened.

"Yeah." I glance sideways at Jack, then look back to Ethan. "You?"

"Yeah, right. I'm more of a last-minute guy, at least when it comes to school."

At the end of the day, Jack and I walk to art together, slow and quiet. I still think Ethan is handsome. I still want to feel his arm around me between classes. But now there's this huge thing that's happened, something that has rocked me down to my bones. And I think Jack knows it.

We get to class just as the bell rings. Mrs. Ely sticks her head out of the door. "Are you two joining us?" she asks. Before I can answer, Ethan swoops in from behind and grabs me around the waist. He swings me around and plants a big kiss on my mouth. Between Jack's glare and Mrs. Ely's staring hard at this blatant PDA, I turn a million shades of red.

"That's enough." She points to Ethan. "You. Get to class." He answers with his best bad-boy smile before he walks off backward, waving to me, down the hall. That smile usually makes me melt. But at the moment, I'm more embarrassed than melty.

Mrs. Ely eyes me as I walk to my chair and sit down next to Jack, who shakes his head and looks to the front of the classroom.

I can't win.

At the end of class, Mrs. E asks me to stick around. She waits until everyone else has left the room, then sits down at her desk. I hope Jack's waiting in the hall for me. We're still going to the hospital. I think.

"Have you finished the project?" she asks.

"Yes!" I say with enthusiasm. It's not even due until tomorrow. "It's right here." I reach into my bag and give it to her. She takes it and flips through the pages, lingering on one or two.

"Hmm." She closes the sketchbook and leans back. "Have you given any thought to the art camp?"

Oh, come on.

"You know, I have so much going on. You know about my dad's show. And my grandmother. It's just been a lot. I'm not sure I'll have time this summer."

"Yes, I know you are busy. I'll give you that. But the application isn't due until the end of May. I'll be happy to help you with it if you like."

I lift my shoulders to my ears. "I don't know."

She huffs and stares at me. "You know something? I know you are the Cake Girl or whatever it is they call you. But you can also draw. These are incredible."

I don't know why she's getting all bent out of shape. I finished the project; I thought that's what she wanted.

"I don't usually nag my students, Sheridan. But you seem to think that the only place you can use your skills is on a cake. Your cakes are remarkable—there's no doubt about that. But I wish you were more willing to step outside of your comfort zone."

She flips the book open to the grape hyacinths.

"I see more than ability in this drawing. I see passion. I swear only someone who loves what they are doing can create something like this."

I cross my arms, not sure what she wants me to say.

"Do you? Do you love it?" She's asking me this with her eyes all turned up and big, like a stray puppy. "It's okay to love drawing, you know, *and* love cakes. You can do both, you know." I am silent. She stands up and sighs. "You don't have to level with me, but at least be honest with yourself."

I shake my head. "I've really got to go. I'll think about it, okay? The camp, I mean."

She hands me the sketchbook. "You know, a true gift isn't something you do because it pleases other people. It's something you *must* do because it fills *you* up inside."

"All right." I hoist my bag onto my shoulder. "Have a good night."

"You, too," she says to my back.

I practically run from the classroom, scanning the hallway, looking for Jack. He's down by our lockers, waiting.

"Art camp again?" He seems to have gotten over Ethan and that embarrassing kiss. I'm glad. I need my friend right now.

"She doesn't know when to give up."

"You gotta hand it to her; she has good taste."

"Whatever."

We walk out to the ancient Corolla that belonged to Jack's dad back in the days of the dinosaurs. It's rickety and scares people because it's so loud, but I'm used to it.

There's another chem lab due tomorrow, too, so I've brought the book with me.

"You want to work as we drive?" I ask.

"Look at you, not waiting until the last minute." Ah. A dig at Ethan. He pulls out of the parking lot and winds through town toward Grand Rapids.

I rattle off questions from the textbook, though I barely pay attention to my own words. I think of Ethan kissing me in the hallway like that and bristle. In front of my teacher. In front of Jack. That was not cool. I wonder if I even have the guts to talk to him about it later, when we meet at the harbor.

As I reach down and grab my notebook from my bag, Jack's bracelet jingles on my wrist. He smiles big. I feel a twinge of guilt. He wouldn't be smiling if he knew about my date with Ethan later.

I stare out of the window and sigh. What am I going to do with these two?

"Why a bird?" I ask, the chem book lying useless on my lap.

"Bird?"

"Yeah, why'd you pick a bird charm?"

He shrugs one shoulder. "Just reminded me of you." He shifts the car, and I listen to the gears grind.

"Why?"

"I dunno." We stop at a light. "I guess even when we were kids, I thought you'd be the one to, you know"—he flaps his hand and laughs—"fly away or whatever. Always seemed like you could do anything, be anything, go anywhere. That's why I got it. It reminded me of you."

"That's weird."

"Why?"

"Because I don't want to go anywhere."

"That's what you say." He shifts again. "But I don't believe you."

"Oh. That's nice."

"Hey." He points to the chem book in my lap. "Lab."

I turn back to the book. We don't say a non-chemistry word to each other the rest of the way to the hospital, and by the time we pull into the parking garage, the lab is done. I even mostly understand it, I think.

The sight of the tall building and the big automatic doors makes me forget all about my romantic issues, and my stomach does a weird jig. I look at Jack.

"You okay?" he asks.

"I'm nervous." The doors open as we walk in.

"Don't be." He grabs my hand. He's never held my hand in all the years that we've known each other. But I don't pull away.

She's on the fourth floor, and visiting hours end in twenty minutes. A cranky-looking nurse asks who we are, then calls another nurse, who seems nicer.

"I'll take you to see her," she says. She looks at Jack. "Only family, sweetheart." She points to a row of chairs behind us.

Jack squeezes my hand, pressing the bird charm into my palm. He lets go and sits down.

The nurse escorts me down a dimly lit hallway. "Lilian?" she calls, and raps lightly on a door. "Are you up for a visitor?"

"Who is it?" I hear her voice, but it's not loud and booming like usual. It sounds weak and watery. I follow the nurse and stop short when I see Nanny. She looks a hundred years old and shrunken to half her size in that big hospital bed.

"Hi." I am stuck to the floor.

"Get over here, girl," she whispers. "You look scared as a wild turkey on Thanksgiving morning. Gosh sakes, come here and give me a hug. I'm not gonna break."

I do what she says, but it seems like just saying those words has worn her out. She smiles big, but when I hug her, I am very careful. There are tubes and wires coming out of her every which way. The nurse has left the room. It's just the two of us.

Since Dad told me that story of the time I stayed with Nanny as a kid, memories have come back to me in bits and pieces. I do remember some of it. Like the fact that I was really confused. I missed Mom and Dad. But at the same time, I always felt safe and totally loved with Nanny.

She pats the bed and I sit next to her. She reaches for my hand. "I'm gonna be just fine, sweetheart. Now you gotta get that look off your face. You're scarin' the bejesus out of me. Do I really look that bad?"

"No. You don't look so bad."

"Oh. Not so bad. Well, that's better than six feet under, I s'pose." She breathes deeply a few times. "Just so you know, they say if I take care of myself from here on out, my ticker'll last a hundred years."

"Good."

I look across the room to the windows that overlook Grand Rapids. It's getting dark.

"Saw your daddy today. Told me he talked to you." She pats my hand.

I nod. "Yeah. We talked all right."

"He's got a bee in his bonnet about you."

"It's not a big deal. I'm not going to New York. It's not something you should worry about."

"Oh, I'm not worried, because I know my girl ain't no dummy. She might be stubborn, but she ain't no dummy."

I turn back to her, look in her eyes, and smirk. "Was that a compliment?"

She laughs quietly, until the laugh becomes a cough. When she finally settles down, she smiles. "I'm sayin' you're bullheaded like your grandmother. But you'd better remember what I've taught you. Darlin', your plans are just plain puny. You can't even imagine the life that is out there waiting for you."

I shrug, unable to imagine anything better than making cakes in St. Mary and having my mother and father in my life at the same time.

"Nanny? Do you think Mom still loves me?" I touch her hand, hold it in mine, will her to say yes.

"Course she does." She is breathing heavier and sounds so tired. The beeping sound behind us is keeping rhythm with her heart. "But you know some people just don't know how to show it."

"You think that's a good enough excuse?"

Nanny pats my hand. "No. It's not good enough. But, sweetie, I can't speak for your mother. All I know is that I adore you. And I want the world for you."

The bracelet on my wrist catches her eye. She touches it. "What's this?"

I lift my wrist and touch the bird. "A present. From Jack."

She reaches out for the charm and reads it as I bring it in closer. "Dream." Isn't that nice? What a sweet gift."

The nurse walks back into the room, starts to mess with a machine by the bed. "Time for your meds, Lilian."

Nanny looks at me. "I am getting a little tired. You should probably go home, baby girl."

"I don't want to leave." I hold her hand tighter.

"Don't worry. These folks say I'll be ready for home on Sunday. Can you believe that? Huh! Modern medicine." She laughs and then winces. "Go and do your TV show. I can't wait to see it." I roll my eyes, but she pokes at my bracelet. "No, no, don't roll those eyes. You've got to dream big, darlin'. Don't be afraid to dream big."

I stand up, lean over, and kiss her soft, sunken cheek. "Love you," I say. But she's already asleep.

Chapter 20

OTHER FISH IN THE SEA

Jack drives me home. He seems to guess that I don't want to talk, which is good, because he is right. That's one of the perks of having a best friend since forever. He turns on some mellow music, and I watch my reflection in the passenger window.

I am trying to make sense of everything that's happened. Trying to understand why Mom hasn't called me back. I am so confused.

We pull up to the house. The parking lot is almost empty, which never happens on a Wednesday night. But the restaurant is closed through the weekend because of the show. I shiver suddenly, afraid that I'm seeing the future: Dad in New York, the restaurant gone, Nanny weak and old. Our little triangle destroyed.

I notice the lights are on in the front room of the house. Jack doesn't make a move to kiss me again, which I think is very gentlemanly. But I lean across with my hand outstretched, touch his cheek, and pull his face to mine. Our lips touch, and once again, my body is zapped with electric charges. So it wasn't a onetime thing. He smiles. But I still don't know what all this means. Ethan's face pops into my mind. If only he wasn't so irresistible.

"See you at school," I say, pushing open the door and stepping from the car. "Thanks for taking me."

Jack grabs my hand. "It's going to be okay, you know," he says across the darkness.

He sounds so sure. I hope he's right.

"Yup. Okay," I say. I close the door, then walk up the front steps and into the house. Dad and the Suits are sitting in the front room. It's like walking into a spiderweb, and I'm a big, juicy bug. My eyes scan the faces, and I notice there are a few extra Suits. Great, they're multiplying.

"Here she is." Amazon stands and walks toward me. "Here's Sheridan. And how is Grammy?"

"Nanny."

"Yes. Nanny. How is she?"

"She's fine." But Amazon is not really listening. She escorts me to the sofa.

"Sheridan, I'd like to introduce you to Bob Fisher, the president of ExtremeCuisine TV."

This old guy with snow-white hair stands up, holds out

his hand. "Ah, the famous Cake Girl of St. Mary. That's what they call you, I hear?"

I nod and force my mouth into a half smile.

"Well, it is a pleasure to meet you." He looks from me to Dad. "Donovan, she's a beauty. Must take after her mother."

Polite laughter follows. Dad's eyes dart to mine. Obviously, no one has schooled Bob Fisher on our screwed-up family dynamics.

"I hope you realize, Miss Wells, that your father is about to change your life forever." He waits for a response. A thank-you? A shout of glee?

I hold the arm of the sofa, tight. "Yes. I do."

Maybe Amazon is picking up on my sarcasm, because she abruptly changes the subject. "So. On to your wardrobe. Olga is here somewhere; she's a seamstress and will be fitting you." She walks over to the chair in the corner. "Here are the dresses. Go ahead and try this one on first; it's my personal favorite." She holds up a melon-colored halter dress with giant hibiscus blossoms all over the fabric.

"For real?"

"Trust me. It'll look like magic once you get it on."

Yeah, like someone magically threw up hibiscus flowers onto my dress.

"Go on, try it on. It's vintage. You'll look stunning." She holds it up to my body. "Just stunning. Maybe have to take in the bust a bit. *Olga!*"

She yells so loud I'm surprised my eardrums don't burst.

I look at my watch. It's only seven. But I hope they clear out by the time I have to go meet Ethan. Because I need to see him tonight, to figure this out.

The fitting goes fast. And yes, Olga has to take in the bust. A lot.

It's only eight thirty by the time we are finished. Dad announces to our guests that he'll cook up a snack if anyone is hungry. Everyone accepts. Thankfully, he has to go to the restaurant to do this because we have no food.

I say no thanks and head upstairs to my room. I reach into my pocket and dig out Mom's heart-shaped note, sit with it on the edge of my bed. My fingers trace the letters, as they have for years. I pull my cell phone out of my other pocket, check for messages. Of course, I already know there are zero.

I throw the phone onto the bed behind me. Then I stand up to get dressed for my "date" and realize that my closet is a black hole of ugliness. Totally inadequate. Nothing to wear. Finally, I decide on the same pair of jeans I wore yesterday. They desperately need to be washed, so I spritz them with a healthy dose of Febreze and hope Ethan won't notice. I add a tank top under the striped hoodie that Lori gave me for Christmas and sigh. This will have to do.

In the bathroom, I look in the mirror and pat at the dark circles under my eyes. I scramble to plug in the flat-iron. I brush my teeth, my tongue, and my gums and even gag myself trying to reach as far back as possible with the toothbrush. This is not a night for stinky breath. A little eye shadow, eyeliner, mascara. It's when I put on the lipstick that I am reminded of Jack's kiss.

Man. What a crazy mess.

It's not even nine o'clock. I should go to the bakery and crank out another hibiscus. But the house is so quiet and peaceful I want to stay. I feel a strange pull, and it makes me lie down in the middle of my bed and dig out my art project. I open to the grape hyacinths.

I see my cake sketchbook on the desk and stretch to grab it. I open it to the first page. There's the sketch of the John Hancock Building, a skyscraper in Chicago that I re-created out of cake last summer. Then a sketch of my Indiana Dunes cake, complete with a dune buggy. That was great. I flip through the pages: wedding cakes, birthday cakes, baby shower cakes—so many over the years.

Then I close that sketchbook and look at the grape hyacinths. Like the cakes, I drew this picture for someone's approval. Mrs. Ely gave me no choice. But there's something about these drawings that makes me feel different.

I love making cakes; I love that they make people happy. And they make me feel closer to Mom. But when I make art, it's not about remembering anyone, or pleasing anyone. I work to please myself. Just me, no one else.

Mrs. Ely's voice floats through my head, trying to convince me that I can make cakes *and* draw. I mean, duh, right? I know I can do both. And I remember Growly talking about how we aren't meant to be exactly like our parents. *We have gifts of our own.* My mother always talked about me following in her footsteps. Wouldn't it make sense, though, that she would also want me to lay some tracks of my own? That maybe she'd want me to do more than she did?

I look up at the clock. It's only nine fifteen. A little early, but I need to get out of here. I stuff a pillow under my bed to make it look like I'm sleeping, pull on my boots, and head out the back door, in case a Suit (or worse, my father) is peeking out of one of the restaurant's windows.

As I swing around Main, the town square is quiet, except for a few people exiting Geronimo's. I skitter into a doorway while they come out, then stick to the shadows. No need for Jack to catch a glimpse of me. A giant-size dollop of guilt hits me head-on. *What am I doing?*

I am on the path toward the harbor. The moon is shining bright on the high bluffs. The air smells like sand and fish, a sure sign that warmer weather is coming. But tonight I stick my hands in my coat pockets and put on my mittens because it's still cold. My eyes follow the line of the water, and I have this terrible thought that it's all going to disappear; that everything is about to change. I memorize everything: every ripple, every sound, every particle of icy air that lands on my face.

What if I did go to New York City? How would I survive without all of this?

I lengthen my stride, and as I near the boathouse, I hear him. "Hey." It's Ethan, early. "What's up?"

He walks up behind me and puts his strong arms around

my waist, holds me tight. He kisses my ear, and the tingle gets going. But I find myself wishing he'd look me in the eye first, maybe ask me about Nanny.

I turn toward him and feel the strength in his shoulders. When I look at his face, I see nothing but confidence. He is sure of me. He leans in for a kiss.

Maybe I'm being paranoid, but the first thing I think is that I taste some sort of flavor on his lips. Like lipstick.

"I can't believe you're actually here," he says. "I was sure you'd cancel."

"Nope." I try to act happy. I know I should be happy. This is what I wanted.

He grabs my hand and pulls me along.

"Let's go down there," he says, pointing to my family's dock.

"That's ours."

"I know."

"How'd you know that?"

"I asked around."

When we arrive, I see a soft-sided cooler waiting. "Shall we?" he says, sweeping his arm down in a low bow. Romantic. He takes a blanket from under the cooler and spreads it out for us.

Once we're settled, he unzips the cooler and lifts out a tiny bottle. "You like wine?" he asks.

"I don't know." I shift uncomfortably; Dad has definite rules about drinking.

"Really?" he says, surprised. "I would have thought you'd have a glass now and then. Nothing better than good food paired with good wine. Not that *this* is good wine." He laughs. "But I wanted to do something special. This is kind of our first official date."

"Is it?" I peer behind me.

Ethan nods his head, brings out a container. When he pulls the top off, the aroma of garlic and basil wafts into the air. Next comes a baggie full of baguette slices.

"Pesto. It's my special recipe."

"You made this?"

"Yes, I did." He spreads some on a piece of bread and hands it to me. "I figured the only way I'd have a chance to cook for you anytime soon was to do it picnic-style." He unscrews the wine bottle, empties it into a short plastic glass. I take a bite of the bread.

"Wow, this is good," I say, trying to cover my mouth. He takes a sip from another bottle and leans over to kiss my neck.

"This is nothing." He kisses me again. "Once I get out of high school, I'm off to Paris. Then someday I'll open a restaurant. Maybe even be on TV like your dad."

I take another bite. This *is* good. "Hmph . . ." I swallow and wipe my mouth with one of the creased linen napkins he's brought. "Trust me, though—you don't want to be like my dad."

"Why not? He's a great chef. That's what I want to be." He is serious.

"Well, he'd probably hire you at the restaurant, if you want to see what it's really like." I snicker. "They're always hiring busboys. He might even let you help in the kitchen after a while, if you're lucky." I roll my eyes.

Ethan shrugs. "I don't want to be a busboy. I just want to cook." He slathers more pesto on another piece of bread, and I am so hungry I completely scarf it down. "And you should be at least a little excited. I mean, you've got it made. Your dad is going to be famous." I look at him; I'm ready to bust up laughing. But he's serious.

"Sounds like you'd rather have him here than me." I smile.

He reaches around my waist. "Not by a long shot." He leans in and runs a finger along my jawline. But all of a sudden, a clear vision of Jack materializes in my mind. I can feel Jack's touch, his kiss, and I pull away from Ethan.

"So. Did Haley stay long? The other night?"

He sits up straight, pulls his arm away. "I thought we settled that." He finishes his mini-bottle in one big gulp. "Look," he says. "I'm sorry. I know you guys have a history. But me and her . . . we're through. So you don't have to worry."

He tries to kiss me, but I back away again.

"Good." I wonder what she's told him. "Because she is not a nice person. I can't stand her."

"Wow, Sheridan Wells actually dislikes someone? And all along I thought you were the town sweetheart?"

"What's that supposed to mean?"

He laughs. "Relax. Haley, she's just wicked jealous of you."

"Of me?"

"Well. You are the most famous person in St. Mary, next to your dad. Everyone knows Cake Girl. She hates that."

"No one *knows* me." I pick up the cup of wine, put it back down. Look up at the sky, where the stars are shining again, like they always seem to do whenever Ethan is around.

"Well, I'd like to get to know you better." He leans backward onto his elbow and tugs at my sleeve until I follow. Now I'm lying on my back, with Ethan gazing down at me like I'm some treasure he's just discovered. He reaches across my body, grabs my hand, laces his fingers through mine. I can see his profile in the moonlight, and I realize that a month ago, a date with Ethan Murphy was a fantasy. I never imagined it could really happen, or that if it did happen, I'd spend the whole time thinking of Jack.

Ethan presses his lips on top of mine. His mouth tastes like wine, which isn't entirely unpleasant, and now he's kissing me harder. I try desperately to focus on the hot boy whose mouth is exploring mine. He moves on to my neck, and I start feeling tingly and floaty. This is nice. He untangles his fingers from mine and touches my stomach, then moves to the bottom of my coat. I feel his hand on my bare skin. It tickles me and then moves upward. When he gets to my bra, I reach up and gently push his hand back down.

"Ethan."

"What?"

"Stop." I laugh.

He kisses me again, more insistent this time. I wonder if he notices that our lips always seem to be just a tiny bit out of sync. "Come on." His hand is searching for skin again. "Let's go to my house."

"And?"

He shrugs, kisses my face. "Let's just see."

No. We can't just see.

"Ethan," I say, surprised by how sure I sound. "I don't think I'm ready for that."

He kisses me again. "Oh, come on. Why not?"

"I don't know. I'm just not."

He stops, leans back on his elbows. "Okay. Fine." He sits up quickly, pulls his knees in against his chest. Like he's having a tantrum.

I sit up next to him and wonder what just happened.

"Look, I think we make a great couple," he says sharply.

"Me, too. I mean, maybe this is just moving a little fast."

"Okay." He takes a deep breath, turns to me. "Why don't you tell me how fast you want to go?"

"I don't know. Not this fast."

He stands up, stretches his legs in that wonderful Ethan fashion. "Well, I can't read your mind. I'm trying here." When I stand up, he grabs the blanket. "Maybe we should do this again after the show."

"Really?" I ask.

"Yeah, maybe the party is making you tense." He moves forward and gives me a quick kiss, a boring one, like we've been married for ninety years. "I'll call you," he says, and walks away, leaving me alone in the dark. I watch those long legs until they disappear.

My mouth hangs open. When it finally closes, I look out onto the water in shock. Maybe Lori was right, and this whole romance thing shouldn't be easy. But should it really be this hard?

Before I start home, I bend down to touch the initials my parents carved into the board beneath my feet, because it always makes me feel better. But this time, I feel nothing.

Just a big empty nothing.

I walk home, the temperature dropping, my face stinging from the cold. Our house is completely dark and unwelcoming, so I pass it and walk toward the alley, digging the keys out of my coat. I let myself into the bakery, lock the door behind me, and grab my supplies. I dump everything onto the table and work a mass of gum paste until I start to relax. Soon the small clump resembles the ruffled edge of a hibiscus petal. I've got about thirty flowers completed already, which is probably more than enough. But I need a distraction, and let's face it, you can never have enough gum paste flowers.

I settle down and let the bakery envelop me. Think of Nanny wanting me to dream big. I look around, at the shelves full of cake boxes, at the pink polka-dotted aprons hanging on their hooks, at the clipboard bursting with orders. I am part of this place. How could I exist without it? *This is where I belong, this is where I belong, this is where I belong.* I repeat this mantra to myself until it is like a song in my head.

This cake will be my best ever. Just spectacular. The Suits will love it. Even Dad will have to admit it's a masterpiece.

It's just after midnight when the doorknob jiggles and I jump. I hear a key in the lock, and the door swings open. It's Dad.

"Been looking for you."

"Here I am," I say, keeping my eyes on my work. I'm glad that I am *here*, and not still on the dock with Ethan, about to get busted with empty wine bottles and his hand up my shirt.

He walks over and inspects my drying petals with a scowl. "You think you need more?"

I grunt. "I'm the cake. You're the other stuff. This is mine. Remember?" I know that sounds rude, but I've had a long day. I just want him to go before it gets worse.

He seems to read my mind, and I am relieved. "Don't stay too late," he says. "And lock the door behind me." Then, instead of heading for the door, he walks over to where I'm sitting, puts his arm around my shoulder, and kisses the side of my head. "Good night," he says, and leaves.

Jeesh. What a day.

Chapter 21

ONE BAD APPLE
SPOILS THE WHOLE BUNCH

A muffled thump from downstairs wakes me. I can't focus.

Bang! Bang! Bang!

I jump up and stumble down the stairs. Through the door I see Lori pointing to an imaginary watch, and I let her in.

"What's going on with you? What are you, alarm-clock challenged?"

"Calm down." I look at the clock and see that, once again, I will have to make a mad dash to school. I run up the stairs and Lori follows.

"I'm sorry. Just go without me. Yesterday was seriously the most messed-up day of my entire life." I pull a bra under the T-shirt I slept in, clasp it, toss on the first shirt I pull out of the closet, and run to the bathroom. "Just when I thought things couldn't get any worse."

My jeans lie in the middle of the floor. Do I dare wear them again? It's nasty, for sure, but I force my legs in, one at a time. There's always more Febreze.

"Yeah, like I'm gonna go without you. I want details, sister."

She has a white paper bag in her hand and thrusts it toward me. "I didn't know what you'd want. They're out of lemon poppy seed, so I got you a blueberry crumble. Roz seems a little overwhelmed over there. When's Nanny coming back?"

"I don't know." I find a pair of socks in my drawer (bonus—they're clean!) and head downstairs. "Maybe I shouldn't go to school today. I could help him."

"Shut up, you have to go to school. Remember? Art project? Chem lab? Any of these things ring a bell?"

"This day is already total crap." I throw my hair up and grab my makeup bag, which will have to wait until I get to the restroom at school.

"Seriously. You're gonna have to repeat sophomore year if you don't get yourself together. Between that nuthouse bakery and this freak-show party and meeting up with lover boy . . ."

I shove everything into my bag. "It's not that bad. And I'm pretty sure that Ethan and I are over."

I reach into my front pocket, where Mom's note has

been stuck for days. I put it in my jewelry box, her punishment for not calling me back.

A car honks out front, and Lori walks to my bedroom window. "Over, huh?" I cross the room and stare out into the parking lot. Ethan's getting out of the Volvo, a bouquet of red roses in one hand.

I'm speechless. Last night was so bizarre; it all happened so fast. He seemed so pissed off. By the time I went to bed, I'd convinced myself that we were over.

"Well, heartbreaker, what's the plan now?" Lori smiles, enjoying this. She runs downstairs, and I hightail it into the bathroom to put on my makeup after all.

I hear Lori fling open the front door. "Ethan! Hey, Ethan!" she calls like a spaz. I watch myself put concealer on a zit. Line my lid with black pencil. There's a stirring in my gut, and it's not hunger. What am I doing with someone like Ethan? He might make me swoon. He *does* make me swoon. When he touches me, there's definitely a spark. But . . . there's always a *but*.

But he left me alone by the harbor last night. But he didn't even make sure I got home safe. But he tried to make out with me in front of my teacher. But Haley Haversham answered his door. But I'm not ready to go to his house and do *whatever*.

I turn off the light. Stand in the darkness. I know what I have to do. I feel it in my stomach, in my head, in my bones. My heart, I think for the first time ever, is speaking clearly.

I grab my messenger bag, walk to the stairs. Ethan is inside now, and he watches me as I descend. His whole face lights up. I swear, it does. It's like I'm the most amazing thing he's ever seen.

"Hi," I say as he holds out the flowers.

"Hey. I'm not sure what happened last night. But I'm sorry."

"Thanks." I take them. "They're beautiful." He gives me a kiss, a nice kiss. But something has changed. My knees aren't shaking. I don't feel dizzy at all.

Lori coughs. "We might want to get to school, kiddies, or it's detention for all of us."

"I can drive us," Ethan says, and looks at Lori like he's seeing her for the first time. "Leslie, right?" She looks at me, then back to him. Her eyebrows lift.

"Close enough," she says, putting her hand on his arm and making googly eyes at me behind his back.

"Just a sec. Let me put these in water." They walk out the front door as I go to the kitchen. The roses are lush and gorgeous. If I wasn't in such a hurry, I'd be tempted to sculpt them out of fondant.

I pull a vase out of the cabinet, take it to the faucet, start to fill it. The flowers are beside me, looking perfect. Flawless. Kinda like Ethan. I turn off the water. *What am I doing?*

Without thinking, I pull out the trash can, flip open the top, and shove the roses to the bottom of the bin. I step back, look at them. Ruined. Too dramatic? Maybe. But somehow it makes me feel a whole lot better.

We get to school and he tries to grab me in the hall, but I see Jack coming from the other direction.

"I'm late. See you later." I step away from him.

"Why are you still mad?" Ethan asks, frustrated.

"I'm not mad. Just thinking. About chem. I can't be late," I say, and walk away smiling.

I slide into Wasserman's class, just in time, but on the way in, I catch Haley's eye in the back row. She flashes her usual sinister grin as I take my seat.

While Wasserman drones on about lab safety (one girl lost an eyebrow to a Bunsen burner last week), I make a mental to-do list: finish cake, wait for my mother to call, take a deep breath and let this show happen. Then break up with the most perfect male on the face of the earth?

At lunch I sit with Lori at one of the round tables that are jammed into the cafeteria. Jack walks over. Since I started going out with Ethan, Jack's been working on some report in the library instead of eating with us.

"Can I sit with you guys?" he asks.

"Moron, you've been sitting with us since first grade and *now* you're gonna start asking for permission? Seriously?" Lori says. Tuba Dude Jim looks at her with total admiration. They may just make it, those two.

"Whatever," he says to Lori.

I smile up at him.

As I eat my salad, I imagine what will happen when I end things with Ethan. No one in their right mind breaks up with someone that popular. It's total social suicide.

Jack nudges me as Lori bosses Jim.

"Are we okay?" he whispers.

I nod. "Yep. Got a lot on my mind is all."

"Yeah. I know," he says. I glance at him. Why have I never noticed how sweet he is? And not just to me. He is just a good guy. His head tilts and he meets my stare. I think of our kiss, which I can't forget, surprised at how much I'd like another one. But that would require untangling myself from Ethan first.

Lori clears her throat. "Ahem, don't let us interrupt or anything."

I sit up and realize that Jack and I are looking at each other all moony-like. He takes a bite of his sandwich and moves his eyes over to the table of black-fingernailed Goths next to us. But Lori doesn't stop. "Why are you two acting so weird?" She looks at me, then Jack, then back to me again. "Wait a minute. . . ." She points a finger at us, and her eyes get wide. "Did you two . . . ?" Her eyes meet mine. "Was that the thing with Ethan this morning? Did you . . . ?" She smiles so wide I think her face might split horizontally. "No! Did you two hook up?"

"Shh!" I whisper, 100 percent mortified.

Lori laughs. "Well, it's about time! And to think, you've

both recently been linked to other people." It's like sitting next to a reporter for the *National Enquirer*.

"Hush," I say. I can't look at Jack.

Lori's eyes focus behind me. "You hush. Here comes trouble."

I turn to see Haley and her faithful followers stomping through the center of the cafeteria and up to our table. The hens stop clucking long enough to let their leader speak. Haley raises her hand like she's about to swear an oath.

"Hello, Jack." She doesn't wait for a reply. The entire cafeteria turns toward us in what seems like one smooth motion. Haley shakes her head. "People who are dating usually sit together at lunch, don't they?"

"Haley," Jack says, "we went on one date."

"Oh, I'm not talking about us. I'm talking about her." She points to me, and there's that evil glint in her eye. "Heather Sanchez was working at the T-shirt shop last night. Taking a smoke break in the alley." Haley's hands are on her hips, and her elbows stick straight out like the east and west of a compass rose. She talks loud enough for everyone to hear. "She swears she saw you two. Kissing?"

Jack and I exchange glances.

"Ethan found that very interesting when we talked this morning. Especially since you were also with him last night."

I look at her and have no idea what to say. I'm just sick of her face, sick of her voice. Everyone around us is dead silent, waiting to hear what Haley's going to say next.

"Of course, they say the apple doesn't fall far from the tree. Looks like making cakes isn't the only thing you got from your mother." She leans toward me and raises her voice just a little louder. "You've turned into a slut, just like she was."

I'm so sick of her I want to scream. I stand up, feel my face turning bright red. "Shut up. You don't know anything about me."

She chuckles with a that's-all-you-got? look on her face.

I wish I could come up with the perfect stinging comeback. But all I can think of is Jack and that he knows I saw Ethan last night. It's killing me.

Finally, the bell rings for fifth period. The crowd disperses; the show is over.

"God, you're a loser," Haley says over the din.

Then she turns on the ridiculous high heels she always wears and pushes her way through the crowd. I think of that Moses movie that's on every holiday, the one with the bad special effects of the sea splitting down the middle. I wish that God would swallow her up right now, just like he did to that nasty Pharaoh. I plop back down into my chair.

Everyone in the cafeteria is off to their next destination, except for Lori, Jack, and me. "Good lunch," Lori mutters, grabs her book bag, and looks at us.

"Hey." She snaps her fingers in front of Jack's face. "*Don't* listen to her. Sheridan had to break up with that asshole sometime, right?"

I look up at her, so grateful I can't stand it. Then I turn to Jack, whose eyes are boring into mine. *Is that the truth?* That's what he wants to know. I force a weak smile but don't say a word. Well, it was almost the truth. But not quite.

Ethan comes to my locker at the end of the day. He's not in my lunch period, and I wonder if he's heard about what happened.

He doesn't reach for me. Doesn't try to kiss me.

"You been seeing someone else?" he asks as I change my French book for history and shake my head. "Is that why you acted weird last night?"

"Ethan." I slam the door with a metallic clang. "It was Jack. Jack is my best friend. I'm always with him."

"Were you kissing him?"

I can't quite get the *yes* out.

"Was this after Haley, at my door? Were you trying to get back at me?"

This is so strange. Three days ago, I couldn't get enough of Ethan. I was wrapped up in him like the filling in a cannoli. But now everything he says sounds wrong.

"I told you, this is going too fast."

"Well, I just *want* you," he whispers. "I'm sorry."

I look up at him. He wants me. And he's so handsome. Unbelievably handsome. I shrug. My brain is so tired it hurts.

"What's that mean?" His eyes are intense. "Are you breaking up with me?" he whispers.

"I don't know." Maybe he deserves more of a chance. Maybe I'm crazy to even consider a romance with Jack.

Ethan slams a locker with his fist.

"Come on," I say. "I just need some time to figure stuff out. A lot has been going on."

"Okay. All right. It's your grandma. And the party, isn't it?" He instantly brightens. "You just need to get through the party. Let's just get through the party." I'm pretty sure it's not just the party, but I nod my head and he seems satisfied.

As I walk down the hall, he keeps pace with me. "You want a ride home? It's pretty cold out."

"No thanks. I have a few stops to make." Which is a lie. But this conversation is starting to get on my nerves.

On the way home, I find myself turning into the harbor. I go and sit on my family's dock, my legs crossed. I need to think.

There's a sailboat coming in, its passengers bundled up and scurrying about on the deck, getting ready to tie up for the day. They're a family: a mom, a dad, and a few kids. They look worn out and cold. But they also seem content, satisfied. I remember that feeling, coming back into the harbor after a long day on the water with Mom and Dad.

Is it too much to ask for one father and one mother who want me to be happy? They don't have to like each other. They just have to like me.

I stand up. It's going to be a long night, with all the preparations for this ridiculous show that I don't even want to be in. I pull out my cell. I dial Mom's number one last time, get voice mail. Surprise.

"Hello. This is Sheridan Wells again. Please have Margaret Taylor call me back as soon as possible. Thank you."

I hang up and stuff the phone into my jeans pocket. I feel it crumple the heart-shaped note, which I pull out quickly and flatten as best I can.

She hasn't called back. And she won't be here to help me with the cake. It's too late. That cake was the perfect reason for her to come home. Now the only reason for her to come back is because I need her. I wonder if that will be enough.

Chapter 22

TWO PEAS IN A POD

Thursday night I dream about Mom. She's standing apart from me, and the closer I come, the farther away she moves.

I wake up at three in the morning and can't get back to sleep. So I take out my cards. I've avoided them the last few days, mad at Mom for not calling. But I need them now.

I dig out number eleven. A cartoon dog on the front. Inside, the card reads *Have a doggone Happy Birthday!* This is *the* card, the one I go back to whenever I feel like maybe she's never coming back.

I open it slowly now, a little worried that the words may have disappeared, or that I imagined them. No, there they are.

Sheridan, eleven on the eleventh. Your golden birthday.
I remember the day you were born. That was a golden day.
They put you in my arms, your fuzzy red hair sticking straight
up. As long as I live, I'll never forget that moment. I hope you
have a happy day, Cupcake. And I wish I could be there. I
love you.Mom.

I flip the card shut and lie down, holding it to my chest.
Shortly before my alarm rings, I fall back to sleep.

At school, I am distracted and tired. I'm thankful Ethan
keeps his distance, especially since I haven't officially broken up with him yet and Jack doesn't know. In the cafeteria,
Lori, Tuba Dude Jim, and Jack chat about the show. They've
had a wardrobe fitting, and Lori has a flowered sarong to
wear. Except she pronounces it "so wrong." When she says
this, I force a laugh so they don't ask me what's wrong. Jack
nudges my shoulder. He knows I'm totally faking it.

After school, I stop by Geronimo's and order a triple-shot
latte, which is necessary if I'm going to make it through the
night. It's Friday, and there's a huge piece of poster board
hanging in our kitchen with a schedule for tonight and
tomorrow. There's not a minute of the next thirty hours
that doesn't have a goal written beside it.

Tonight it's rehearsal, at five o'clock sharp, and we'd
better not be a minute late, Amazon threatens, or the entire
schedule will be thrown off.

I go to the restaurant and stand in the center of the dining room. Dad is by the kitchen door, talking to Amazon and Gray Hair. He looks tired and worried.

Amazon gazes at Dad admiringly whenever he speaks. I wonder if they've moved from just going to a jazz club to something more. They're acting so *together*. Oh man, if she ends up being the first woman he introduces to me as his girlfriend, I just might vomit.

Enough. I don't have time for this now. I need to focus on finishing the cake. It *will* be perfect; it has to be the most perfect thing about this lame party. And it's almost done, but of course, there's something still bugging me. Something's missing, and I can't figure out what it is.

I step into the kitchen, head out the back door, and walk to the bakery, which is quiet and dark.

The cake stands like a glowing beacon of awesomeness in the center of the worktable. It's gorgeous. Three tiers covered in turquoise fondant, without a crack or a crinkle. Perfect. Bright hibiscus flowers wind their way up to the very top. Tasteful. Colorful. Beautiful.

Still, I fuss with the flowers for ten minutes. *What is missing? God, I wish that Mom would call right now. She could tell me what to do.*

And then, like a lightning flash, it hits me. A butterfly. This cake needs a butterfly—the one that Mom was supposed to make—perched on the top tier. No big deal. I can make butterflies. Not as good as Mom's, but I don't see her around here to do the job.

I whip out the gum paste and work like a maniac to finish a beautiful bright yellow butterfly. It needs time to dry, but it will look perfect. Seconds after I'm done, my cell phone starts to wiggle out of control.

Come to restaurant now.

It's Amazon. I've been here a while, and rehearsal is about to begin. I leave the butterfly to dry.

When I get back to the restaurant, I hear Amazon barking orders and see Surfer hopping around inspecting the room, coffee in hand. He's in charge of the set.

The main dining room is a mess. I hope they have time to finish, because it looks horrible. There are big potted palms being wheeled in and buckets of bright flowers that have been delivered, but nothing has been put together.

I spy Jack and Lori standing against the far wall, their arms crossed, looking horrified. I walk over to them and try to avoid Amazon's laser glare.

"Don't look so excited, guys," I say. Lori laughs nervously. Jack doesn't say a word; just stares at me, dumbfounded. "What is it?"

"Um. Sheridan? Who exactly did you invite to this little shindig?" Jack asks.

"Well." I shift from one foot to another. "Just you guys, basically. I didn't know who else to ask."

"Oh." Lori squints at me, twists her mouth funny. "Well, it looks like someone went ahead and added to your guest list."

"What?" I say. "What are you talking about?"

Jack points a finger up to the ceiling. "Ethan's here. In wardrobe."

"Yeah, well, I invited him . . . before."

"And Haley." Jack's mouth seems to be moving in slow motion.

"Haley? No. That's impossible."

They shake their heads in unison. I turn away from them and dash across the room to find Amazon. She'll fix this; she has to. There she is, yelling at one of the crew. "No! The lights go here, not there!"

"Excuse me?" I say, trying to keep my cool.

She doesn't seem to hear me.

"Excuse me?" I say again, louder this time.

"Yes?" She turns to me. "Oh good, you're here. Listen, I need you to do a final fitting upstairs."

"Um. First, there are some people here who I didn't invite?"

"Well, yes, Sheridan." She chuckles. "You didn't exactly give me much of a guest list."

"But . . . those aren't my friends. Not even a little."

"Really? Sheridan, come on." She puts her hands on her hips and looks disgusted. "Can't you make nice for one day? You seem like the kind of girl who can be friends with any-one. I had to ask the drama teacher at the high school if she had any students who might make attractive extras." She picks up a potted plant, and I follow her as she carries it to a long table. "That's it! Don't think of them as friends; think of them as extras. That'll help."

She sees someone doing something wrong across the room. "You! There! That doesn't go there!" And she hurries away.

That's when I see Haley walk down the staircase, surrounded by her entourage. Lori and Jack stare at me and shrug. They're no help at all.

Dad walks into the room, a tray of hors d'oeuvres in his hand. He's passing them out to the crew, smiling and laughing. But something's wrong. He's nervous? Tired?

Haley waits at the bottom of the stairs, and I look up to see Ethan making his way down. He looks marvelous, and maybe a little bit sad when he sees me. A part of me wants to run to him, grab him, kiss him, and give this another try.

But Haley gets to him first. He stands back, avoids her, gives me a see-I-told-you-we-were-through look. And then . . .

"Okay, people!" Amazon yells in a strong, loud voice. "We need to get the basics down here. Cast, remember this is reality TV; this is not staged. But certain things have to happen, and that's what we're here for now."

This not-staged rehearsal has us serving fake food, cutting fake cake, opening fake gifts. There's even a deejay coming tomorrow, so we have to practice fake dancing on a fake dance floor. Surfer bounds over to my side, pulling Ethan along behind him. He lowers his voice and whispers, just to us, "I want you two to dance with each other. Give me snuggles, kisses, the whole nine yards—got me? I'm counting on you two to bring the sexy to this party."

Um. Okay.

Ethan is smiling like he just won the lottery.

By seven o'clock, we've got the drill down. During a break in the action, Lori and I sit down at a round table in the middle of the room.

"How's it going?" she asks.

"I don't know."

"Trouble's brewing, methinks."

"You're telling me." I look around for Haley and see her sitting in a circle of chairs with her coven of witches.

"By the way, Jack's freaking out. He thinks he's blown it with you, big-time."

"What? No." I lean forward and lay my head in my hands. "I just haven't figured out what I'm going to do yet. With him. And Ethan."

"Really, Sheridan?" She stretches her arms. "You and Ethan? Come on, you guys are like Coke and Pepsi. Both tasty, but they don't go together. You and Jack, you're like peas in a pod. Both totally OCD, both cranky as hell. And it's slightly disturbing to say this out loud, but you have got some chemistry with that boy. Seems like a no-brainer."

"Coke and Pepsi?"

"You know what I mean. If you asked for my advice, which you did not, but I'm giving it to you anyway, it's you and Jack. I've seen it coming for years." She sits back, crosses her legs, and sighs.

"Really?"

"Oh, yeah."

"But what if it doesn't work?"

She shakes her head. "Can't think like that. You know who thinks like that? Chickens. Are you a chicken, Sheridan?"

I shrug and drop my head to the table. "Bawk, bawk," I cluck.

"Okay, dinner break, people! But we're doing another run-through after!" Amazon shouts. "Be back at eight!"

There's a tap on my shoulder. I look up and Ethan is behind me, glowing. Seriously, his glowing blond hair frames his glowing face, which is connected to his glowing neck. I try not to want to kiss those lips. Try not to want Ethan Murphy.

"Hey. Sheridan." It's Jack, from my other side. "Let's go eat."

I look from Ethan to Jack. They glare at each other, and I find myself wishing that Sheridan & Irving's was equipped with a trapdoor. Wouldn't it be nice if I happened to be sitting directly over it?

I push a stray hair from my eyes. Smile at them both. No idea what to say.

"Sheridan!" Dad approaches. "Let's eat up at Nan's. I'm cooking."

"I should probably go work on the cake," I say, thinking of the butterfly that will hopefully make it perfect.

"No, come on. You've got to eat something."

I peer at him, suspicious. Why in the world does he want to eat dinner with me when Amazon is here, or the Suits, or anyone else, for that matter? Being with me stresses him out. Stresses me out, too.

"Come on, I'll make you anything you want."

Jack and Ethan fidget.

"Anything." Dad is really trying. "Salade Niçoise? I can grab some fresh tuna, or filet. You want filet? You love filet."

Dad pays no attention to the boys who flank me. He just waits for my answer.

"Fine," I say. "Pancakes. I want pancakes."

"Pancakes?"

"You said 'anything.'"

"Just plain pancakes?"

"No." I stand up and cross my arms. "With chocolate chips."

Dad stares at me, and I wait for him to argue. He'll want to make me an omelet, or at least crepes. But instead, he says, "You know, that sounds really good." He puts his arm around my shoulder. "Excuse us, gentlemen." He nods in the general direction of Ethan and Jack as he leads me away from the entire mess.

We head out together into the cold night. I am speechless. I think my dad just saved my butt.

He walks ahead of me and doesn't say a word as we make our way up Nanny's back stairs and into her kitchen. The apartment is quiet and smells empty. It makes me sad.

He goes straight for the mixing bowls, grabs a griddle from Nanny's arsenal. I sit down on the nearest stool and watch him.

I decide to get right down to business. "Okay, so I can see you're trying to be nice, but if you think that I'll change my mind about the show, you're wrong."

"Sheridan." He turns around, places the griddle on a burner. "Can we just not talk about the show? For like forty-five minutes? Can we just eat dinner together?"

"Fine with me," I say coolly.

"Why don't you switch on the radio?" he says. Chef Donovan Wells does not cook to music, but okay, whatever.

He pours some cream into the mixing bowl while I switch on Nanny's stereo. There's an oldies station on. I'm not a big fan, but I don't feel like hunting for something good. And I'm not turning on that ABBA CD. So we listen to Johnny Cash instead.

"Ah. A classic," Dad says as Johnny sings about a ring of fire. "You know where she keeps her chocolate chips?"

I walk to the cabinet next to the fridge, throw him the bag.

"You know," he says, "I remember making these for you when you were little. Really little." He cracks two eggs into the mixture. "I have no idea when all this time went by. I swear you were just four years old, sneaking chocolate chips out of the bag."

I remember that.

He adds flour, baking soda, and vanilla; mixes it all up; then dips a ladle into the pancake batter and drops the liquid onto the griddle. Maybe it's the way he looks so worn out tonight, or maybe I just want to pretend that there's some hope for us, but something inside me cracks, like the eggshells he just threw away. I feel like the Grinch at the end of the story, when his heart grows. It's not like mine's gonna burst out of my chest or anything, but something is different—for now, anyway.

I walk up to the stove, stand next to him. "You're doing it wrong. Don't you remember the bears?" I grab the spatula and pick up the four lame, round pancakes that he's made, then pile them onto a plate.

"Oh, yeah," he says, and watches as I scoop up a good bit of the mix, let it fall into a big circle, then drop two smaller dollops on top of the large one. I grab the bag of chocolate chips and strategically place two eyes, a nose, and a crooked smile on the teddy bear face.

"You remember?" I ask him again.

"Remember? I *invented* these suckers." He gently nudges me out of the way, taking the spatula back.

The song changes on the radio from something I don't recognize to a tune that is vaguely familiar.

"Hee-hee!" Dad laughs. "It's 'Henery'!"

Before I know what is happening, he is humming, then singing along with this totally ridiculous song—"I'm 'Enery the Eighth, I am; 'Enery the Eighth, I am"—in this goofy English accent.

I sit back down on the stool. I'd forgotten how this used to be; how we used to have fun together, cooking and listening to crazy music. I remember doing this even after Mom left. But then the restaurant, his travel, his social calendar—it all butted in, and the time we spent together just fizzled out.

And maybe my cakes had something to do with it, too. I think of the times he asked me to go for a bike ride, watch a movie, or just sit and talk, and instead I went to the bakery and made someone a cake.

When he starts dancing around, waving the spatula, I burst out laughing.

"I'm her eighth old man, I'm 'Enery; 'Enery the Eighth, I am!" he sings. At the same time, he serves me up a bear on a plate, slaps the syrup and then the butter dish down, and finally takes a bow.

I try to stop myself from smiling too big, but the memories are oozing out of me. They flood my brain and submerge my heart. I feel like a crazy mile-wide dam has broken open and I can't do a thing to stop it.

The song ends. "These are good," I say as I swallow an ear.

"Good. I'm glad you like them."

He stares at me. His eyes narrow like he's trying to remember something.

"What?" I ask.

He turns back around and flips the next bear. "Nothing."

I take another bite. "Dad? Are you dating Amaz— I mean, Jacqueline?"

He shakes his head. "No, not really."

He flips the conversation around. "Are you dating that blond jock?"

"No. I don't think so."

"Good. I don't like him." He raises an eyebrow. "What about Jack?"

"Don't know."

"Jack I like. He's a good guy."

I shrug. He shakes his head. "Of course, any guy'd be lucky to date you. You've got so much going for you."

I am surprised, hearing him talk like this. And I wish he'd tell me what exactly I have going for me.

When I am halfway through the bear's face, I look at Dad and think of him living in New York City without me. He drives me crazy, but the idea of him not being around fills me with a dark, empty feeling. Like if that happened, our family would officially be over.

"Do you still love Mom?" I'm not sure why this particular question pops out of my mouth, but now that I've asked it, I really need to know the answer.

He looks surprised and turns to check on a pancake. He puts it on a plate and grabs the butter, taking a moment to spread a pat and dump some syrup on top of his bear. When his fork is poised, ready to slice into it, he stops.

"In the beginning, it was great. But a few years after you were born, something changed. And then I was miserable. And worried. A lot. But at the start, she was a lot of fun; she made me laugh." He slices off a bite, puts it in his mouth, chews. I can tell it's hard for him to swallow. "But that wasn't enough."

His eyes are shiny. With tears? And I feel a lump rising in my throat.

"So is that a no?"

He smirks. "I love that I got you out of the deal."

He takes another bite, puts his plate down, lays the fork on top. He walks over to me. "You want another?" I nod and he takes my plate. I wipe my mouth with a napkin, take a swig of the ice-cold milk he's poured for me.

After I devour another innocent bear, Dad looks at his watch. "We'd better get back, so the wrath of Jacqueline won't fall upon us." He rinses the dishes, and I put away the butter, the chocolate chips, and the syrup, then turn off the radio.

Dad gets the lights behind us and locks Nanny's door. "We should do this more often," he says. "That was the best dinner I've had in a long time."

I laugh. There's no way that chocolate chip bear pancakes beat his gourmet cuisine. But still, I know what he means.

Chapter 23

YOU HAVE TO TAKE THE
BITTER WITH THE SWEET

I wake up, look out the window. Snow. On May 7.

It's only six thirty in the morning, but the house is alive with noise. I shower and get dressed. Amazon warned me to wear a button-down shirt so that my hair and makeup won't get ruined when I change into my Hawaiian vomit dress. I find an old blue oxford in the back of my closet, button up, and take a deep breath.

Downstairs, I see that the front room has been transformed into a one-chair beauty salon. Amazingly, my father is sitting in front of a floor-length mirror, and some big guy dressed all in black is putting makeup on him.

Now I've seen it all. I head to the kitchen.

"Sheridan?" Dad calls me back.

"Yes?" I walk into the room and look at him like he's

some incomprehensible piece of modern art.

"Don't give me that look. Your time will come." He's smiling this morning. I had a nice time last night, but I'm not ready to be all rainbows and sunshine with him. Besides, I haven't had coffee yet.

"You must be the birthday girl?" That's the big guy in black. I also notice he's got black fingernails and a pierced lip. Not the kind of dude you see often in St. Mary.

"Sort of," I say, smiling.

"Well, you couldn't be more gorgeous." He walks over to me and touches my chin, angling my face upward. "Would you look at those cheekbones. And those eyes. Yum-yum, dee-licious." He shuffles back to Dad. "No offense, Mr. Wells," the man in black says. "You're a handsome man and all, but I think she got her looks from her mama."

It's not exactly a smile I see on Dad's face. And not exactly a frown. Something in between. Something bittersweet.

"You're right about that, Frank. A hundred percent."

After I grab some coffee, Frank calls me to the chair. By the time he's done with my hair, I've been sprayed, twisted, brushed, teased, and sprayed again. My nails are painted by a nice older woman, and then Frank starts slapping goop on my face. He stands right in front of me so that I can't see my reflection in the mirror, and I have the feeling that I'll look like the Bride of Frankenstein by the time he moves out of the way.

"How's it going, Frank?" Amazon walks in. I start to turn my head.

"Don't you dare move," he says to me, totally serious. "She'll be ready soon, Your Majesty."

"Good. They need your help with the extras over at the restaurant as soon as you're done. And, Sheridan, thank you for humoring me with the guest list. I tend to agree with you; those girls are—what's a nice way to put it?—prima donnas. They're driving hair and makeup crazy." She leaves without another word.

After what seems like a very long time, Frank announces that he is "*finis*" and steps back, away from the mirror. "Voilà!"

Wow. I touch my hair.

"Don't touch!" Frank screams.

"Sorry."

My auburn hair is shining, hanging down in loose curls around my face. My makeup is perfect. I don't look like an undead monster's bride; I look like me, with a hint of Greek goddess thrown in. One of the nice goddesses who don't turn people to stone or eat them alive.

"Perfection," Frank says.

Amazon storms in. "Oh my God!" she says, so loud that at first I think she's angry. But no, this is Amazon happy. "Sheridan! Who knew there was a supermodel under that cake-covered exterior?"

I roll my eyes. That might be taking it a bit too far. She puts her arm around my shoulder, leans down, and looks at me in the mirror. "I'm serious. You look gorgeous. Now go upstairs and get that dress on."

When I get upstairs, there's a stranger in my bedroom smoothing wrinkles out of the dress with a steamer. It looks different in the bright white sunlight of my room. Almost pretty.

"Hi," I say to the stranger.

"You Sheridan?" the woman says in a thick New York accent.

"Yes."

"Good. I'm Miriam. Go ahead and change." She looks me up and down. "There's a bra built into the top, with a little extra added for good measure, if you know what I mean."

"Okay." So I turn away from the woman and drop my shirt and jeans. I pick up the dress and pull it up over my hips. There she is, at my back, zipping before I have a chance to take a breath. It falls over the curves of my body perfectly. I look in the mirror in the corner of my room.

"God, that's just gorgeous," Miriam says, smoothing the skirt. "A little weird on a snowy day, sure, but it looks like it was made for you."

She turns, starts digging in a small case on the dresser, and pulls out a bright pink hibiscus flower. She clips it above my left ear.

"And that is the icing on the cake, my dear."

Who is that girl in the mirror? She looks good. I wish Mom could be here today to see me.

When Miriam is finished, she leaves my room, and I

grab Mom's heart-shaped note and stick it in my cleavage, since there are no pockets on this dress. I grab my cell phone and don't try to stick it down my bra. My boobs look big enough already. Extra padding? They totally gave me the Dolly Parton model. Last, I fasten Jack's charm bracelet on my wrist for good luck, the little bird charm jingling.

I make my way to the restaurant, hidden under my parka, my feet stuffed into boots. Frank almost wouldn't let me wear a coat, but I warned him that a frostbitten birthday girl would not be very attractive. It's colder now than it was a month ago, and even though I'm only crossing the parking lot, there are ice patches here and there and I have to walk flat-footed and slow. I can feel my perfectly lined lipsticked lips turning blue.

When I enter the kitchen through the back door, no one even looks up. Lights and equipment are everywhere. I tiptoe over cords and push through to the dining room.

Oh wow. I turn in a circle to take it all in. The huge potted palms have transformed the room into a tropical garden. Yards and yards of silk, in turquoise, chartreuse, and orange, are draped along the walls. Fairy lights are strung everywhere, glinting off the crystal chandeliers, and enormous tropical flower arrangements seem to sprout out of nowhere, all purples, pinks, yellows, and bright, vibrant greens. A waterfall gushes in the corner, and long tables with bamboo legs fill the space. Dad's already filmed the cooking segments, and the premade food is out: carved watermelons filled with small fruits, pineapples, trays of shrimp, and piles and piles of crudités. Totally mouthwatering.

It's spectacular. Just what I'd expect from an Extreme Sweet Sixteen.

And then, of course, there's the cake. It's been brought over from the bakery, and it looks like a jewel in the center of all that food. Despite the fact that I don't want this party to happen, I can't help the smile that's creeping across my face.

I hear Lori's laugh and spin around to find her. Jack, Lori, and Jim are walking down the stairs, all made up and dressed for a party. They stare at me in my parka, which is making me hot under all these lights. I take it off and lay it on the chair next to me. And seriously, their eyes pop out of their heads.

Lori floats across the room in a supercute aquamarine halter top and her flowered sarong, which is tied expertly around her waist.

"You are stunning!" I say to her, but all three of them just stare at me. Lori backs up a step, puts her fists on her hips.

"Well, glory be! Our little girl, all grown up!"

Jack doesn't say anything. He's got on a pair of long shorts and a Hawaiian shirt. As I look closer, I notice that instead of hideous barfy flowers and random palm trees, his Hawaiian shirt has baseballs, pennants, and random Chicago Cubs paraphernalia.

"What the heck is that?" I ask.

"What, this?" He picks at the shirt. "They said we could wear any tasteful Hawaiian shirt. This is the most tasteful one I could find."

"Tasteful?"

He tilts his head and winks. "Go Cubs?"

I shake my head, but he's looking at me all serious.

"You look really . . . beautiful."

"Thanks." His eyes on me are making me blush.

"Oh, good Lord. Get a room." That's Lori.

I'm about to shoot her a dirty look when my eyes travel up the staircase and I see Ethan descending with Haley at his side. Her friends follow like baby chicks behind a mother hen. She's got on a dress that's way shorter, lower cut, and tighter than mine. And her boobs aren't sewn in, either.

"Give me a break," Jack says.

"Oh, brother," Lori adds.

Ethan glances in my direction, but he sticks with Haley as the group pools at the bottom of the stairs.

He looks good, like he just stepped off the beach in Hawaii. Natural, tan, so cute I can't stand it. Why does he have to be so cute?

He steps in front of Haley, waves an arm. But she walks around him and over to where we're standing.

"Good morning," Haley says, the chicks in formation behind her. I stand up a little taller in my boots and stick my chest out just a bit farther. "I've come to make peace."

She smirks. "Thanks for asking me to your party." She sticks out a hand. I don't reach for it, because I don't believe her for a minute. She grins her wicked grin and looks me up and down. "Sheridan, you're so . . . totally vintage."

I think of all the years that Haley has gone out of her way to be wicked to me. I am so sick of her. "I did not invite you."

"Oh." She puts a finger to her lips. "That's right. Poor thing, had to pay fake friends to come to her party."

The girls behind her snicker.

"Wait—you're getting paid?" Lori interjects.

I glare at my friend, who clamps her mouth shut.

"You've got a lot of nerve even coming here," I say, and I notice a few of the production crew have stopped to watch us.

"Oh, relax. You know I was telling the truth before. Your mother *did* get around; it's no secret," she says matter-of-factly.

I take a step closer to her.

"What are you gonna do, Sheridan? Hit me?"

I've never hit anyone. But I want to so, so bad. "What are you so jealous of, Haley? I don't get it," I say.

Amazon steps in. "This isn't funny, girls. My nerves do not need this today."

Out of the corner of my eye, I see that Dad has entered the room.

"Then send her home, and you won't have anything to worry about," I say.

Amazon looks at Haley. I know that Haley is the last person she wants to send home. I mean, look at her: if anyone can get teenage boys to watch some lame cooking show, it's her.

"Jealous?" Haley says sharply, like she's about to lose it. "*I'm* jealous? Try that the other way around. I guess Ethan didn't tell you that we never stopped seeing each other. And you were too dumb to figure that out when I opened the door of his house." She flashes that evil grin. "And it's so funny that you never wondered why he was so interested in someone like you." She lifts her arms. "This. This TV show. Ethan's got big plans, baby." Her face is scrunched up and she actually looks really ugly. "Duh, Cake Girl!" She cackles as Ethan moves forward.

"Shut up, Haley." He turns to me, a deep wrinkle between his perfect blue eyes. "She's a liar."

Amazon crosses her arms. "Okay, you need to leave." She points to Haley, who puts her hands up to her chest in fake shock.

"Whatever." She raises a hand, beckoning to her brood. But they don't move. Haley flips her hair, leans in to me, and whispers, "You think you're *it*. Ha! Even your own mother can't stand you."

Amazon is the only one close enough to hear that comment. She puts her hands on my shoulders. I guess she's afraid I'm going to jump on Haley and start pounding, and she's not wrong. I want to, in the worst way.

"Go," Amazon says firmly. And Haley sashays off in her high heels, all by herself.

Amazon looks at me. "A word, Sheridan?" She sounds like some scary school principal. I follow her to the corner by the staircase.

She stands up straight and circles her shoulders backward. I'm making her tense. "Sheridan, I don't know what that was all about, but I am going to suggest to you that you stay focused on the show. This day is very important to your father. I can't stress that enough. I'm sure you want to pull that girl's hair out, but clearly she is delusional. You are an amazing young woman. Anyone can see that. Now. Can you regroup?"

I look up at her and nod. "Yes. I can."

"Good. Don't let me down." She walks away, shouting last-minute instructions to a cameraman.

I sit down on the bottom step, take a few deep breaths. I look over at Jack and Lori, who are talking to some of the other guests, as if they know that I need a few minutes on my own to cool down.

Amazon has crossed the dining room and is talking to Dad, but they don't look my way.

There are cameras everywhere, people checking equipment and lights. This is really going to happen. I sigh. It wasn't supposed to be like this. Mom should be here.

There's a tap on my shoulder from behind. I turn and see Mr. Roz. I can tell right away that he's coming down from makeup—he's got an orangey glow—and he's wearing the brightest Hawaiian shirt I've ever seen. Tasteful? That's questionable. "Sheridan." He smiles big, as usual.

"Hey, Mr. Roz." I stand up.

"You look like angel," he says, and puts his arms out for a hug.

"Jesus, Mary, and Joseph!" Frank is on me like white on rice. He pulls a pick out of his suit jacket and begins to fix my hair. He looks at Mr. Roz. "Please, man, not the hair!"

I smile apologetically. Frank walks away, shooting Roz threatening looks.

"What is *that* and what that thing in his lip?"

"That's Frank and . . . don't ask."

Dad crosses the room and joins us. "Hey, guys."

"Donovan!" Mr. Roz shakes his hand. "Look at our Sheridan! What a grown-up lady she is become!"

Dad's eyebrows lift, and he nods. "Tell me about it."

"All right, people." Amazon only has one volume today: Obnoxiously Loud. "We'll get started in about ten. Do not wander off, do not ruin your makeup, do not leave. If you have to sneeze, don't. If you have to pee, hold it. No one move."

And that's when I remember. The cake. I never went to the bakery for the butterfly.

"Oh God!" I run toward Amazon, but Dad stops me first. "What is it?"

"The butterfly. I need it for the cake. For the top."

290

"What butterfly?"

"I made one. For the top. It's at the bakery." I know Amazon will kill me, but her back is turned at the moment. I look at Dad, then make a run for it, grabbing my coat on the way out.

So I'm running across the parking lot in boots, struggling into my coat but not quite making it. I'm blue all over.

The bakery door is locked. I reach into my coat pocket, pull out my cell phone, grab the keys. Jack's bracelet gets caught on a stray thread. Damn! I wrench my hand out of the pocket and drop my cell phone. Shoot! I stick the key in the lock and swing open the door.

When Amazon finds out I left, she will go ballistic. *Hurry, Sheridan, hurry.*

I bend to pick up my cell. One missed call? I run into the bakery's kitchen, see the butterfly on the worktable. It's not 100 percent dry, but it will be fine through the shoot. Who called me? I hit the Select key. Grab the butterfly. Put the butterfly back down.

SSM. 8:00 A.M.

Sault Sainte Marie.

She called, an hour ago, and I missed her.

I can't believe I missed her. I lean against the back counter. My breathing feels a little scary, my throat just a little too tight. *It's okay, it's okay, it's okay. Do not panic.*

It's Saturday morning; she must be at the bakery. What if she is there? What do I say?

I circle the kitchen, walk into Nanny's office. Think about sitting down. Can't. Walk back into the kitchen, then to the front of the bakery, so quiet and empty. The phone practically throbs in my hand. I go back into the kitchen.

I take a deep breath. I can do this. I've been waiting for this moment for years. I hold the phone and hit the Call button. Okay. Another deep breath. I'm ready.

The number dials. I gulp. What if I cry? I think of how mad Frank will get if he sees my eyeliner smeared. *He'll get really upset, so don't cry, Sheridan. Do not cry.*

"Sweetie's Bakery."

It's her.

"Hi." I suddenly wish I wasn't alone. Suddenly wish I had a hand to hold. "This is Sheridan." My voice is high-pitched, almost giddy.

"Oh. Hi." This is followed by a very long pause. "Did you get my message?" She sounds like she's at a funeral, talking in low, hushed tones.

"No. I saw you called. And wanted to call you right back." *Why isn't she saying anything?* "Mom?" I am smiling. She's right there, on the other side of this phone call. "Oh my gosh, I'm so glad you called!" She actually called.

"Sheridan." A big sigh. I hear her sniff. She's crying? "Honey," she says, "I'm so sorry."

"No, Mom." See, I knew she was scared to come back. "Mom, I'm not mad. Forget everything. I don't care. I just . . . would really like to see you again."

"Sheridan. God, you deserve so much better than me. I wish you'd listened to the message."

I brush a few stray crumbs off the counter. "But I didn't. Why, what'd you say?"

She's quiet.

"Mom . . ." I laugh. If she's not going to talk, I will. "This TV show is crazy. Mom? They're filming it today. Dad might move to New York. But I was hoping you could come home, like you said in the card. We could work together in the bakery. You said you wanted to come home."

She doesn't say a word. But she hasn't hung up, because I can still hear her crying.

I keep talking. "So come on, come home. I've been looking all over for you. How cool is it that I found you? Or if you can't come home right now, maybe I could come and visit you?"

"Sheridan, please. Stop. I can't come back," she says.

"But why not?"

"Because I can't. Sheridan. I have people here."

"It's okay. I get along with people really well. Ask anyone."

"Not just people."

"It's all right. I like everybody."

"A husband. I have a husband."

"Oh." My head begins to spin as the word rolls around inside of my brain. A husband?

"Mom." I gulp again. My hands are shaking so badly I can barely hold the phone. "I thought you said you were single. In the last card."

I can only hear her breathing.

"But that's okay." I don't want to scare her off. "I'm okay with that." A husband is fine. It's not like her and Dad getting back together was even a remote possibility.

"It's not that simple."

She sounds so businesslike all of a sudden.

"Well . . . what's not so simple?" I rub at a spot on the stainless-steel counter with my thumb. It's not going away.

"Because . . . he doesn't know about you."

Doesn't know about me? "What? Why doesn't he know about me?"

"Because. Sheridan, it's complicated. I met him, I got pregnant. Everything happened so fast. I didn't have time."

"To tell him you have a daughter?"

"Sheridan . . ."

Wait, wait, wait. What did she just say? "Wait, pregnant?"

"Sheridan, let me go now. The bakery is busy. I can't talk from here."

"Pregnant? You're pregnant?"

"No. I'm not." She pauses. What, did I imagine she said that? "I had the baby. I *have* a baby."

"Oh." There's this taste in my mouth. Heavy, metallic, nasty. "I don't understand."

She sniffs, starts crying again. "I'm sorry. It's just the way life has worked out, Cupcake. . . ."

"What?"

"I'm so sorry. But Sheridan . . . I'll always be your mom,

no matter what. I'll tell him, someday. But I can't. Not right now. And I'm sorry about the card. If I had known you'd hold me to it, I wouldn't have sent it."

"Hold you to it? It was all I had." I feel hot; my stomach is churning.

"Honey . . ."

"So that's it?"

"I should go."

"Mom." My voice shatters into a million pieces. "*I'm* your daughter. I need you."

"I've got to go." Her voice is broken, too, and I am having a hard time making out her words. "I don't deserve you, sweetheart. You're better off forgetting about me." At least I think that's what she said.

"No . . ." I can taste my own tears, mixed with anger. They're bitter. She wants to hang up. Go on pretending I don't exist.

"You're my *mom*. How am I supposed to forget you? I think about you all the time."

"Sheridan. I'm so sorry. I think of you all the time, too. Your cakes, they're beautiful."

My cakes?

"I'm sorry."

"Mom . . . no, no, no!" Tears stream from my eyes. Frank will kill me. "Don't go."

"Sheridan. It's not forever; just for now. I need you to understand."

"How am I supposed to . . . You are my mother. Don't go. You can't leave me again! Please don't go! Mom! Mommy!" I am screaming. I sound like a crazy person. When I don't hear her, I quiet myself, afraid that she's hung up.

I inhale a sob. "Mom?"

"I'm sorry," she says in a tiny voice.

And then she's gone. Poof. Just like that.

I straighten up. Drop the cell phone. My tears are flowing from some well of infinite sadness deep down inside. And then somehow I make them stop. In another minute, my breathing evens out, my body stops shaking.

I pick up the butterfly, still sitting pretty on the worktable, and walk out of the bakery into the crisp white air. I don't have on my coat, but I can't feel the chill. I walk into the parking lot and throw the butterfly as hard as I can into the sky. I can see its bright yellow wings against the cloudless blue. It falls and shatters.

Then my feet find a patch of ice, and I slip and land hard, my head thunking on the slick concrete. I lie there, on my back, whimpering to no one, watching the cold sky falling down on top of me until I am floating in black emptiness, all alone.

Chapter 24

THE APPLE OF MY EYE

$\mathcal{I}$ smell lilacs, see the tiny green buds waking up on the trees.

"Sheridan!" Nanny calls me from the dock. I look toward her and smile. She's got a nine-inch round cake in her hands, and there's a SWEET 16 candle on top. Mr. Roz is with her, and so are Jack, Lori, and Dad. They walk toward me and sing, "Happy birthday, dear Sheridan."

There's a woman with Dad. She's holding his hand, wearing a flowing yellow dress, her wavy golden hair hanging loose on her shoulders. My mom. She is so pretty.

When we meet, Nanny hands me the cake and topples into the water. One by one, they all fall off the dock and into the water. They flail, they can't swim, they scream for help. But I'm holding the cake. I can't help them.

My mother, she's the only one left. She stands in front of me with her arms crossed; a sweet smile flashes across her mouth. "Come on, Sheridan. All you have to do is let go."

I wake up in a cold sweat, in the back of an ambulance. Everything is fuzzy, and sounds are muffled.

"Sheridan! I'm here, I'm here." It's Dad. I feel his hand in mine, but I can't talk.

When I wake up again, I am in an emergency room. There's something on my finger, and a machine counts off the ticks of my heart. My head throbs and my legs feel heavy.

"Sheridan." It's Dad again.

"What happened?" I ask, trying to adjust my eyes to the light.

"You slipped, on the ice. You have a concussion. Just relax, sweetheart." I feel his hand, gentle on my hand. "Don't worry, I'm here."

A man comes in—the doctor, I guess. "Hello." He doesn't sound very friendly. I force my eyes open and see that he is looking at a clipboard.

"The scans look good. It's not the worst concussion I've ever seen." He lowers the chart to his side, walks over to me. "Do you remember what happened prior to the accident?"

I look down at the blanket on top of me. "I don't remember slipping." My brain works hard, thinking back. The image of a butterfly in the sky. My mother.

My eyes dart to Dad.

"I remember some."

"Well, that's a good sign."

No, it's really not.

"I'll be back," the doctor says, and walks through the split in the curtain.

Dad scoots up on the stool. "You really scared us."

"I talked to Mom."

His head drops. "Why?" The word comes out as a breath.

"Because she is my mother."

"Sheridan. Did she call you? She promised me she wouldn't call you. What did she tell you?"

"She told me that she has a husband who doesn't know about me. And a baby."

I don't take my eyes off him, even though the light in this room is too bright and I just want to sleep.

"Sheridan. I wish she hadn't spoken to you."

I squeeze my eyes closed. My whole body hurts. "So you know?"

He looks at me like he's the one in pain. "I'm sorry, Sheridan."

"Stop!" I shout, the word echoing painfully in my head. I lower my voice. "Don't say you're sorry. Just tell me the truth."

Dad nods.

"Why didn't you tell me?"

He's still nodding. I would beg him to stop the nodding and answer me if my head didn't feel like a ticking time bomb.

"Can we talk about this later?" he pleads.

"No," I whisper. "Just tell me."

Then my father, Mr. Supercool Reality TV Celebrity Chef, cries.

"Stop it. Stop crying. Tell me."

He looks up, breathes deep. I watch as he pulls himself together, his look of sorrow replaced by the serious, down-to-business face that I know so well. He looks at me, and his eyes are just like mine. Brown, wide, honest, scared.

"All right . . . Okay." He sits up straight on the stool, wipes his eyes again, crosses his arms, and lowers his head. "A few years ago, she called; told me she was having a baby and getting married."

My head is pounding, but I am determined to find out the truth. "You didn't tell me." I flinch. My head hurts.

"Sheridan, just listen."

I look at him and sigh.

"No. I didn't tell you. Things were going so well. I thought we were okay."

"That why I didn't get my card?"

"She hadn't told the guy about you or me. She was afraid."

"So she wrote me off?"

"Sheridan. Let's talk later. You need to rest."

"No. Not later. Now!" I practically growl at him.

He leans closer to me. I want to move away. "Not until you hear me. Are you listening?"

I don't respond.

"Sheridan?"

He reaches over, and his hand surrounds mine in a firm, unyielding grasp. Like when he used to help me onto the boat. I was never afraid that his grip would fail me.

"Before I tell you, you have to hear me."

"I'm listening." I feel tears ready to fall, drops of heartache building in the corners of my eyes.

"I will *never* leave you," he says, his gaze intense. "I know my job has been hard on you. And this show"—he shakes his head—"has been crazy. But no matter what happens, I will not leave you. *Ever.*"

Oh, he's making my head pound. I clench my teeth. "Just tell me."

He sighs. "She told me she was going to stop the cards; she couldn't communicate with you. He doesn't know, and she thinks he'll leave her if he finds out." I can tell he's furious with her. "Look, I know this is bad. But I do believe she still loves you, somewhere in her heart."

No. I'm pretty sure denying my existence means she doesn't love me, anywhere in her heart.

I look away. "She doesn't love me. I could tell."

"Well." He grabs my hand tight again. I'd pull it away if I could. But it hurts to move. "*I do.* I do love you. *Believe* that."

I don't know what to believe. As I close my eyes, I think of God and the plan for my life. The plan sucks.

I spend the night in the hospital, for "observation." I'm in and out of sleep. At one point I wake up and Dad is there. "Have some water," he says, and puts a straw in my mouth. The water is icy, and I don't think I've ever tasted anything so good. "Jell-O?" he asks, but I shake my head and drift back off to sleep.

When I wake up later, I hear a voice: ". . . like to scare me half to death. And I've already been half dead once this year." It's Nanny.

I open my eyes. A nurse stands above me, laughing. "You have a visitor."

I turn my head an inch, try to smile.

"Hey, sugar pants, it's me." She's in a wheelchair; the color is back in her face.

"Are you okay?" My voice sounds far away, out of focus.

"Am I okay? What about you?"

"I'm fine. But you should be resting."

"Nah. Goin' home tomorrow. You, too."

I blink. Now I'm crying. The realization has hit me head-on: I don't have a mother. She gave me up, like an old car or a cake she made. How could she?

"Oh, baby," Nanny says.

I want to crawl into her lap, like I did when I was little. Instead, the nurse wheels her closer, and Nanny grabs my hand, tight.

"You let it out, girl. I know you're hurtin'. You cry all you want, baby doll. You just let it out. But"—her tone changes, to her strong voice, the one that can convince me of anything—"you never forget who loves you. You are God's child, a blessing to me, a blessing to your daddy. You are the doggone apple of his eye. He would die for you. Don't you ever doubt that, Sheridan. Not ever."

I cry and cry and cry, and Nanny doesn't say another word. She doesn't have to. Even after I fall asleep, I know she's there.

It's Sunday morning. I'm feeling better—physically, anyway. They tell me my ankle is badly sprained, but my brain is fine. Which is good, I guess.

I hear a knock at the door. Jack steps in, a white bakery bag in one hand, a bouquet of tulips in the other.

"Hey."

"Hi," he says. "You up for a visitor?"

"Be quiet," I murmur. "I was starting to wonder if you'd ever come."

He hands me what I assume is a lemon poppy seed muffin, puts the tulips on the bedside table. "Steal those from Growly?"

Jack raises his eyebrows and pulls a chair close to the bed. "Maybe." He leans forward and puts his hand on the blanket. I dig my hand out from under the covers and grab on to him. His bracelet still hangs on my wrist.

For a long minute, we stare at each other without a word. I love that about Jack. I can kind of read his mind. "My mother doesn't want me. Hasn't for a while."

He closes his eyes and nods his head. "Your dad told me."

"Sucks, huh?"

"Totally."

"And she had a baby . . . a girl," I said, wondering if maybe someday I could meet her. A sad smile crossed my face. "I have a sister."

"Wow."

"Yeah."

We stare at each other, reading each other's minds. I know he understands how I feel. I don't have to describe how my heart is not only broken, but ripped apart and stomped on.

He breathes in sync with me. I squeeze his hand.

"I love you." I say the words without measuring what they mean first. I just say them.

He leans toward me. "I love you, too."

"Jack." He tilts his head. "What happened with the show?"

"Nothing. When we saw you in the parking lot, everything kinda shut down."

"Great. He must hate me."

Jack leans on the bed, kisses my hand. "He doesn't hate you. But I think he's pretty pissed at your mom."

I shake my head and cough out a laugh. "Feel free to run away now. Your family is so nice and normal. And mine is totally screwed up."

He smiles. "It *is* kind of like watching a soap opera. But

if anything had been different, you wouldn't be the same. And that would suck. 'Cause you are pretty incredible. And you've met my brothers. If you think it's normal to live in the midst of a fart cloud, you really are crazy."

I laugh out loud now, and my head only hurts a little. A nurse comes in to check my vital signs. She says my broken heart is beating just fine. Apparently, I'm going to survive.

My ankle throbs under the tight bandage. Before I am released, a nurse comes in and gives me a pair of crutches. She shows me how to walk with them.

Dad pulls the car around front and meets me where they've wheeled me out. He's overdoing it, treating me like a little kid. Trying to make up for what's happened with my mother. He hasn't said a word about the show. He grabs Jack's flowers from my lap and helps me out of the wheelchair and into the car, all smiles.

Nanny said he would do anything for me. But I ruined his big chance, so I doubt that's still true. We drive away. His eyes are on the road. He's still smiling, but it seems awfully forced.

"You mad?"

"Not at you."

"At Mom?"

His mouth tightens. "Yes. And at myself." He stops at a red light and looks at me. "I should have been there for you more. I should have been honest with you. But I was scared."

Right. How do you tell your child that her mother doesn't want her? I look straight ahead.

"I'm sorry." He says the words and they fill up the empty space in the car, each syllable surrounding me with sadness. Mom said she was sorry, too, though. Who do I believe?

At home, the parking lot is empty. No limos, no trucks. I look toward the bakery, where Mr. Roz is most likely holding down the fort, again. Dad helps me out of the car and up the front steps. He opens the door to the house, and I limp over the threshold. I look around the front room and see no signs of the Suits or Frank, of hibiscus flowers or Hawaiian shirts. Almost like it was all a dream.

"Well, you'll want to be in your room. So I'm gonna have to carry you."

"Dad, really. I weigh like a thousand pounds."

He rolls his eyes. "Give or take." He holds out his arms.

"Okay, but if you get a hernia, don't say I didn't warn you."

"I'll take my chances."

He lifts me off the ground and makes his way onto the first step. A memory flickers in my mind, of him doing this when I was little, carrying me up to my bed in his arms. I look at him sideways. His face is getting red; I am no lightweight.

Then I remember how he'd go away for business and send postcards. I still have them stashed away, somewhere. He always called to say good night. And he made me special dinners at the restaurant; let me sit in his office and eat behind his desk.

By the time we get to the top step, my mind is washed in a steady stream of memories that I had left buried somewhere, like the box in my closet. I recall those first weeks after Mom left, going into his room and sleeping next to him in their big bed, wondering where she had gone. He must have been so mad. But he never showed it. He just threw back the covers when I came in all scared and restless. "Come on," he'd say, "you need your rest." When he was next to me, I could sleep. I felt safe.

I think of us singing in the kitchen, and bear pancakes. And our weekly dinners, and his stupid rules. It's like I've spent the last eight years working so hard to remember my mother that I forgot my father.

We finally make it to the landing, and something comes over me. I grab around his neck, just like when I was little, and hug him tight.

He puts me down gently, on my good foot. Without a word, he goes into my room and turns down the covers. "Come on, you need your rest," he says quietly, without looking up.

He takes off my shoe, and I slide into bed, which feels like heaven. "Okay," he says. "Get settled. I'll come check on you. I'll be in my office if you need anything."

He pulls the quilt up to my chin and then brushes the hair off my forehead.

"Thank you," I say. And I mean it.

When he leaves, I pick up my cell phone. There are texts from Lori, Jack, and Ethan.

Hope u r good, Ethan says.

Doing good. Home, I text back. In a few seconds, he replies.

Come c u?

Not 2day. Rest only.

Soon?

Sure.

I know I need to tell him it's over. I'm such a chicken.

I'm staying home from school the entire week, and by Wednesday, I am officially stir-crazy. Dad pokes his head into my room in the morning and asks if he can go to the farmer's market in Grand Rapids.

"You don't have to ask me, Dad. Just go."

"All right. Well, Mr. Roz is at the bakery. And Nanny's at home. Maybe I shouldn't go."

"Dad. Go." I look at him. All his attention is starting to get on my nerves. "Please."

"I'll only be gone for an hour, hour and a half max."

"Go!" I yell so loud that my head hurts.

As soon as he leaves, I get up. I am so out of here. The sun is shining. All the snow and ice from the weekend are gone. Hopefully, we can have a spring now, before summer gets here. I sit on the top stair and then descend on my butt, dragging my crutches along with me.

I step out onto the front porch and do the same butt-slide down the front steps. No one is around and I feel free. The pain pills they gave me at the hospital have taken the edge off my headache, and my ankle isn't throbbing anymore.

I suck in the fresh air, wobbling along on the crutches, across the parking lot toward the front of the restaurant. I know exactly where I want to go. I head to the rectory at the end of the street and the brick wall surrounding the garden. I want to see the flowers; see if they survived the freeze.

By the time I make it to the gate, I'm exhausted, but I hobble inside, work my way around to the little bench, and sit down, out of breath from the effort. I really need to get serious about running again, once my ankle heals.

I see the tulips, which are in full bloom now. The daffodils, white and yellow, sway back and forth in the breeze. But my grape hyacinths, they are fading and dying.

I hear footsteps on the path again. Oh crap.

"We meet again."

I start to rise. "I'm just leaving, Father. Sorry."

"Why must you leave? I have a feeling it took you a good while to get here." He nods toward my crutches.

"May I sit?"

Double crap.

"Sure."

I scoot over to make some room. He sits. "Have you been admiring the tulips?" he asks.

"Yes, and the daffodils."

"And if your crutches allow, go to the lilac bushes; they're about to spring forth."

"Maybe, I'll try."

"And so, how is your recovery going?"

"Fine."

"Praise the Lord."

"Right."

"Ah." He turns to me. "Do I detect a bit of sarcasm?"

I actually think before I answer him. "No." A breeze sweeps across the garden, creating a beautiful, fragrant wave of color. "I just don't get it. I mean, I just wonder . . ."

"What?"

"If God is so into us, how can he let a mom leave her kid?"

"Ah. That's a loaded question." He sits forward again, crosses his arms. "You want to know what I think?"

I shrug.

"It's just free will. The ultimate blessing and curse. God might lead you one way, but if you choose a different path, what can He do? Nothing, of course; that's why it's called free will. But I also think if someone makes a choice that hurts us, that's when we need to notice what's left—the blessings that have always been there, right in front of our eyes. I think we almost always will find a few."

He claps his hands together and laughs. "Now, I don't know all this for sure. It's not like we've ever had a face-to-face, He and I. But it's something to think about, eh?"

I shrug again.

Growly shakes his head, stands up.

"Well, Sheridan. It's always a pleasure. If you ever want to visit again, remember, the garden is always here for you." He stands tall. "Changing and growing, a little more every day."

"Okay," I say tentatively. "Thanks." He lifts a hand and walks away.

I sit for a while longer, thinking on his words. Squinting in the sunshine, noticing the loveliness right in front of my eyes.

Chapter 25

THE CHERRY ON TOP

Between Nanny's recovery and my injury, Mr. Roz and Dad have had to hire a new cake decorator. She's not bad; she has good technique and excellent references. I'm not happy about having someone else fill my shoes, but at least our reputation won't go totally down the toilet.

I've been drawing a lot, since I'm stuck at home. I even decide to apply for Ely's art camp. Still scares me, the idea of being stuck in the wilderness with a bunch of art geeks. But Mrs. Ely gave me an A-plus on my project and even called to remind me that the deadline was approaching.

On Monday morning I'm back at school and Ethan ambles up to my locker. I haven't seen his smile for ages. I am glad to see him, but afraid of what I know I have to do. I avoided him all last week, so I imagine he knows something is up.

He stops next to me. "Can I still kiss you?"

I smile. Look at those lips. Yes . . . No.

"Ethan." I hate the idea of using a stock speech. Let's take a break. It's not you; it's me. I really think you're nice. Let's just be friends.

"Ethan," I say, deciding to go with total honesty. "I think maybe you did want to be on the show more than you wanted to be with me. I mean, maybe not on purpose, but deep down."

He shifts feet. "Sheridan."

I close my locker, lean up against it, and wait for him to talk.

"I'm sorry, about everything." He runs his hand through his awesome hair. Which I will probably never touch again. "I meant what I said. You're different than the other girls." He reaches for my hand. "I probably don't deserve you."

I let him hold my hand; I savor that warmth. He's crazy good-looking, so funny, so popular. But he's right. He doesn't deserve me. I give him a kiss on the cheek.

"So that's it?" he says.

I smile. "Friends?"

A look passes over his face. I don't think Ethan's ever had a girl friend. And I don't think he's about to start now.

Our hands feel so perfect together. I remember the first time he held mine, the day we tried to skip school, and the thrill I felt.

"If you ever change your mind, let me know." He leans down and kisses my forehead, then walks away, his hands in his pockets and his golden hair glinting under the fluorescent lights.

I see Jack down the hall by his locker. He slams it shut and smiles when he sees me coming. We walk toward each other. I can read his mind right now, and I'm hoping he can read mine. We are face-to-face and then his arms are around me and our lips are touching and I feel myself floating free. Yes, this is exactly what I was thinking.

It hits me. That's the difference—why I always felt so clumsy and awkward kissing Ethan. He could have been kissing any girl. But Jack and I, we just fit together right. Not that I've forgotten about the possibility of temple defacement. In fact, I think of it even more now, and I know this isn't going to be easy. But at least I know Jack will be patient. Because if he isn't, I'll smack him.

Jack drives me home. When he swings the Corolla into the restaurant parking lot, we both gasp. There's a black limo in front of the house. Oh no. They're back.

"Jack." I look at him as he helps me out of the car. "This could be bad."

"Yeah, maybe. But it could be good, too. You never know." He holds my school bag and helps me with my crutches. I look up at him. Jack. Tall and dark and handsome. And I kiss him again, because I can.

I push open the front door. The house is dark and quiet.

"Maybe they're at the restaurant?" I say to Jack.

"Sheridan?" Dad sticks his head out the kitchen door. "Join us, please."

I'm scared. The last time I saw these people, I was just about to ruin their big show.

"You want me to come in?" Jack asks.

"Yes, but you better not. I'll call you after," I say.

"Okay. Well, break a leg."

"Ha-ha."

He walks backward slowly, smiling the whole way to the front door.

Dad stands waiting. I limp in on the crutches, ready for the firing squad.

"Hello, Sheridan." It's Gray Hair, sitting across from Amazon. They've got coffee cups in front of them.

"Hi," I say.

"It's good to see you again, Sheridan." Amazon stands and walks over to me. "Can you maneuver yourself over here to sit down?"

"Uh. Sure." I look at Dad, who seems uneasy.

When I sit, they all sit. I am overwhelmed with guilt and begin to confess. "Look, I'm sorry. I know I ruined the show. I didn't mean to."

Gray Hair smiles. "You know something, Sheridan— in television you learn pretty quickly that you can't plan for everything. And yours certainly was an extraordinary circumstance."

"I'm not going to lie to you," Amazon chimes in. "Cancelling the shoot was quite a blow. That was the crucial scene for the pilot episode; the rest of it didn't make much sense without the party. When we left here, we talked about cutting our losses and scrapping the show altogether."

"I am really sorry." I look at Dad.

"Sheridan, don't apologize." Gray Hair takes a sip of coffee. "There's no need. The reason we're back, in fact, is that once we reviewed all the footage, we realized that we'd be foolish to let your father go."

"Oh."

"We're offering him another chance. But this time, our offer has a condition," Gray Hair says, looking directly at me.

"Actually, the condition is that you will be part of the show with your father. We like your personalities so well that we want to put you on together. It'll be a mix of cooking, cake decorating; we even love the idea of sending you on a few trips a year, to try out new restaurants and find interesting things to do together. So there would be some travel. Lots of fun," he says.

"Are you serious?" I say.

"Completely," Amazon replies.

"Just for the summer?"

"No," she says. "This would be a series. We'd need you based in New York year-round."

"New York? What about school? What about the bakery?" I look at Dad, wondering how I could possibly leave Jack, Lori, my cakes, Mr. Roz, Nanny. I even think of art camp; after all this, how could I miss art camp?

"There are great schools in New York, and when you travel, we'll provide a tutor," Gray Hair says.

I can't believe this.

"I don't know what to say."

"Well, take some time to think about it," Gray Hair says. "Discuss it with your father. It's a big decision."

He stands up and Amazon follows.

"I hate to run, but we've got a plane to catch," Gray Hair says, holding his hand out to my father. "Don't get up, Sheridan." He shakes my hand from across the table.

Amazon gives Dad a hug and looks at me. "Sheridan, this *is* a big decision, but I've been watching you the last few weeks. You are smart and talented. This is a wonderful opportunity for a girl like you."

She holds out her hand and gives mine a firm shake.

I am speechless.

Dad walks them to the door and comes back into the kitchen. I am still in the same place, reeling. He sits quietly back down, folds his hands in front of him.

"This is entirely your decision. If you don't want to do it, I'll stay here, run the restaurant. I'll make it work.

Something like this *will* change our lives completely."

I watch him as he gets up, gathers the coffee cups, and takes them to the sink. I touch the bird charm on my wrist. How can I leave my home?

That night, Dad and I have dinner with Nanny. She's still not getting around easily, but a steady stream of her friends have been spending the night at her place, making sure she's not overdoing it. Because if anyone is going to overdo it, it's Nanny.

Dad comes over from the restaurant to eat with us. He brings grilled salmon and a wild field salad. Delicious.

We discuss the deal. Dad wants this to be my choice. That doesn't help me at all. I text Jack to come over later. I'm hoping he'll make it easier to decide. Or maybe he'll make it harder.

At the end of dinner, Dad stands up. He has to get back to work. "Come on, Sheridan, I'll help you get home."

"Wait," Nanny says. "Don't y'all get to goin' so fast."

Dad puts his keys on the table. "What is it? You okay, Mom?"

"I'm fine, just fine. But I have something to say."

Dad sits down. "Go on."

"Well, I will, thank you." Nanny rolls her eyes at Dad. I've got a bad feeling about this. "I have decided to sell the bakery and go live in New York City." She says this matter-of-factly, like she's telling us the weather.

"Mom?"

"What?" I say.

"What are you talking about?" Dad says, staring in shock.

"Yes. I asked Jakup if he was in any position to buy the place. And of course, that man never spends a dime. He's gonna buy it. No better candidate."

"Nanny." I stand up, angry. "Why would you sell the bakery? Why would you want to go to New York? You've lived here forever."

"Well, I'm thinkin' it's time for a change. Always wanted to live in the big city. Course, I won't lie to you; I'm nervous as a long-tailed cat in a room full of rockin' chairs. But as recent events have proven, I am not getting any younger. And then if you decide to go, Sheridan, you can keep an eye on me. Wouldn't that be the cherry on top?"

I sink back down into my chair. This is so weird.

"All right. I've dropped my bomb. Now I need my beauty rest." Dad helps her into bed and we walk home, shell-shocked.

Once Dad's back at the restaurant, I sit on the sofa with my laptop and wait for Jack to show up after his shift at Geronimo's. For the last hour, I've been researching New York City. There are bakeries there; lots of world-class bakeries. Their Web sites are gorgeous; their cakes are stunning. And art? I could take classes in painting, pottery, filmmaking—anything I wanted.

Then I look up the St. Mary town Web site. The

lakeshore, the town square. Sweetie's, Sheridan & Irving's. How can I desert this place that I love? I feel like a big traitor just thinking about it. And then there's Jack. How can I leave him now?

I see him walking across the parking lot and hobble over to the door, opening it before he can knock. "Hey," he says, closing the door behind him. "Hey." I raise my eyebrows. Then he grabs me around the waist and kisses me. And that's it. Fireworks. Electricity. Thunder and lightning. Every time. Guaranteed. I don't want to stop.

But we need to talk.

"So . . ." I back away.

"So? What's the story?"

He takes my hand and helps me into the front room. We sit down side by side on the sofa and rest our feet on the big ottoman.

"What a week," I say, leaning against his chest as he throws his arm around my shoulder.

"What did they want?" Jack asks warily. "The Suits."

"You sure you want to know?"

"Yes. I want to know."

Before he showed up, I rehearsed what I was going to say. I'd declare my love and tell him I could never leave. Something like that. But in the end I just spit it out as fast as I can.

"They want me and Dad to do a show together. In New York City." He sits up and I turn to look at him. "And

Nanny says she's coming with us. But they are leaving it up to me. So I'm saying no."

Jack is quiet, thoughtful. He sits back, and I lean into his chest again. The room is so still and cozy, and I know that I will remember this moment forever; that's how perfect it is.

For a long time, neither of us says a word. The clock ticks, the house settles. And then Jack speaks. "No. You shouldn't say no, Sheridan."

I don't move. "Why not?" I say quietly.

He reaches down, grabs my wrist, holds it up, and touches the bird charm. He's the one who thought I would want more, who thought I would fly away. "Because," he says, "we've only got two more years of school. Then we'll be in college, anyway. Who knows—maybe I'll go to college in New York City. Maybe you'll come back here. It doesn't matter; no matter what happens, you're not going to lose me."

"I'm not?"

"You're not."

"Promise?"

"Promise."

After a while, my phone rings. It's the warden.

"Hi, Nan."

"Sheridan, I think it's time for Jack to be gettin' home." She pauses.

"Fine." I think of what will happen if she does go to New York. I might as well become a nun.

I hang up the phone. "Nanny doesn't trust us."

Jack looks into my eyes. "Smart woman." He kisses me, then sits back, holding on to a lock of my hair.

"I don't know about this, Jack."

"You're going."

"But . . . how can I leave you? It's too much like . . ." I glance at him, not wanting to finish that sentence.

He shakes his head. "No, Sheridan. It's nothing like her. *You're* nothing like her. You have to know that."

I nod, hoping that he's right.

"I better go before your grandmother ends up back in the hospital." He stands but still holds my hand.

"I wish you could stay."

"Me, too."

We kiss once more, and after he leaves, I hop up the stairs and get ready for bed. I lie in the dark for a long time, wondering what to do. I am silent, waiting for the voice in my heart to speak to me. To tell me what to do. But I have a feeling that this time the answer won't come out of the blue. This time I might just have to close my eyes and jump.

Chapter 26

HAVE YOUR CAKE AND EAT IT, TOO

I head out the door first thing in the morning. It's a sweltering July day, and I'm not sure I'm prepared for what's about to happen. I hope I made the right decision.

Tomorrow is my Sweet Sixteen, the real one this time, and the day after that, I leave for art camp. Today, I need to finish the portfolio I'm supposed to bring for critique. I've got my messenger bag, filled with supplies, and the sketchbook where I've drawn a series of my favorite spots in St. Mary. Sweetie's on one page, Sheridan & Irving's on another. Geronimo's, too, and Father Crowley's garden, of course. For my last piece, I walk toward the harbor, and I end up on our dock. I pull a flimsy piece of onion paper out of my bag and place it on top of the initials my parents carved into the wooden board. With a charcoal pencil, I make a rubbing of the letters and the heart that surrounds them.

The black charcoal stains my fingers, and when I'm done, I put everything away and lean back on my hands. There are tons of people out on the water today, enjoying the weather, enjoying St. Mary. I will always love this place. It will always be my home.

When I get back to the house, I cut out the onion paper rubbing and reach for a painting I've already finished. Swirls, hearts, curls, teardrops, all the shapes I use on my cakes, only this time in watercolor.

In the center of the piece I've glued a red paper heart. It's the lunch box note, from my mother. I run my fingers along its surface, nearly worn through after all those years of wishing. Then I attach the rubbing of their initials on top of it. I can see her writing through the crude *DW + MT. Love you, Cupcake.*

I don't hate her. I can't. But I find myself hoping that, even if for only a split second, these hearts meant something to her once, something real.

I might never know for sure.

When I am finished, I close my portfolio and stick it in my book bag. I answer a text from Lori, who is mourning her breakup with Tuba Dude Jim. Then I text Jack.

You ready for 2night?

Within seconds he texts back.

See you at 7.

***

He knocks on our front door at 6:55. Jack is never late for a date. I've got on a new dress and new shoes, and my hair is long and loose. I even met Lori and got a manicure. Not even a trace of food coloring left on my hands.

"Hello," Jack says gallantly, holding the door open and kissing me on the cheek. "You look gorgeous."

"Thank you." I blush. He looks so handsome, dressed in a neatly pressed blue oxford and khaki pants. His hair is long and a little shaggy. I love it and can't wait to run my fingers through it tonight. I can do that. He's my boyfriend.

We walk hand in hand across the parking lot and into the back door of Sheridan & Irving's. Dad is there, working alongside the new chef he's hired to take his place. He looks up as we walk through the kitchen.

"You guys couldn't come through the front door?"

"What, like all the regular customers?" I tease. "No thanks. We're *special*."

The crew laugh and say their hellos as we pass through. I wonder if they're sad that Dad is on his way out. But he's got a huge future ahead of him, and they all know it.

We're seated in one of the private dining rooms upstairs. This room is big enough to sit fifty, but tonight it's just the two of us. The lights are dimmed, and there's a bouquet of roses waiting on the table. Jack pulls out my chair and I sit.

We sit close together, holding hands, talking and laughing. It's odd how easy it was for us to move from best friends to this. And scary to think that he might not have had the guts to kiss me that first night if I had never dated Ethan Murphy.

"You all packed?" he asks me.

"Pretty much, I guess." The movers have been stashing our stuff in boxes all week. The new chef and his family will be renting the carriage house, and our things will be on their way to a brownstone in New York City—Brooklyn, to be exact. They have some killer bakeries there.

"I'm going to miss you so much," I say. We've been together almost every day since we were five. I'm still not sure I can do this.

"We *can* do this." He's reading my mind again. "I'll be out to see you August first. After that, we just need to get to Thanksgiving. It'll work, I promise."

"Okay." I squeeze his hand and he gives me a kiss. "I don't know how I'm going to survive not kissing you," I say.

"Yeah, that's gonna be tough."

A lot of things are going to be tough. Like not making cakes every day, and not running down to the lake, and not seeing Lori or Mr. Roz or even Growly.

We have an amazing dinner, cooked by my father, and when we're finished, Jack reaches into his pocket and pulls out a box. Pink metallic wrapping paper, shiny pink bow.

"For you." He pushes the box toward me. I grab it immediately and start to unwrap it. There's a small blue velvet box inside, with a tiny card on top.

I open it and read.

Happy Birthday for real this time. Hope you get what you really want. I did. Love, Jack.

When I look at him, he's smiling. "Open it." I flip back the lid and see another charm. It's a small silver cake, with three tiers. Beautiful.

"That's to remember St. Mary by, and also me, because I'm so sweet."

"And modest."

"And in love with you."

I snap the box closed and give him a kiss that he will never forget.

The next morning, even though it's my birthday, I'm in the back of the bakery, finishing up an engagement cake. I've been trying something new—painting on my cakes. This one I'm doing in the style of *Starry Night*, by my old friend Vincent van Gogh. It's not a copy; I put my own twist on it, adding a few hearts in the swirly night sky.

I want this cake to be perfect. It's my last as an employee of Sweetie's Bake Shoppe. The front doorbell rings, but I don't hear Mr. Roz greet anyone.

"Hi! Just a second, please," I shout, and put down my brush. When I walk into the front, the singing begins. Oh God.

"Happy birthday to you, happy birthday to you . . ." No way.

It's Jack, holding a round cake decorated with a clump of pink buttercream roses and a bunch of lit candles stuck into the center. Lori follows, then Nanny, Mr. Roz, and Dad.

They've got weird smiles on their faces. Lori is holding a big box with a red bow attached to the top, and Mr. Roz has a picnic basket.

"What's this?" I laugh.

"It's your birthday. You didn't think we'd let you go without a celebration, did you?" Lori says as we walk into the back.

"Oh. Thank you, but first I have a cake to finish." I pick up my paintbrush.

"Well, at least blow out the candles," Jack says. So I close my eyes and blow.

Mr. Roz stands next to me and inspects my work. "What a beautiful cake. The best one yet." I glance at him and smile. But I'm serious. It's not done.

"I know, I know. It takes the cake," I say.

"Sheridan, darlin', this cake looks done as can be," Nanny says, sidling up to me.

My eyes scan it from top to bottom. No, something is definitely missing. But they are crowding me, and I can't think.

Lori thrusts the giant box at me. "*Open* it," she says.

"Fine." I take it from her, rip at the paper, flip back the cardboard top. I look up at all of their faces. "Um. Thanks?

It's a life jacket," I say, stating the obvious as I pull it out and turn it around in my hands.

"I rented a sailboat for the day," Dad says. "Thought we could take a quick trip up the coast."

"A sailboat?" I am shocked. I look at the engagement cake. "But this is due soon. I've got to finish."

"Sheridan, the cake is done," Dad says. "Let's go out and enjoy this beautiful day. I made us a picnic."

"Sheridan Wells, you are coming." Lori looks at me, dead serious. "I took a Dramamine for this."

"But . . ."

"Come on. Let's go." Jack catches my hand. "We've only got you for a few more hours."

"Sheridan, I say cake is done! You must take morning off!" Mr. Roz insists.

"No, wait. Come on." I stop, stare at the cake. I am right. There is something missing. If they'd all just be quiet, just for a minute, I could figure this out.

I concentrate and block their voices out, and then she pops into my head. My mother. The mother I remember, anyway. I can almost smell her perfume, like the honeysuckle that's in bloom right now. I can still feel her with me. Will she tell me what's missing?

And then I hear something. Only it's not her. It's me. A voice starts in my heart and flows like a buttercream swirl up to my brain.

Nothing's missing. It's done.

I give the cake another look, not sure I should trust what I've just heard. But I look around the room, at my friends and family, and I know that the cake is perfect just the way it is.

So I let go. Finally.

I push the cake to the middle of the table, take off my apron, and hang it on a hook. Dad has put my birthday cake into a pink bakery box. We'll eat it on the boat. I'll have a big piece, one with lots of icing and a big fat rose.

I can almost taste it now, each bite sweeter than the last.

ACKNOWLEDGMENTS

$\mathcal{A}$ first book necessitates a list of thank-yous a mile long. This is, after all, the culmination of a very long journey that started in something like the third grade. But I'll do my level best to keep it short and sweet.

To Michael Stearns, you are extraordinary, talented, and kind. Thank you for finding me, honing my story, and turning me into a published author. Danielle Chiotti, thanks for shoring me and my book up in countless ways. I am blessed to be represented by such competent and caring people.

Many thanks to the wonderful team at Egmont USA: Regina Griffin, Elizabeth Law, Douglas Pocock, Mary Albi, Katie Halata, Nico Medina, and Alison Weiss. Heartfelt thanks to my editor, Greg Ferguson, for respecting my words and pushing me to go deeper, and for just being a really nice guy. And for my copy editor, Ryan Sullivan—I owe you, big-time.

A huge thank-you to my friends in the children's writing community but most especially to my critique group, Will Write for Cake: Laura Edge, Doris Fisher, Miriam King, Lynne Kelly Hoenig, Monica Vavra, and Tammy Waldrop. Where would I be without you? Your thoughtful insights are woven into this book, and I couldn't be more grateful.

To my SCBWI-Illinois friends who have supported me over the years, especially Esther Hershenhorn and the founding members of the Springfield Scribes. And to my dear friend Kimberly Hutmacher for asking me a decade ago if I had ever considered writing for children. I thought you were off your rocker. But that was a life-changing day, truly.

Love and thanks to: Holly Gillice and Lori Warda, steadfast friends. Paul and Kerry Hegele, for giving my main character a hometown to love. Friends near and far who have helped me get to this point with loving support and a ready glass of wine, especially Kara Trotter, Michelle Bretscher, Erin Conley, Jill Holliday, and Maryanne Walker. And a very special thank-you to my first teen reader, Ashley Nail.

My stories often center on family, and this is not by accident. Thanks, with all my heart, to my parents, Richard and Carman Durr, for insisting that I follow my dream and not accepting anything less. You have championed me every step of the way and I love you. Thanks to my creative and talented siblings, Rick and Jeanne, for putting up with me despite my rotten middle-sister tendencies. To all of my amazing in-laws and to four remarkable young people who inspire me daily to write good books for teens: Libby, Matthew, Zofie, and Ricky. Thank you.

To my darling daughters, Lily and Cate, whose affinity for cake sparked the idea for this story. You make my life beautiful and truly are the sweetest things. And to the best man I know, who has cooked more dinners and handled more bedtimes than the average husband so that I could write. Mickey . . . I love you to pieces.

Last, I am so grateful to God for giving me the heart of a writer. It's such a gift to sit down every day and do what I love and I will never take it for granted.